Readers love *Double Indemnity* by MAGGIE KAVANAGH

"*Double Indemnity* is a fast paced murder/mystery with a well developed plot that twists and turns from start to finish."
—Carly's Book Reviews

"This book is one wild ride! I could not put this down."
—MM Good Book Reviews

"…this book is filled with twists and turns that keep you interested all the way through. I had a hard time putting this book down."
—Hearts on Fire

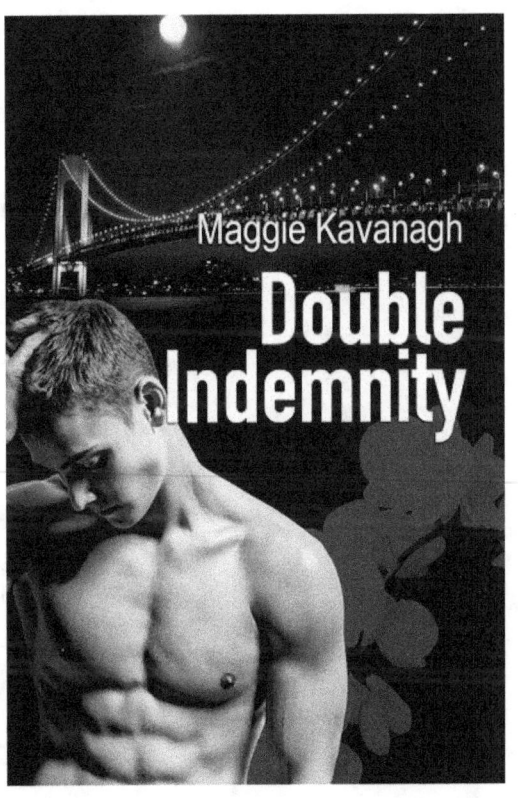

"I really enjoyed *Double Indemnity* and wouldn't mind reading more from Maggie Kavanagh."
—The Novel Approach

By Maggie Kavanagh

Taking Flight

The Stonebridge Mysteries
Double Indemnity
Inner Sanctum

Published by Dreamspinner Press
www.dreamspinnerpress.com

Inner Sanctum

Maggie Kavanagh

Published by
DREAMSPINNER PRESS

5032 Capital Circle SW, Suite 2, PMB# 279, Tallahassee, FL 32305-7886 USA
www.dreamspinnerpress.com

ISBN: 978-1-63476-404-9
Digital ISBN: 978-1-63476-405-6
Library of Congress Control Number: 2015945756
First Edition September 2015

Printed in the United States of America
∞
This paper meets the requirements of
ANSI/NISO Z39.48-1992 (Permanence of Paper).

To my partner in crime, always.

Acknowledgments

WRITING DOES not occur in a vacuum, and I'm incredibly grateful to have the support of so many people. I would like to extend thanks to the friends and readers who have encouraged me to continue this series. Thank you, in particular, to Olivia, Michela, and Asya—dear friends who have offered their insightful feedback and cheerleading at all stages of the drafting and editing process. This novel wouldn't exist without them.

Prologue

THE FIRST splash of gasoline over the upholstered car seat sent a wave of fumes into the air. No one was there. No one would notice until it was too late. The small box rattled, filled with a hundred tiny sticks. It would only take one.

Headlights suddenly flashed at the end of the road and disappeared, a momentary inconvenience as the car turned down another street. This was the time. This was the place. This was the beginning.

The match rasped against the side of the box and hissed to life. The tiny flame flickered in the darkness.

It would only take one.

Chapter 1

SAM FLYNN bolted upright in bed. He ran a hand through sweat-damp hair and glanced at the time. Only ten, which meant he'd dozed off waiting for Nathan at his apartment. The light was on, and next to him on the king-size bed was a tiny white kitten. Nathan recently rescued it from a feral bunch of strays. The once-clean duvet was covered with potting soil, and a telltale trail of blame led from the floor plant near the window across the beige carpet. Sam shook his head and frowned. "You're nothing but trouble," he said to the cat.

The details of the dream had already faded—thankfully—but Sam wasn't eager to fall back to sleep. After his near-death experience the previous winter, the nightmares were bad, but he hadn't had one in a while. He supposed he was overdue.

A noise from the other room—keys unlocking the door.

"Sam?" Nathan called.

"In here." Sam's pulse picked up—this time with excitement.

Moments later, Special Agent Nathan Walker appeared in the doorway, looking edible in the suit he chose that morning for a meeting at his New York field office. He pulled at the tie to loosen it and gave Sam a sexy smile. Even after six months together, he was still the handsomest man Sam had ever seen.

"Hi," Nathan said. "I'm glad you came." The smile faded when he noticed the dirt. "Oh no. Again?"

Sam fought a grin. Nathan was one of the most fastidious people he'd ever met. That he hadn't given the little pest away yet was a testament to his patience.

"Afraid so. Hey, you're the one who thought getting a kitten was a good idea."

Nathan sighed, but his exasperation gave way to a shrug. "I guess I'll just have to get rid of the plant." He removed his suit jacket and discarded his tie and shirt. Sam watched the undressing process appreciatively, drinking in Nathan's defined arms, broad shoulders, and trim waist—a swimmer's build. He stood up and crossed the room to help.

His fingers met the warm skin of Nathan's flat belly, and he worked the black leather belt open. "How was your day?"

"Better now." Nathan's dark eyes raked over Sam, who was clad only in a pair of tight, red boxer briefs. They were Nathan's favorite, and they made Sam's ass look fantastic.

Once the belt was off, Sam coiled it neatly and set it on the mahogany dresser. Before he could turn to face Nathan again, arms wrapped around him from behind. He leaned into the embrace.

"You're all sweaty." Nathan nipped at his ear. His breath tickled, and it smelled faintly of cigarettes covered up with mint. "Bad dreams?"

Sam swallowed. He shook his head. "I don't remember."

They both had bad dreams sometimes. And though Nathan didn't smoke often, he sometimes did when he was stressed... or when he was thinking of the wife he lost the year before.

Emma was murdered when she uncovered a rotten scheme among some colleagues in the police department who were working with the mob to bring drugs into Stonebridge, Connecticut. Nathan was a main suspect, though he'd been helping the FBI get dirt on Chief Dan Sheldon, an old friend of Sam's family and the ringleader of the whole operation. The trial shook up the Stonebridge Police Department, and Sheldon was behind bars, along with his accomplices.

Nathan didn't talk much about it, but Sam understood his need for privacy. After his parents died in a car accident that left his brother comatose, he learned enough about grief and recovery to last a lifetime. On a more selfish note, he didn't want to bring Emma into the bedroom he'd been sharing with Nathan. As much as Sam liked Emma, competing with ghosts was pointless.

The kitten meowed. She arched her back into a stretch and regarded them with a wide, blue-eyed stare.

"She is cute, though, you have to admit," Nathan said. He still hadn't named it.

3

"So were the gremlins, and look what happened after midnight." With Nathan's warm skin against his back, Sam didn't care about the cat.

"I think you like her. Admit it."

"Call me paranoid, but I believe what they say about cats taking over the world. Haven't you ever seen *Life After People*?"

Nathan huffed a laugh against Sam's neck and chased it with a soft brush of his lips. Electricity sizzled between them as Nathan pressed his trouser-clad erection into Sam's ass from behind, and Sam ground back against it. Though he was tired from a long day of landscaping work in the business he co-owned with his friend Yuri, one part of Sam certainly wasn't tired. His cock thickened and pushed against the front of his boxer briefs, looking for something more solid to press against. Sam turned around so he and Nathan were chest-to-chest, or as close as they could come with the five inch difference in their height. Sam preferred tall guys, and Nathan fit the bill to a tee.

"Mmm, you feel good." Nathan ran his fingers along Sam's sides to tickle the sensitive skin of his waist. Sam batted him away and grabbed two handfuls of Nathan's firm ass.

"So do you." Sam nosed the stubbly skin of Nathan's jaw. He smelled like fresh cologne and only a slight hint of cigarette smoke. "You're not going to tell me how the meeting went?"

"It was fine."

"That's not very specific."

"Well, I found out I'm going to be traveling to DC soon."

"For how long?" Sam's stomach dropped. Nathan's work on a special FBI human-trafficking task force took him all over the country, sometimes for months at a time. Before they got together, one operation required Nathan to go undercover at a sex club. It was only part of the job, but if a similar case arose, Nathan would do what was needed to save innocent lives.

"Only a few days."

The sinking feeling didn't go away.

"What's wrong?" Nathan obviously felt the change in Sam's body language.

"Nothing."

"It's not that kind of case. This is strictly educational training for the local PD. I'm going to be leading a seminar."

"Teaching?" The warm flood of relief made Sam dizzy.

"Yeah. Apparently my boss thinks I'm the perfect guy to school a roomful of rookie cops about warning signs to look for when dealing with homeless juveniles." Nathan frowned and released Sam. He brushed the dirt off the bed, and the kitten attacked his hand. "If it goes well, he's going to have me teach other seminars up and down the east coast. It's not exactly what I would have chosen for myself."

"What about the rest of the team?" Sam climbed onto the bed after Nathan and got to work removing his trousers. Nathan put his hands behind his head and lifted his hips to assist.

"So far as I know, I'm the only one they asked."

"Well, that means you're the best, doesn't it? I think you'll be great." He straddled Nathan's thighs and leaned down to kiss him, but Nathan didn't seem as responsive as usual. Something about the teaching gig was bothering him, and Sam had a feeling they were going to do a lot more talking before sex happened. At one point, with another guy, maybe it would have annoyed him. But he was getting better at the whole relationship thing—at least he hoped he was.

Nathan raised a skeptical eyebrow. "Do you really?"

"Yeah. I do. You've got what it takes to be a good teacher."

"What's that supposed to mean?"

"It means you're patient but strict when you have to be, and you look hot in dress-up clothes." Sam liked the idea of Nathan in front of a classroom of students, though he wasn't sure what, if anything, the rookie cops would learn. If he were in their shoes, he'd be too distracted to do anything but stare, especially when Nathan got authoritative. Sam's mind ran wild with various scenarios—being bent over a desk while Nathan fucked him hard from behind. Nathan's dark eyes flashing, his mouth curling in a sexy, arrogant smile as he forced Sam to his knees. He ran his hands down Nathan's chest for emphasis and swiveled his hips provocatively.

"Hmm." Nathan still didn't seem convinced, though his cock started to perk up again.

"What? Are you nervous about standing in front of a roomful of cops?" Sam tried.

Nathan shook his head. "No. That part is fine. I actually might even enjoy it. I don't know why, but I can't help feeling this is some sort of retirement job. I haven't been assigned to a real case for months."

Ah, so that was it. At thirty-six, Nathan had eight years on Sam, but he was hardly geriatric. Sam didn't want to be dismissive, but he knew Nathan was only projecting his anxiety. Sam had a lot of experience with that kind of shit—they both did.

"You're not old enough to be put out to pasture yet," he said.

"Ha." Nathan gave him a halfhearted smile.

"I think you should feel flattered. It means you're smarter than everybody else. I'd have thought that would make you happy."

"Now you're calling me a know-it-all?" Nathan rolled them over so they were side by side, facing one another on the bed. He kissed Sam hard, but just as he seemed to be getting into it, the kitten decided to pounce. She insinuated herself between them and curled into a ball. Nathan cooed and scratched behind her ears.

"Cockblocked by a white, fluffy monster," Sam muttered with a sigh. He knew when he was beaten.

IN THE morning, Sam woke at the crack of dawn without his alarm—a new thing for him. Not being hungover was another. He stretched and smiled at the ceiling, glad he'd slept the night through without his nightmares returning. He contemplated whether to slip out of bed and make coffee or wake Nathan and finish what they'd started the night before, when the kitten rudely interrupted them.

Seizing the opportunity, Sam pressed his morning wood against Nathan's bare ass and kissed his neck. With their busy schedules, they rarely had the same day off, but that day they could spend hours in bed if they wanted. Nathan murmured something, on the border between sleep and wakefulness, and then he came fully alert with a slow blink and yawn.

"Hey, you."

"Oompf," Sam grunted as Nathan rolled on top of him. "Good morning, Professor. You don't mind if I call you that, do you?"

"If you do, I'll throttle you." Nathan sought out Sam's hard dick and gave it a squeeze.

"Is that a promise, Professor?"

"Do you want it to be?"

"Maybe." Sam's breath quickened in anticipation. They often kidded about Nathan dominating Sam in bed, but aside from some occasional roughhousing and dirty talk, they hadn't done anything about it. Sam wasn't sure why Nathan was holding back, since he obviously relished being in control. From what he told Sam about his undercover sexual experiences, he'd enjoyed being dominant when his job required it.

And Sam was growing certain he wanted to do more than joke. The idea of letting Nathan take charge of his pleasure got him so fired up his cock twitched and leaked against his belly as they kissed. He wasn't exactly sure how to ask, though, given Nathan's reticence. And from the covert Internet research he'd done on the subject, Sam felt out of his league.

"God, Sam." Nathan interrupted his wandering thoughts. "You're so damn sexy." He ran his thumb over the wet slit of Sam's dick, making Sam shudder.

"You're not so bad yourself."

"The things I want to do to you." Another slow stroke.

"I'm yours." He blushed after he said it, feeling cheesy. But Nathan smiled with a devilish glint in his eye, pushed the covers back, and kissed his way down to Sam's cock. His lips hovered an inch from the sensitive flesh, and he licked a hot stripe down the underside toward Sam's balls. Sam propped himself up on his elbows. He loved watching Nathan go down on him. Though he hadn't done it much at first, he seemed to enjoy sucking cock as much as Sam did—and Sam liked it a lot.

Sam's phone rang.

"Don't answer it." Nathan looked up at Sam from beneath sooty eyelashes.

Sam almost didn't, but the switch in his mind flipped from sex to panic once he recognized the ringtone. "Shit, it's Shady Brook. It must be about Tim."

"Of course." Nathan understood Sam's younger brother's life hung in a precarious balance. He released Sam, who leapt off the bed to search for his phone.

He answered with numb lips. Shady Brook rarely called unless it was an emergency. "Hello?"

"Hello, Sam? This is Lisa."

His stomach twisted when he heard the voice of his brother's nurse. Nathan sat naked on the bed, watching him with growing alarm.

"What's going on?" Sam asked.

"I'm sorry to call so early, but there was a fire in the building late last night, and we had to evacuate all our patients to local hospitals. Tim's at St. Mary's for the time being."

Sweat broke out on his brow. "Was he injured?"

"His vitals are steady, but we're keeping him under observation and treating for smoke inhalation to be on the safe side. So far, so good."

"What does that mean?" Sam's heart rate spiked again, and he felt sick. He reached for Nathan's hand. Tim was already vulnerable in his comatose state. Any additional complication might be enough to kill him.

"There was a lot of smoke in the building, and fine particulates can be damaging, but we'll be watching for infection over the next couple of days. I promise we'll do everything we can to make sure he's okay." As Lisa spoke, her voice cracked.

"What is it? There's something you aren't telling me."

"One of our nurses died." She sniffed. "He was sleeping in the break room, near where the fire broke out. By the time we figured out someone was missing, it was too late."

A lump lodged in Sam's throat. He needed to get to St. Mary's immediately. "Do they know how it started?"

"No idea, but it spread quickly. Luckily emergency services responded fast." Her voice broke again. "John was so young. He had a family. It's such a shame."

Sam frowned at Nathan, who squeezed his hand. "Fucking hell. Pardon my language."

"Sweetheart, if you had the kind of night I've had, you'd be saying much worse," Lisa said.

"I appreciate you letting me know. Can I visit him?" He'd planned to spend his morning off writing his blog, but until he saw his brother safe and sound, he wouldn't get anything done. Lisa let him know the visiting hours and assured him again the treatment was a purely precautionary measure. Sam started to relax, though his mind was still whirling.

After he hung up the phone, Sam filled Nathan in on the bits of conversation he'd missed.

"But Tim's going to be okay?" Nathan asked, his voice full of concern.

"He better be, or I'm going to sue the rest of the shingles off that place." Sam was already up and getting dressed. Something wasn't right. He had a bad feeling deep in his gut.

Nathan's expression seemed troubled. "What's up?"

"I was thinking about those other fires. Do you think they could be related?" There had been several car fires in the downtown area, and one in the suburbs of West Stonebridge. Most people thought it was teenagers, maybe gang related, but no one had been arrested. "I mean, think about it. When's the last time there was a major fire in this city, and now there's, what, four in a couple weeks?" There were small fires all the time in

Stonebridge, a mid-sized city of about 90,000, but few were big enough to make the evening news. Maybe Sam was paranoid, but he didn't like the sudden increase.

Nathan crossed his arms. "Well, they're different types of crimes. A car fire is property damage, and this fire, if it was arson at all, was intended to harm. Though I suppose it could be a sign of escalation."

"You mean whoever's responsible could be looking to make a bigger statement?"

Nathan nodded grimly. "Or get a bigger rush. I know you're concerned about Tim's safety, but I don't think you should jump to any conclusions yet, okay?"

Sam contemplated Nathan's words. Maybe he was right about Sam's emotional state. In any case, his main concern was lying helpless in a hospital bed across town. "Well, whatever it was, they better figure it out quick, or they'll have me to deal with. Tim could have been killed."

"You're going now?"

"Yeah." Sam buttoned his jeans. His erection had deflated as soon as he heard Lisa's voice. "Sorry for running off when things were getting interesting, but I need to see him."

"I'll come with you." Nathan pushed back the sheet around his waist.

"Nah. It's okay. I'm gonna head back to my place after to shower and change. I'll call you if there's any news." He came toward the bed and leaned down for a good-bye kiss. Nathan threaded his fingers through Sam's hair and held him close.

"Give him a hug for me?"

"Of course. I'll see you later?"

"Yeah. At the housewarming tonight."

"Dammit." Sam grimaced. He'd completely forgotten about Yuri and Michael's party—which was shocking because Yuri couldn't shut up about moving in with his boyfriend. He checked his cell phone. October third. "I didn't even get them anything yet."

"Don't worry about it. I'll have time to pick something up today."

"That would be great." Sam got a secret thrill at the idea of bringing a shared present, but he didn't let it show. Sometimes he worried their relationship was progressing too quickly. Even though they'd spent several months apart before they started dating—time to allow Nathan to grieve for his wife and to let Sam get his head on straight—he worried Nathan might realize he'd made a mistake. The intricate orchid tattoo on Nathan's shoulder was a beautiful, melancholy reminder of what he'd lost when Emma was murdered. Sam couldn't help feeling it was only a matter of time before something went wrong and broke them up.

He didn't know what he'd do if that happened. It was best, in these intimate moments, to play it cool. "I'll meet you there," he said, doing one last check for his wallet and keys. "Eight o'clock?"

"Eight o'clock." Nathan grinned. "And remember to play nice."

"What do you mean?" Sam grumbled. "I'm always nice."

"I mean you've been making comments about Yuri moving in with Michael for weeks."

"Only to you." It was no secret Sam preferred the city to the 'burbs. Even the street had an annoying name. Belleview Drive sounded like something out of a Disney film. He did hope Yuri would be happy there. He never would have been happy with Sam.

Chapter 2

SAM LOATHED hospitals. They reminded him of his parents' accident—long nights spent pacing the corridors, unable to sleep as his mother succumbed to her injuries. And then there was his own recent visit. He'd gotten a concussion and a pretty nasty scalp laceration from a run-in with the guys who killed Emma. He would be set for life if he never had to go back to St. Mary's.

His brother seemed paler than usual, even a little green, and Sam stared uneasily at the oxygen mask on his face—just as a precaution, the attending doctor said. Sam wasn't convinced.

"Heya, bud," Sam said, squeezing his brother's limp hand. "I was so worried when I heard what happened. You okay?" Tim stared at the ceiling. According to one of the on-duty nurses, several months before, Tim had made sounds in the middle of the night, but nothing else had happened since then. Sam almost hated that they'd told him about it. Every time he visited, his chest tightened and filled with painful hope. He hadn't heard Tim's voice in almost seven years.

He leaned down and smelled Tim's hair. It was fresh and clean—baby shampoo. No trace of smoke.

"Everything all right?" Lisa poked her head in and smiled wearily when she saw Sam. She wore brightly colored scrubs covered in blue and pink dolphins, but the dark circles under her eyes were evidence of a long, sleepless night.

"Hey, what are you doing here?"

"I didn't want to leave my patients until we're sure they're okay. I'll probably be here until the building's repaired and we can move everyone back."

He was so happy to see her, his voice caught in his throat. "That's great. I'm… I'm glad." At least complete strangers wouldn't be tending his brother.

Lisa crossed the room with her clipboard and wrote down some of the vitals from the bedside monitors. "Where's your handsome man?"

Nathan had bonded with Lisa when he took it upon himself to pay—behind Sam's back—for Tim's continued private care. Since then, he'd become a regular fixture on visiting days.

"At home. I wanted to spend some time with Tim alone."

She nodded sympathetically. "I sure hope they catch whoever did it—fast."

Sam's shoulders tensed. "So they confirmed it's arson?"

"It seems to be. I don't know any of the details yet. But Tim is doing well, sweetie. He's in good hands. Let me know if you need anything, okay?"

"Thanks, Lisa."

She patted him on the arm and left.

Sam looked at his brother's peaceful form, and a fierce, protective urge welled inside of him. He wondered what it would be like to have Tim at home, where he could watch over him. The idea of constant, round-the-clock care had once seemed terrifying. He was afraid of leaving Tim alone, of something happening. The guilt would be unbearable. But if he got a bigger place and hired a nurse when he was working, he could probably manage. For a moment, he indulged himself in a fantasy—living with Nathan and Tim, together as a family. Maybe it would be the stimulation Tim needed to finally wake up.

"How would you like that, bud? Living with me? We could have some awesome parties." Sky blue eyes stared blankly, clear and trouble free. He decided he'd table the idea and do some cost comparison. Letting Nathan pay the care center bills still made him uncomfortable, but he would do whatever was necessary to make a safe, stable home for his baby brother.

Sam opened the book he brought and settled on the chair next to Tim's bed. He was in the middle of *Moby Dick*. It seemed like the kind of book his brother would like. As an added bonus, Sam suspected Ishmael and Queequeg were gay for each other. "Sharing a bed for warmth, my ass," Sam said, and got down to reading until visiting hours were over.

AT A little after eight, Sam met Nathan and the rest of their friends at Yuri and Michael's place, a two-story Cape Cod in the suburbs of West Stonebridge.

"There you are." Rachel, one of Sam's best friends, strode across the room with a glass of wine in hand. She was punked out with streaks of purple in her teased Afro and sporting her favorite black leather vest. Her girlfriend, Alex, was talking to Michael's family on the other side of the room, and she waved and smiled at Sam. Rachel wrapped him up in a fierce hug, and her wine sloshed dangerously. "I didn't know if you were coming—because of what happened."

"I wouldn't have missed it," said Sam, hugging her back. His eyes met Nathan's over Rachel's shoulder, and Sam's breath hitched. Dressed in all black, Nathan looked edible—and slightly dangerous.

Finally Rachel released him, and Yuri joined the group. His dimples deepened and his dark eyes flashed warmly as he greeted Sam. "I appreciate you being here. Is Tim okay?"

"He seems to be. They're giving him some precautionary antibiotics, but they don't expect any complications." Still, Sam couldn't quite shake a feeling of unease. He gave Yuri a small smile and punched his muscled arm. "The place looks good."

The house had a home-furnishing catalogue vibe, like everything had been purchased all together. It was still mostly Michael's stuff. A framed Yankees World Series poster, autographed by the '09 team, was the only thing in the living room Sam remembered from Yuri's old place. He refrained from commenting, however. Mentioning it would only give Yuri another reason to gloat about the Sox's shitty last season. "You've done a great job with the—" He glanced around. "Couch pillows."

"Congratulations on your color coordination. And your new life together." Nathan smiled conspiratorially at Sam and handed Yuri the bag he was holding.

"Let's see the place," Rachel said to Yuri, linking her arm through his. "Where's Michael?"

Michael was with a young woman he introduced as his sister Katherine, a history major at the local college. She was a plain, shy girl who mumbled a greeting and went back to sitting quietly next to her boyfriend, an older man with glasses and an academic air. Michael's parents, the Smiths, and Yuri's mother were present as well. Several work friends from both sides rounded out the party.

Those who hadn't yet had the pleasure of a tour snaked their way up the staircase and down the hall toward the master bedroom, and Sam and Nathan went along. This wasn't the first time they'd visited Michael's house, but Sam could tell Yuri was excited to show them around more formally.

"So this is where the magic happens," said Rachel, poking her nose into things. "Where do you guys keep the lube?" Alex elbowed her in the side when Michael's parents exchanged an uneasy look.

Sam found it difficult to focus on his friends' banter while his mind kept drifting back to Tim and his visit earlier in the day. He took a long walk afterward to clear his head, but he still wasn't completely sorted. Almost unconsciously he reached out for Nathan's hand. If anyone would understand, he would.

DOWNSTAIRS, SAM hung to the side as glasses were refilled and people chatted. He was starting to get the hang of being in social situations without drinking. He could even ignore the cravings, if he tried hard enough. Nathan joined him, handed him a seltzer, and gave him a quizzical look.

"Is there something you're not telling me about Tim?"

"No. He's okay." He fought for words that wouldn't make him seem paranoid. On the other side of the room, Michael talked with Katherine and her boyfriend, who laughed loudly at something one of them said. "But it gave me the heebie-jeebies seeing him at St. Mary's. I couldn't stop thinking about what might have happened if they didn't get him out in time."

Nathan rubbed his arm. "I understand."

Even so, Sam wanted to change the subject. "So what did we get the happy couple? Not a set of Mr. & Mr. hand towels, I hope."

Nathan smirked. "*We* got them a Red Sox throw blanket."

Sam's mouth dropped open. "I knew there was a reason I was dating you."

"I thought you'd approve."

"You are a perfect man."

Nathan bowed. "Thank you. By the way, I spoke to Tony earlier today, but he doesn't have any information yet." An FBI buddy of Nathan's, Antonio Rivera, had been assigned to help sort out Stonebridge's police department after the trial put the old police chief behind bars. The feds wanted to make sure the same kind of rampant corruption didn't take root again. Sam had only met the guy a couple of times.

"I was thinking of writing something about it. Especially if it turns out the fires are related."

Nathan smiled, and one corner of his full mouth lifted. He was supportive of *Under the Bridge*, Sam's blog, where he reported on local and, increasingly, national news. "Sounds good."

"What are you guys plotting over here?" asked Rachel, joining them. "You look so serious." She put her hand on Sam's arm, and her silver bracelets jangled.

Sam had given her the brief version on the phone, but he hadn't mentioned his concern that the fires might be connected. Instead of seeming skeptical, as he expected, she nodded thoughtfully.

"You know, when I heard about this latest one, I thought the same thing."

"You did?" Sam asked.

"So many, in such a short period of time? Made me wonder if the person is getting more, I don't know, adventurous."

"That's exactly what we were talking about this morning," Sam said. Nathan wrapped his arm around Sam's waist to pull him closer, and Sam's stomach flipped at the affectionate gesture.

"You don't think it's a coincidence?" Rachel asked Nathan.

"Well, I can't say I'm as convinced as Sam, but arsonists are like other criminals. If they're not caught, they're unlikely to stop, especially if they're thrill seeking. At the very least, it could be a copycat."

A few of the other guests had caught wind of their conversation and gathered around.

"Did you know the nurse who was killed?" Rachel asked Sam.

"No, he worked in a different ward," Sam said, slightly ashamed to be thinking so much of Tim when someone had died.

"I'm sorry to hear your brother was involved," said Michael's mother. "What a horrible thing to burn a hospital." Mrs. Smith was a short, gray-haired woman with a tremulous voice. Her husband stood next to her holding a glass of whiskey, and the smell made Sam's mouth water. He tried not to inhale too deeply.

"He's fine. Well, he's in a coma, so he's not exactly fine, but he wasn't badly hurt either."

"I'm glad to hear it," said Katherine's boyfriend, who joined the group along with Katherine. He wrapped a protective arm around her, and she seemed to shrink against him. "They don't have any idea who might have done it?"

"No. Not yet, unfortunately."

"It's scary, when you think about it," said Alex. "This guy could be right under our noses. He could be anyone."

Michael looked from guest to guest, an uncomfortable expression on his face. The party had certainly taken a turn for the depressing. "Well, what do you all think? Anyone up for a friendly game of poker?"

Various murmurs of assent and relief echoed through the room.

During the game, Sam found himself on the couch, wedged between Yuri and Katherine. Sam folded early in the round, and then it was down to Nathan and Alex. The latter turned out to be quite the card shark. Nathan, Sam was learning, had an obvious tell. He liked to think it wouldn't have been noticeable if they weren't lovers, but every time Nathan had a good hand, he looked at Sam.

Nathan concentrated intently as Alex reraised. Even though his face was carefully blank, Sam could tell he wasn't happy with his cards. Later Sam would have to tease Nathan for being a shitty poker player, maybe give him a reason to go further with their own personal game—the one they'd been skirting around for months. The thought gave him a semi in his jeans, and he shifted in his seat and hoped no one would notice.

Nathan was more observant. Almost as though their brains were connected, he glanced over and arched an eyebrow. He had a teasing, knowing look in his eyes, and as corny as it sounded—even in Sam's head—for a minute, there was no one else in the room.

"You two want to use the bedroom, or can you make it till you get home?" Yuri whispered in his ear, not loud enough for anyone else to hear.

"I think we'll manage." Sam's cheeks warmed at being caught staring. Given his past with Yuri, talking about his sex life wasn't the most comfortable topic, but he knew Yuri was happy with Michael. His own relationship with Yuri had been strained for a while. What Sam thought was a series of casual encounters to blow off steam had meant more to Yuri, and Sam's insensitivity had almost ruined their friendship. But it was all in the past.

"How's married life?" Sam asked.

Yuri looked over at Michael, who was fiddling with his phone. The hand folded with Alex as the victor yet again, and when Nathan went to deal another round of cards, Yuri and Sam declined and got up to continue their conversation in the kitchen.

It was a bright, newly remodeled space with an island and a set of gleaming silver pots suspended from the ceiling. Even Sam, who was a terrible cook at the best of times, could appreciate the improvement from Yuri's old place.

"Speaking of married life, I should ask you the same question," Yuri said with a gleam in his eye. "You two seem like you're spending a lot of time together. Thinking about taking the next step?"

Sam almost choked on his drink. "You mean moving in together? No, it's way too early. It's different than with you and Michael," he amended.

Yuri shrugged. "It's weird, isn't it? You, me, Rachel. All of us coupled up. I never thought I'd live to see the day when you were off the market."

There seemed to be a wistful note in Yuri's voice, but before Sam could confirm it, Katherine entered the kitchen with two empty bottles. She didn't seem old enough to drink—but maybe Sam simply perceived her shyness as youth. Yuri gave her an encouraging smile. "Hey, Kat. You need something?"

"Yes, thanks. Benedict wants another beer." She resisted meeting Sam's gaze, though he gave her a friendly nod.

"Help yourself."

"Okay," she said again, flushing as she darted around Sam and Yuri at the kitchen island.

"Anyway," Yuri said, continuing the conversation. "Maybe you two should move in together. Nathan's apartment is nice, and yours is a shithole. It's a wonder you haven't been robbed. Your windows don't even lock."

"Only the one in my bedroom." Sam stuck his tongue out. "Besides, I live on the fourth floor. If anyone wants to rob me, they're welcome to my old shit. And since when did you become a Real Housewife?"

His comment earned him a shove, and Sam shoved back. Both of them laughed just like old times. It was good to be like this with Yuri without the weight of unrequited feelings between them. Katherine hurried out of the kitchen like a scared mouse.

"She's shy," said Yuri, once the kitchen door swung shut and they were alone.

"I've noticed. What's her deal, anyway?"

Yuri ran his finger over the rim of his glass. "Michael's been trying to get her to come out of her shell, but the past year has been hard. She took some pills a few months ago."

"Shit." He felt a pang of empathy for her.

"She's doing better now. Enrolled in some classes at Stonebridge College to finish her degree. We're letting her crash here until she finds a job and gets her own place."

"And that's okay with you?" Sam raised his eyebrows.

"It's only temporary. She doesn't get along great with the parents, you know? They hover too much and they don't like Benedict. He was her professor last year and he's a lot older. So she's staying in the guest room."

"Michael seems like a good brother."

Yuri blushed like the compliment had been directed at him instead of Michael. "He's great."

Sam slapped his friend's arm. "Let's go save Nathan before he loses all his money to Alex."

POKER TURNED into another card game, and then another, until most of the guests left. Sam kept mulling over his brief conversation with Yuri in the kitchen, particularly the casual way he asked whether Sam and Nathan were getting serious. He'd seemed so nonchalant, like it wouldn't have surprised him at all if they moved in together. Sam didn't need a shrink to figure out why the idea, though appealing, made him nervous. These things always came to an end. What if, when it didn't work out, Sam couldn't pick up the pieces?

"You want to come back to my place?" Nathan asked as they headed toward Sam's parked truck.

Sam hesitated. He was in a weird mood and wasn't sure he would be good company. "I've hardly been at my apartment the last couple of weeks. There're some things I need to catch up on," he said lamely, not even sure why he was saying no.

Nathan's smile grew slightly thinner. "All right. Give me a call."

"Of course. Maybe tomorrow. I'm sorry, I'm just—the fire, and Tim…."

"It's okay. Seriously. Go home. Do what you need to do."

The cool, fall night was crisp, and leaves crunched under their feet. It reminded Sam they had made tentative plans to go camping in the Adirondacks but had never solidified them. He imagined a small cabin in the woods with no electricity and only Nathan for company, days of hiking and building fires in the evening to warm their food, which would taste even better after the time outdoors. He wondered if Nathan still wanted to go.

They said their good-byes and kissed. Sam climbed into his truck alone.

He sat for a while in the darkness, until the headlights of Nathan's Mercedes disappeared from view.

Chapter 3

"AREN'T YOU going to be late?" Nathan asked. He strode into the living room and buttoned his crisp white shirt. Sam glanced at the time. *Shit.* He snapped his laptop shut.

He'd been doing some research for his latest piece and wound up looking at some kinky porn sites instead. His hard-on was probably pretty obvious. Nathan paused and arched an eyebrow.

"Working *hard* or hardly working?"

"Ha ha. Very punny. You're right, though. I have to get going or I'm gonna be late for my interview."

"Are you sure you need to go? I can call in sick." Nathan's eyes glinted provocatively as Sam stood and adjusted himself.

Whenever Nathan's voice took on that deep, sexy edge, Sam found it nearly impossible to resist. He hesitated and then blew out a breath. "I can't."

"Won't you at least tell me what you were looking at?"

"Maybe later." He slipped his computer into his bag. It wasn't time to get into the conversation he wanted to have with Nathan. Though round two was incredibly tempting, he'd told Shelby Newton, the YMCA volunteer-program coordinator, he'd be there by 9:00 a.m. He wasn't running away—not at all. He evaded Nathan's gaze and slung his bag over his shoulder. "I'll see you tonight for dinner?"

Nathan snagged him by the back of his jeans, and Sam's erection pulsed with excitement as he found himself manhandled back into Nathan's arms. His dick wasn't interested in keeping appointments.

"Are you sure everything is okay?" Nathan asked.

Sam plastered an innocent expression on his face. "Yeah. I'm sure. But I should probably wipe my browser history before I open my laptop at the

Y." He thought of one particular video he'd found—one guy gagged and tied up on the bed, unable to move as his lover edged him almost to orgasm and then backed off again—and again and again—until he finally got permission to come, and he exploded, whimpering *thank you thank you* in a muffled voice. Fuck. Sam had to get it together, or he would never leave.

"All right. Clearly you're not ready to talk about it. You're driving me crazy, though. Just so you know." Nathan palmed Sam's hard cock through his jeans. Sam groaned, and his body started to melt. He supposed being a little late wouldn't hurt.

SAM HOPPED in his truck and drove to the old Y near the docks. He wondered why he was having such a hard time telling Nathan what he wanted in the bedroom. Maybe it was because he was used to taking without talking.

He wasn't shy, but he'd been drunk during most of the sex he'd had before Nathan. Aside from the basic conversations about position preferences and what felt good, he hadn't talked about sex much with those guys. He knew it should be easier with Nathan, because they cared about each other. When they first got acquainted, Nathan admitted he'd almost become addicted to the thrill of anonymous sex—and the dominant role he'd performed in his undercover work. Maybe he preferred to keep that part of his life separate. Maybe he didn't want that sort of relationship with Sam.

And Sam didn't want to fuck up what they had. He didn't want Nathan to see him as less than an equal. What did it mean for him to want to be bound like the guy in the video… to submit? He hated the idea that Nathan might think he was weak.

Preoccupied with these thoughts, he almost missed the turnoff for the Y. He had to slam on his brakes and make a sharp right turn, pissing off the guy behind him. He got the finger and a whole lot of expletives shouted out the open car window, and as he coasted into a space in the mostly full lot, he hoped there weren't any kids around to hear.

Shelby Newton's office smelled of glue and stale donuts. She was a recent college grad with a round face and a pug nose, and her excitement about the program was clear from the moment they started walking toward the rec room.

"The incentives seem to be working," she said. "And eventually we hope the participants will come to see the benefits inherent in their volunteer work and won't need to be rewarded. Intrinsic motivation is more powerful in the long run."

Sam nodded and glanced at the colorful artwork lining the halls. As part of Mayor White's "Streets Clean for 2015" plan, high school students who spent their afternoons tutoring and playing with younger children received "credits" at participating stores for discounts on clothing, music, food, and other stuff teenagers wanted. Adult volunteers, many of them from the local college, provided tutoring for high school dropouts studying for their GEDs and helped with job placement. The whole thing used bribery to get bored kids off the streets and into more productive social roles.

When he first heard about it, he was skeptical, but after checking out the newly refurbished rec room and tutoring space, he reexamined his previous stance on the mayor's plan. At least thirty teenagers of varying ages were hanging out with the younger kids. While Sam had imagined they would be phoning it in to get the discounts, he was surprised at how engaged they seemed. One girl, maybe around fifteen, sat in a corner with two little kids, reading them a book. Their eyes were wide as she turned the page and leaned forward with a conspiratorial whisper.

"That's Lakshmi," said Shelby. "She's a great storyteller." Sam nodded and jotted down some notes. Maybe, after she was finished with the book, he'd talk to her.

Another teenager wearing a Red Sox T-shirt and jeans watched as he passed by. He had a wary look on his face, and he paused in whatever he was saying to the little blond boy on his right, who was drawing a picture. The two of them would have been a great advertisement for the program—one light, one dark—a perfect display of racial unity. Shelby grabbed Sam's arm and thrust him forward. The little kid appeared to be drawing a giant Technicolor walrus.

"Damon," Shelby said to the teenager, "this is Sam Flynn. Sam, Damon Blake. Damon, Sam's doing an article on the program for his news blog, *Under the Bridge*. Isn't that great?"

"Nice to meet you," said Sam. "You a Sox fan? Man after my own heart."

Damon's eyes flicked over him, assessing, and he gave a quick nod of his head. He leaned back in the undersized chair at the art table and spread his legs wide.

"Can I ask you some questions?" Sam asked.

Damon shrugged. "Guess so."

"Will you excuse me for a minute?" Shelby asked.

An argument had broken out among some of the other kids, and Sam nodded and watched as Shelby turned to address the situation. Once he was alone with Damon, he dragged up a tiny chair and got out his recorder.

"Do you mind if I use this?" Sam asked.

"Whatever," said Damon. The little blond boy had gone back to his drawing.

"So, how long have you been volunteering?"

"Dunno. Couple months."

"And how did you first hear about the program?"

Damon sighed. "My foster parents made me. I'm taking some classes to study for my GED."

"But it seems like you've wound up volunteering your own time, as well? How come?" Sam gestured to the little kid.

Damon gave Sam a challenging look. "Because they give you discounts on sh—stuff," he said. "Why do you think?"

Sam realized he wasn't going to get anywhere with Damon. He scrubbed his hand over his face, flicked off his recorder, and figured he'd try his luck elsewhere. The little boy tugged on Damon's arm.

"D, look what I do."

"Look what I *did*," Damon said patiently.

"Look what I *did*," repeated the little boy. He smiled and held up his picture. "Do you like it?" he asked Sam.

"Yeah. It's great. What is it?"

"It's a doggy."

Sam glanced at the picture. It didn't look like a walrus anymore. In fact, with the smoke coming out of its nostrils, the massive horns—were they ears?—and the red eyes, it looked more like a demon.

Sam stifled his laugh behind his hand and cleared his throat. "Oh yes, I can tell now. That's… a pretty awesome dog. What's its name?"

"Spot."

This time Sam couldn't hold back. He laughed as his eyes met Damon's over the table. Damon was biting his bottom lip to hold back his own laughter. He tousled the little kid's hair. "Nice one, Patrick."

Patrick beamed.

Sam talked to a couple more teenaged tutors and one adult mentor, and by the time he left the Y, he was feeling pretty optimistic about this aspect of the mayor's plan. Beyond the cash incentives, most participants seemed genuinely engaged in or helped by the program. Shelby asked him to come back anytime, and he said he would.

HE SPENT the rest of the afternoon writing, until Nathan showed up with a steaming bag of Thai food. After they ate, they cuddled on Sam's hideous floral couch and watched stupid reality TV. Nathan rested his head in Sam's lap, and Sam dragged his hands through Nathan's soft, almost black hair, which was only subtly peppered with premature gray. Nathan closed his eyes and nearly purred when Sam rubbed his scalp. Sam chuckled.

"What's so funny?" Nathan murmured.

"I was thinking. It's no wonder you like cats so much. You practically are one."

Nathan opened one eye. "Then I hope you like cats more than you pretend to."

"I like this one." He scritched again, and Nathan sighed and nestled closer. His long body took up the entire sofa.

After a few minutes, Nathan said, "My mother used to massage my scalp when I was sick." The show they'd been half watching ended, and Sam flicked off the TV. It was nice being alone and quiet with Nathan. He could smell Nathan's aftershave and his sandalwood-scented shampoo as he scratched.

"Were you sick a lot?"

"Not really. But some of my favorite memories are of being sick. Like the time I had chicken pox, and I had to stay home from school for a week. I don't remember how awful it felt, but I do remember my mother singing to me in Italian and stroking my hair. Isn't that strange?"

Sam held his breath. Nathan rarely spoke about his childhood. "No. I don't think it's strange. You never told me you were Italian." He had often suspected it, though, in spite of Nathan's English-sounding last name.

Nathan nodded. "My mother is Italian and Lebanese. She lived in Rome until she was fifteen."

"That's awesome. Have you ever been?"

"A few times. My grandmother lives in Switzerland, but she has a house in Rome." Nathan wrinkled his nose like he expected Sam to chastise him for coming from a wealthy family. Sam's family hadn't exactly been poor, but there was no denying the difference in their backgrounds. And Nathan wasn't one to flaunt his money—much.

"Any time you want to whisk me away to a sunny Roman villa, I'm A-OK with it," Sam joked.

Nathan turned to look up at him. His content expression softened his patrician features, making him seem vulnerable. Sam's heart swelled again, thinking how lucky he was that Nathan trusted him. He figured he might as well ask another question while he had the chance.

"What was it like growing up in California? I've never been."

Nathan seemed to weigh his answer. A line formed between his dark eyebrows. "It was always perfect. The weather, the people. At least on the outside. I grew up thinking everyone had a comfortable life."

Sam remembered the boy with the sad eyes in the few photographs Nathan kept from the country house he shared with Emma. There was definitely more to his story than he'd admitted.

"And your father traveled a lot?"

"He was in the import/export business, always flying to Tokyo, Hong Kong, Dubai. I stayed home with my mother. She didn't work. I think she wanted a bigger family, but after me, she couldn't have any more children." Nathan sighed. "I should call her." He sounded guilty.

"You don't visit much."

"It's difficult. My father and I don't have a very good relationship, as you've probably guessed. I don't think he ever forgave me for not going into the family business. He's retired now, puttering around the house and irritating my mother."

"He can't disapprove of your job."

Nathan snorted. "My father disapproves of everyone and everything, except himself. But I wanted to be like him when I was a kid. He always seemed important, with his fancy car, his fancy clothes."

Sam hesitated to point out Nathan's car wasn't exactly a junker—nor were his clothes—but Nathan must have caught his expression. He smirked. "I never said I wasn't like him in some ways. But my mother and I were only accessories to him. He could point to his colleagues and say he had a wife and a son—two marks off the 'successful man' checklist."

Sam hadn't always had an easy relationship with his father, but he'd never been treated like an adornment instead of a person. At least he never doubted his father's love, even when they fought.

"Maybe it's cliché, but I wanted him to be proud of me," Nathan continued. "So I went to Yale, like he did, and I enrolled in the business school. I hated it." He grabbed Sam's hand and kissed each of his fingertips, then let it go, presumably so Sam could continue the scalp massage. "During my sophomore year, my father got audited by the IRS. They didn't find anything, but I knew he'd broken the law. He wasn't even sorry about it. I confronted him, and he called me a hypocrite... which I was, of course... using his money for school. But I was taking classes in political science and sociology, meeting new people and hearing about injustices all over the world. It made me realize I wanted to help people. I figured, once I graduated, I could make a difference."

Hearing Nathan talk so passionately of the things he learned in college was incredibly sexy. Sam wondered if he should suggest taking their conversation to the bedroom, but he didn't want Nathan to stop. "Don't tell me you joined the Young Democrats."

"Worse," said Nathan.

"Not the Socialists." Sam pretended to be shocked. "Wait a second, the Communists?" He gestured dramatically with his hand to his head. "Dear heavens."

They laughed. Sam pushed all of his recent worries to the back of his mind and leaned down for a kiss. He felt lighter and closer to Nathan than he had in days.

Chapter 4

SAM SIPPED his morning coffee and booted up his laptop. He'd stayed home alone the night before because he needed a good night's rest for the major landscaping project he, Yuri, and the crew were starting that day.

The headline of the *Gazette* caught his eye. Another fire. He started to read and frowned as the grim news got worse.

A fire broke out in the early morning hours and destroyed a duplex in downtown Stonebridge, leaving two people dead and one firefighter seriously injured. The four-alarm blaze began on the first floor and quickly spread to the rest of the structure. Firefighters responded quickly and stopped the flames from consuming nearby homes. Aided by police, the fire marshal is investigating the fire as a suspected arson, the latest in a string of fires in Stonebridge and the surrounding community.

Eighteen-year-old Lindsey Krause, a senior at East Stonebridge High, and her father, fifty-two-year-old Scott Krause, both died in the blaze. Citizens are urged to use caution and report any suspicious activity to the hotline set up by the Stonebridge Police Department....

The article concluded with details about a memorial service for the victims, set up by their surviving family members. Sam's gut curdled like he'd eaten something rotten. It had been over a week since the fire at Shady Brook, which had been ruled arson because of traces of accelerant found at the scene. Sam had hoped, perhaps foolishly, it would be the end. But this new fire erased any hope they were going to get off so easily. Three people were dead, and if the culprit wasn't caught, it looked like more deaths might follow. Sam reread the text with increasing horror. The destroyed building wasn't very far from where he lived.

Sam stared out his window at the building on the other side of the street. Either one of them could have been burned. He knew people over there. He knew people all over the city. He thought of all the patients at Shady Brook who might have been killed. Some had suffered more severe smoke inhalation than Tim.

If the cops had any leads, the new chief of police wasn't talking, nor were they forthcoming with details of either fire. When Sam called him on the way to work, Nathan explained that the police were trying to avoid copycats. As with any crime, the more specifics relayed to the public, the greater the chance another person might try his hand for a share of the attention. People did fucked-up shit.

SAM TOOK the next day off to do some research. He couldn't find anything to connect either of the new victims to the Shady Brook fire or to the first fatality, the nurse, John Berringer. On social media, people were talking about how lovely Lindsey had been—she was a track star, a cheerleader, and a good student. Scott Krause had been a janitor until he'd recently started collecting disability. Thankfully the other side of the duplex where he lived with his daughter had been vacant at the time, or else more people might have died.

And then there were the comments Sam read in the online group in support of the fire victims. The arsonist had to be brought to justice, and people needed an outlet to vent their frustrations and express their support for those affected. But some posts made Sam bristle.

"Listen to this one," he exclaimed, turning from his desk to face Nathan, who was lounging on the bed, reading. He was still shirtless after their morning sex, but Sam was too angry for distractions.

"What now?"

Sam cleared his throat and read aloud. "I think it's the work of Muslim extremists. No red-blooded American would ever do such a terrible thing. We should've bombed those bastards off the planet."

Nathan closed his book and sat up on the bed. "Sadly it doesn't surprise me one bit."

Sam nodded. "And there's more. I mean, no one knows who set the fires. It could be anyone, but this forum is an easy way for assholes to let their persecution fantasies run wild."

"It's disgusting," Nathan agreed, frowning. "I hope not all the comments are like that?"

"No. There are some people objecting. Not enough, though." Sam turned back to his computer and started typing. "At least my rage has me inspired. I really need to talk to some people. You wanna go for a walk down to the station?"

"That doesn't sound like much fun." Nathan's voice darkened.

The feds had played a major role in cleaning things up at the precinct, but tensions had grown between the agents who were brought in and the local police officers, who felt their toes were being stepped on. Nathan's close connection to Antonio Rivera, the federal agent in charge, made Nathan an unwelcome entity.

Sam glanced away from his monitor. "Yeah. I figure the chief dislikes you enough we might get in to see her, just so she can tell you off."

Nathan raised an eyebrow. "Well, when you put it that way." He swung his feet over the side of the bed. "If she starts in on me—"

"I'll protect you. I think she likes me."

"As far as she likes anyone."

He thought he might have to come up with some more convincing rationale to get Nathan to agree, but Nathan surprised him by shrugging on his shirt. Sam couldn't hide his grin. He liked the idea of looking into the case with Nathan, and he wondered what it would be like to be Nathan's work partner for real. Of course it was a mere fantasy. He didn't have the training or the credentials, and Nathan would never put him in danger. The idea held an allure, all the same.

They finished dressing while they shot theories back and forth. Then they left Sam's apartment and fell into companionable banter on the cracked, leaf-covered sidewalk. A clear, blue October sky arched over the city, and the bracing wind coming from the Sound made Sam glad he wore a sweater. As their arms brushed together, Sam glanced appreciatively at Nathan, who hadn't shaved. His strong jaw was covered in dark stubble. The small lines etched into his skin at the corners of his eyes deepened as he squinted into the sunlight and laughed at something Sam said. And then, only seconds later, his mouth curved seductively, and he looked like he might want to pull Sam into the closest alleyway and ravish him. There was something slightly dangerous about him, even after all their months together.

Sam couldn't lie to himself. He would probably go for it.

The station came into view, and he put the thought out of his mind. Time to get down to business.

THE CHIEF was in a meeting when they arrived, but they loitered long enough to catch her on her way to grab a coffee. A few minutes later, they found themselves on the other side of a desk that had once belonged to a man Sam believed was a friend, but who turned out to be the worst kind of enemy.

Donna Howard was nothing like her predecessor, the corrupt Chief Sheldon. She had a brusque, businesslike manner and didn't beat around the bush. Her steel gray hair complemented her eyes and was cut in a sharp, angular bob to match her personality. But that didn't mean she had nothing to hide, or that she couldn't manipulate people for her own ends. During their few interactions over the past months, Sam concluded that she simply found it tedious.

She certainly seemed to find their presence tedious as she stared them down from behind trendy wire-rimmed glasses. When she spoke, she directed her attention at Sam.

"You're here because of the arsons. I get it. Believe me when I say I wish I had something to tell you, but we've got nothing. Nada. Zip." Her thick Brooklyn accent, evidence of the city where she'd lived and made a name for herself before moving north, almost made Sam smile. He stopped himself in the nick of time.

"Have you made any arrests?" Sam asked.

"No arrests, but we've questioned about everyone in town, feels like. We've got the best fire guys on the beat. Shouldn't take long to turn something up. And God help me, we better, before someone else gets hurt."

"You think they're gang related?" Sam leaned forward in his chair. "That's what they're saying online."

The chief shook her head, and her hair swooshed. "Doesn't have the markings of a gang turf war. I've seen enough of them to know. This isn't about pissing on a hydrant, but I don't know what it *is* about. The only one who knows is the person—or people—lighting the fires, and they're not talking." She pursed her thin lips, and they paled to match her skin.

"Look," Sam said. "This case has hit close to home for me. My brother's at Shady Brook, and he suffered from smoke inhalation during the fire."

"I'm sorry to hear it."

"He's okay, but it could have been much worse. I don't want him going back there until whoever's doing this is caught."

She folded her manicured hands on her desk. "We're running analysis on burn patterns, fuel sources, and ignition techniques to look for similarities, but those reports won't be ready for another week, at least. We've combed surveillance vids from near the duplex down on Pine. Nothing out of the ordinary has turned up so far, and nothing from over at Shady Brook. Looks like their cameras were down."

"It could have been an inside job, then. A disgruntled employee, maybe?" Nathan hadn't said much during the conversation, aside from a politely strained hello. Chief Howard met his remark with an icy smile. Nathan, always a consummate professional, didn't seem fazed by the treatment. He kept his expression neutral.

"Yes," she said simply.

"Or a disgruntled patient," Sam added to get her attention back on him. According to what Nathan heard from Rivera, the Shady Brook arsonist had specifically targeted the nurses' overnight break room, and whoever was responsible for the crimes was certainly unstable.

"We're looking into both avenues. Yep."

"But what's the connection to the Krause duplex, or the car fires?" Sam was turning over all of the options, trying to connect dots that resisted connection. It was possible the seeming randomness of the targets could simply be a matter of the investigators missing a crucial link. Or the fires could be arbitrary, set for nothing more than the enjoyment of a pyromaniac. "Seems to me there are three options. Either the victims are connected, the targets are connected, or it's entirely random." Sam snorted. "I guess that's not very helpful."

"No," Nathan said. "It is. Maybe it was a former tenant who lived in the duplex, someone trying to get back at the landlord. The cars could have been practice. Anyone used to live in the building who has a connection to Shady Brook? What about Lindsey Krause's mother?"

"She's dead. Leukemia. A few years ago," said Chief Howard.

"Hmm."

They continued to talk, and Sam's attention split as he surveyed the room and noted how changed it was from the cluttered and homey office of Dan Sheldon. The walls had been repainted, and aside from a cactus on her desk and a photo Sam couldn't see, there were so few personal touches it verged on antiseptic. In some ways, the differences were comforting. Sam fought a shudder as he remembered the way Sheldon had stared at him from where Chief Howard sat, lying through his teeth about Nathan's involvement in his wife's murder. He balled his hands into fists and took a deep breath as anger made his pulse speed. Times like this, he really wanted a drink.

"You all right?" Nathan asked under his breath. The chief—obviously reaching the end of her tolerance at their intrusion—had taken a phone call and sat with her swivel chair facing away.

Sam nodded, though his heart was still hammering. Since he'd made up his mind to stop drinking, he'd only slipped once—and no one knew but Rachel and Alex. He'd shown up at their place one night, drunk off his ass, about three weeks after the trial ended. He was ashamed enough not to tell Nathan.

Most days he could ignore the thirsty devil clawing at the back of his mind, the one that said having a beer couldn't hurt—not just one. But then he remembered how hard it was to stop once he started. He remembered all of those days going to work hungover, and all of the men he'd never called back. All of the times he'd told himself he didn't have a problem with alcohol and pushed down the troublesome doubts. He didn't want to be that guy anymore. He liked himself much better now—and he had a feeling Nathan wouldn't stick around if he started drinking again.

"You don't look all right," said Nathan. "What's wrong?" It sounded like the chief was wrapping up her call, and Sam didn't want her to see him losing it.

He forced a smile. "Nothing. Nothing's wrong."

After she hung up, Chief Howard stood and faced them. "This has been interesting, gentlemen, but if you'll excuse me, I have an arsonist to catch."

The matter-of-factness of her tone got Sam back on track. He shook off the panic and rose to his feet.

"So you don't mind if I do a bit of digging around?"

She arched a perfectly manicured eyebrow—another difference between her and Sheldon. "I'm not saying anything official, but the more eyes and ears open, the better. If you do turn up anything, call me immediately."

"Will do."

"And you—" She turned to Nathan. "If you see him, you can tell your friend Rivera to stop sniffing around my crime scenes. This case is still under my jurisdiction. We have it under control."

Later, once they'd been seated for lunch at a nearby pizzeria, Nathan brought the conversation back to Sam's reaction at the station. "It was being in Sheldon's old office, wasn't it?"

"It was a little weird."

"Do you want to talk about it?"

Sam closed the menu and sighed. "I'm okay. I promise."

"It's okay to not be okay sometimes." Underneath the cover of the table, Nathan brushed his ankle against Sam's. "If you want to talk about it, I'm here."

"Thanks. That means a lot to me." He relaxed, and warmth spread through his chest. For the rest of the lunch, as they munched their thin crust, extra pepperoni, Sam let the memories go and allowed himself to feel content. They talked about their Adirondack trip, which looked like it would have to wait until November. Nathan loved hiking and fishing, and his face brightened when he described one particular stream—perfect for rainbow trout—where he had exceptional luck a couple of years before. Sam knew Nathan had been there with Emma, but the thought didn't make him jealous, only vaguely sad.

Nathan's phone rang, interrupting their conversation. "It's my boss. I've got to take this."

He excused himself from the restaurant, leaving Sam to wait for the check. Once he paid, Sam went to find Nathan hanging up from his call. He smiled when he saw Sam, but the expression didn't quite reach his eyes. Sam steeled himself for the worst.

"What is it?"

"I have to go down to the city tonight. The local PD made an arrest this morning—looks like some trafficking in Queens. Not sure of the scope of it yet, but they want me to run the questioning."

"So you're not out to pasture after all." Sam checked his shoulder as they started to walk.

"Doesn't seem so."

"You're not happy about it?" For a guy who'd worried a couple weeks before that he was going to lose his job, Nathan didn't seem very enthusiastic. His smile slipped.

"Well, I'll be going straight to DC for my seminar afterward. You're not going to do anything dangerous while I'm gone, I hope."

Sam rolled his eyes. "I don't think I'm next on the arsonist's personal hit list."

"I worry about you, given your track record."

"I'll be fine," Sam said, raising his voice in annoyance. "When you get back, this will all have blown over. Then we can get back to the important stuff, like what sort of bait and tackle to bring on our mountain getaway. And I'm not talking about fishing gear." He winked.

"Hmm." Nathan pulled Sam into an embrace on the street corner. "That's a weird innuendo, but I like the sound of it. Hey, would you mind taking care of the kitten while I'm away?"

Sam fingered the key ring in his coat pocket, which included Nathan's, strung together with the rest. He'd never exchanged keys with a lover before, and he still got a secret thrill whenever he used it to open Nathan's door. "Yeah. I guess I don't mind." He kept his tone nonchalant, but when Nathan took his other hand in plain view, for anyone to see, his heart felt like it had grown ten sizes.

Chapter 5

WITH NATHAN gone, Sam turned his attention to work and his blog. The next couple of days he wrote late into the night, until he had two pieces finished—one on the after-school program and one about the arsons. He was especially proud of the latter and hoped others would find it thoughtful and provocative. As soon as he hit Publish, he rubbed his eyes and looked at the time stamp—2:00 a.m.— with surprise. It had been a while since he'd been up so late, and he looked forward to the oblivion of sleep. He had an early start on Friday.

When he woke, it wasn't to his alarm, but to sirens.

"Shit." He glanced at the clock. Only an hour had passed since he dozed off. Another siren screeched past his apartment building. Not stopping to think, Sam threw on his clothes and shoes, grabbed his phone, and pocketed it as he ran out the door.

The street was filled with bleary-eyed onlookers. Fear and a strange sort of morbid excitement appeared on nearly every face.

"What's going on?" Sam asked the closest body, who turned out to be the asshole from 512, his hot-water nemesis.

"What do you think, dumbfuck?" he said, cigarette hanging from his fleshy lips.

Without bothering to reply, Sam turned to another tenant from his building. She clasped her robe closed with one hand and looked startled when he spoke to her. "I don't know. I always sleep with my window open, and the wind must have carried the smoke. Oh God. Can this be happening again?" Her eyes were wide and nervous.

Other interactions yielded similar results. No one seemed certain what they were doing out of bed, and most people were either in their pajamas or as hastily dressed as Sam. The night was blustery, and the air smelled like

35

acrid smoke, but the location of the fire wasn't immediately apparent. Once Sam got his bearings, he checked Twitter and discovered the fire had broken out about six blocks away, in a section of the neighborhood consisting mainly of single-family homes.

Sam made his way down the crowded sidewalk, toward the cross street, only to find it blocked by several emergency vehicles.

"Can't go down there," said a broad-shouldered police officer Sam didn't recognize. He eyed Sam critically. "We've got a four alarm in progress and it's dangerous. Streets are blocked off for pedestrians and anything but emergency access." He puffed up his chest.

"I'm a reporter," Sam said. "Has anyone been hurt?" He could see the glow of the fire lightening the sky with an orange haze, but it was far enough away that he couldn't make out any details. The fire trucks were quiet, and in spite of the commotion of bodies on the street and the flash of emergency lights, the entire scene had a surreal, slow-motion feel. Sam wondered if he'd stumbled onto a film set.

"There's nothing I can tell you, and I advise you to go home and get out of the way so we can do our jobs."

Sam's temper flared. "I'm not trying to stop you from doing your job, but this is my neighborhood. I have a right to know what's going on."

An ambulance rushed past seconds later, and Sam's blood ran cold. He hoped the person inside wasn't too badly injured. Another cop distracted the first, and Sam used the opportunity to slip past and walk quickly down the street, giving the emergency workers a wide berth. The fire made the October night feel like August.

Flames engulfed the entirety of a two-story home while firefighters sprayed the neighboring buildings to lessen the chance the fire would spread. Nearby, a diverse assortment of people of various ages and ethnicities clustered behind wooden-horse barricades. All of them glowed with unnatural light. Sam hoped the occupants of the destroyed home were among them as well—it would mean they'd managed to escape before the fire got out of control. He came closer, and as a member of the group met his eyes, the surprise of recognition passed between them. It was one of the teenagers Sam had met down at the Y. Damon Blake.

He stood slightly apart from the other observers, neither talking to them nor taking part in their rituals of comfort, and his body language reminded Sam of a bird poised at the edge of flight. His eyes were bright with unshed tears. Sam nodded at him, but Damon had already turned toward the fire.

Maybe he knew the people who lived there. A pang of sympathy throbbed in Sam's chest. Tim had been lucky.

Sam recognized another familiar face. Antonio Rivera, wearing a black leather jacket and FBI baseball cap, stood not twenty feet away, talking to some of the responding officers. He gestured sharply with one hand and held a walkie-talkie in the other. Chief Howard would shit a brick when she found out.

Sam scanned the crowd again for Damon, but didn't see him. He shot a quick text to Nathan on the way back home. *Another fire. I'm not hurt. I miss you.*

NATHAN: *YOU okay? Worried about you. Call me.*
Sam: *In a bit. Think I'm onto something.*
Nathan: *Sam…*

Sam could almost hear Nathan's heavy sigh, but he avoided replying. A day after the fire, news broke about the identity of the latest victims. Robert Jones, 42, and Veronica Jones, 38, succumbed to burns at St. Mary's. Their three minor children had been staying with relatives at the time of the fire, thankfully. After some basic research, Sam made an interesting discovery. Veronica had been a nurse at Shady Brook.

Two nurses from Shady Brook were dead in less than a month. Out of a body count of five, it seemed an unlikely coincidence. For whatever reason, the police weren't making the info public. Sam printed out a map of the town and hung it on the corkboard above his desk. He marked each crime site with a colored pin, red for cars, blue for buildings. He glanced over his notes again.

John Berringer, nurse. Age 37. Fire: Shady Brook
Scott Krause, janitor. Age 52. Fire: duplex on Pine
Lindsey Krause, high school senior. Age 18. Fire: duplex on Pine
Veronica Jones, nurse. Age 38. Fire: house on Washington
Robert Jones, carpenter. Age 44. Fire: house on Washington

The victims were listed as white and African American, male and female, so it wasn't a pattern related to race or gender. They were mostly middle-aged, but that didn't mean anything—aside from several leaving kids behind. Sam shook his head and tried to focus. Perhaps Nathan's theory about a disgruntled patient or former employee made the most sense. It still didn't account for Scott or Lindsey's death, since neither of them had a connection with Shady Brook, so far as he could find, but Sam made a mental note to talk with Lisa as soon as possible. Maybe she would have some insight.

Lisa. He worried about her. If the perp had it out for Shady Brook's nurses, she'd be a walking target. He was glad they'd decided not to reopen until the arsonist was caught.

But then there were the car fires.

Hyundai Elantra, red, 1998 model. Terrace Ave, West Stonebridge
Ford Explorer, black, 2011 model. Grant St, Stonebridge
Toyota Camry, gray, 2008 model. 5th Ave, Stonebridge

Wealth didn't appear to be a motive, since none of the cars were particularly expensive. They didn't seem to have any connection to the other crimes, but Sam didn't have all the facts. Maybe it was the lack of sleep, but he felt hypersensitive, aware of every strange noise. Earlier in the morning, when he went to Nathan's to feed the demon beast, he was sure someone was following him. It must be an effect of the fatigue. He missed Nathan.

His article on the troubling racism in the community arson support group received tons of hits and a substantial number of comments, both supporting and criticizing what he'd written. He'd even been contacted by *Slate* to run the piece on their site, which bolstered his spirits even as it made him feel a bit like a profiteer. He told himself it wasn't wrong to take some pride in his work—that was what Nathan would say.

His phone rang, flashing Nathan's name.

"Why didn't you answer my text?" Nathan's voice was calm, but the barely veiled irritation made Sam wince.

"I'm really sorry. I was about to call you. How's the case going?"

"Don't try to change the subject. After what happened last night, I think you should leave the city."

"I think you're overreacting a little." Sam shrugged his shoulders to release some of the tension.

"Maybe, but I don't like you up there all alone."

"I'm not alone. I'm hanging with the gang tonight." In fact, he had to get a move on or he'd be late.

"That's not what I mean."

While Sam appreciated Nathan's concern, he also knew Nathan still carried a lot of guilt over Emma's death. Sometimes that guilt leaked into their interactions and made him overprotective. "I know. I'm sorry. I can't leave, though—not in the middle of all this."

"I thought you'd say that." Nathan sighed. "And what's this about being onto something?"

Sam filled Nathan in on what he discovered about the connection between the nurses and Shady Brook. "So, what do you think?"

Nathan sighed. "I think there is a connection, definitely. I heard from Tony today—"

"I saw him there last night, by the way," Sam said. "He looked like he was having the time of his life."

Nathan ignored his sarcasm. "He's been given the go-ahead to help with the investigation. Anyway, they're about to announce a warrant for the arrest of the Jones' foster son. Wait a second—what do you mean you saw him last night? Sam—"

"I was perfectly safe. Seriously. And never mind about that. Tell me about the foster son." Sam frowned at his laptop and started typing. He hadn't heard or read anything about a foster son. As far as he knew, the Joneses only had three biological children, all girls.

"He's been living with them for about a year. Name's Damon Blake. He's got a history of behavioral problems, and setting fires on school property is among them. Been in and out of foster homes since his parents died eight years ago."

Sam's stomach dropped to his feet and then sank even lower. "Wait a second, did you say Damon Blake?"

"You know him?"

"He was one of the teenagers I interviewed at the Y." Sam was planning on returning in a few months for a follow-up. "I saw him in the crowd at the fire."

"Well, you better call the police and tell them."

"Are you sure it's him?"

"Tony sounded pretty certain. They found some empty gasoline canisters in the backyard too. Leaving behind evidence is sloppy. Seems an amateur was probably responsible."

"Why would he want to kill his foster parents? Or the Krauses?" Sam thought back to his conversation with Damon. Sam had gotten the impression that, while his foster parents had encouraged him to join the program—a fact he might have resented—he was enjoying himself. He seemed to like little Patrick. And the night before, Sam was certain he'd seen tears in Damon's eyes.

"I don't know. Could be any number of reasons. Obviously Tony couldn't share all the details with me, but he doesn't jump the gun without cause."

"You trust Rivera?"

Nathan cleared his throat. "Of course I do. I've known him for years. He's a good agent."

"How old is he? Blake, I mean."

"Seventeen." Nathan sounded reluctant.

"Shit." Sam rubbed his hand over his face. Not much older than Tim had been at the time of the accident. "I don't know what to say."

"Stay safe, okay? You'd better report the sighting."

"All right. Come home soon?"

"As soon as I can."

Other words froze on Sam's tongue as they said their good-byes. By the time they hung up, Sam felt sick to his stomach. He wasn't looking forward to a night of socializing without drinking.

Sam got up and flicked on the evening news. He sucked in a breath when the story began and a picture of Damon Blake appeared on the screen. His skin looked darker than Sam remembered him being, and he was frowning at something in the distance, his eyebrows drawn together. The headline under the picture read *Suspect at Large, Considered Dangerous*.

"While the suspect is a minor, the police have decided to release his identity based on the severity of the crimes. Please report all sightings immediately." The reporter concluded, and Sam shifted uncomfortably on his feet as the screen flashed a tips hotline.

He wandered into the bathroom and turned on the cold water, followed by only a splash of hot—the combo he'd worked out would keep him from being scalded, so long as the asshole upstairs didn't turn on his shower. He undressed and stared at himself in the mirror. His hazel eyes were clear, almost green, blinking back at him from his tanned face, which was still boyish, in spite of his being nearly thirty. He rubbed his dirty-blond hair. A few leaf particles fell into the sink—evidence of the minor leaf fight he and Yuri had earlier in the day.

He got into the shower and scrubbed his body clean, wondering about Rivera's evidence. What happened to Damon Blake to turn him into an arsonist? Orphaned as a kid, he'd probably seen more foster homes than he could remember. But to kill five people? And to threaten an entire building filled with incapacitated, helpless patients, including Tim?

In an effort to distract himself from his gloomy thoughts, he tugged his dick, but he couldn't get more than half hard. He wanted a drink. He wanted a drink so badly he almost considered heading to a bar instead of to

Michael and Yuri's, where his friends waited with their ritual takeout and Friday-night movie.

He reminded himself that Tim was safe. Tim was still safe, and nothing would ever hurt him again.

SAM ARRIVED at the same time as Rachel and Alex.

"Thanks for the ride, babe." Rachel leaned into the car window and kissed Alex good-bye.

"You're not staying?" Sam asked Alex.

"Got to work on some layouts tonight, unfortch," said Alex. Her white-blonde hair almost glowed in the darkness. Sam wondered what color it really was. "Have fun, kids. Don't do anything I wouldn't do." She winked and pulled away from the curb.

They ordered Chinese. The three of them sat in relative silence, eating their dinner and watching some movie Yuri picked out. He rarely got the chance with Michael and Rachel, the film experts, in constant competition. None of them discussed the arson, though it was probably on all of their minds.

"Where're Michael and Katherine?" Sam asked, to break the silence.

Yuri set his plate on the coffee table and picked up his beer. "Michael's out with colleagues for someone's promotion, and Katherine's upstairs with a cold."

"She doesn't want to come down and hang with us?" asked Rachel.

"I invited her, but she said no." He shrugged and swigged his beer again. Sam hadn't exactly been keeping track, but it seemed like Yuri was drinking more than usual.

"So what's going on in your life, Rach?" Sam nudged her arm. He hadn't spoken much to her in the last couple of weeks, which was unusual in the timeline of their long friendship.

"Oh, you know. Same old, same old. Bar's been pretty slow lately." She rolled her eyes. "I need to get out of there. It's sucking my will to live."

Sam hesitated. "What about opening your own bar?"

"It's just a dream, kid." She tousled Sam's hair, and he batted her away. "Maybe someday."

Yuri had gone to snag another beer, and this time Rachel and Sam exchanged a look.

Sam punched Yuri's arm when he sat back down.

"Ouch. That hurt, asshole."

"Where's the present we got you?" Sam feigned indignation. "Nathan picked it out especially. I've heard it's a beautiful blanket."

"Yeah, right, Sam. I know you were behind it."

"Nope. I'm totally innocent. It was all Nathan."

Rachel grinned. "He must know you pretty well, then. I'm almost jealous."

Sam couldn't help smiling back. "You had your chance."

"Please. You wouldn't know what to do with a vagina if one fell on your face."

"Eww." Sam shuddered.

They continued joking as the movie ended and the credits began.

"This one was a real winner," Rachel teased Yuri. "What other cinematic masterpieces do you have up your sleeve for us to enjoy?"

Yuri gave her a wan smile but didn't laugh, and Rachel's expression grew concerned. "Are you all right?"

"I guess. I don't know." He lowered his voice. "Katherine's parents want her to move back in with them, and she won't. And Michael's being sort of distant. I think he can tell I'm not thrilled about Katherine living here. He said it would only be for a couple of weeks, but she's not really looking for a job. She's doing a lot of volunteering for school and hanging out at her boyfriend's. I don't know why she doesn't move in with him, since they're together all the time anyway. It's frustrating, but we can't exactly kick her out, you know? Anyway, I'm starting to get the feeling he wishes we'd waited to move in together." He flipped open his beer with his Yankees bottle opener.

"I had no idea," said Rachel. "That sucks."

"Yeah." Yuri flicked back to the main Netflix menu and picked another random movie. His heart didn't seem to be in the selection. "Every time I bring it up, he changes the subject. Reminds me of someone, actually." Yuri's full lips twisted into a smirk as he glanced at Sam.

"Hey," said Sam. "I talk about my feelings and shit." Rachel and Yuri both snorted. "Well, I'm a lot better than I used to be."

"True," said Rachel. "Anyway, I'm sure Michael will come around. Everything will work out, in time."

Yuri didn't seem convinced. He downed a long swig of beer. "This is TMI, but we haven't had sex in two weeks. And we used to do it twice a day." He did seem a little sexually frustrated.

"Sounds to me like he's depressed." Rachel snagged a fortune cookie from the coffee table. She raised it up. "Here's hoping this is a good one."

Yuri tossed a cookie to Sam, and they all spent a moment rustling open the packaging.

"You go first." Rachel nodded at Yuri.

"*You will conquer obstacles to achieve success,*" Yuri read aloud.

Rachel sniggered. "In bed."

"Sounds pretty accurate." Yuri sighed.

She turned to Sam. "What about you?"

He flushed as he read it over to himself. Then he repeated it to his friends. "*Your life will be full of magical moments.* In bed."

Yuri snorted, and Sam shot him a glare. His friend's eyes were dark and teasing.

"I don't even want to know," Rachel said to Sam. "Seriously though, you guys. Listen. *A great pleasure in life is doing what others say you can't.* In bed." She shook her head and slipped the fortune into her pocket. "I gotta show this to Alex."

They all admitted Rachel had won.

LATER THAT evening, Yuri caught Sam's arm in the front hallway while Rachel was in the bathroom. He smelled of beer and swayed on his feet.

"Are you all right going home tonight?" Yuri asked. The quiet concern in the words made Sam smile.

"You mean back to the big, bad city with a suspect on the run? He's probably halfway to Canada by now."

"You can always crash here. On the couch." The qualification came a second too late to ring entirely true, and Sam wondered if Yuri was coming on to him.

Yuri was undeniably handsome. His vulnerable expression—brought on by some combination of Michael's distance and the booze—tugged loose a protective emotion in Sam. True, they hadn't worked out, but Sam hated seeing his friend in pain. For a couple of weeks, he had wanted to broach the topic of selling back his share of the business. He'd already cut back some of his working hours at Manella's, and he'd been getting more offers for freelance reporting from some reputable online news outlets. But it wasn't the right time, not with Yuri so upset about Michael.

"He won't be back until later," Yuri whispered, leaning closer. His fading Greek accent got thicker when he was drunk. Sam had always found it sexy.

Before Sam could register what was happening, Yuri closed the distance between them and pressed his mouth against Sam's. It was a tentative gesture, questioning, waiting to see if Sam would respond. For a second, it was tempting. Yuri's breath tasted good—like beer—but Sam recognized the craving for what it was. He wanted another man.

He made a quiet noise of protest and put his hands on Yuri's shoulders to end the kiss. "Yuri—"

A creak from nearby made him freeze, but they were alone. It was only the house settling. Yuri stepped back. His movements were slow, impeded by alcohol, and the words sounded thick on his tongue.

"I shouldn't have. I'm sorry."

Even in the dark hallway, Sam could see Yuri's face flush with embarrassment. "It's okay. Listen—"

"No. Please don't. It didn't mean anything. Just go." He grimaced.

The doorbell rang.

"Shit," said Yuri, pushing past Sam to open it.

"I'm here to see Katherine" came a voice from outside. Sam shuffled uncomfortably, wondering what was taking Rachel so long.

Yuri widened the door and stepped aside. "She's upstairs."

A man entered the foyer, and Sam recognized him from the housewarming party as Katherine's boyfriend. Ben something. Bendy-dick.

"Hi," said Sam, grinning at his own unspoken joke.

"Hello," the newcomer said. He glanced between Yuri and Sam. "Am I interrupting something?"

"Nope. Just heading out in a sec." Sam tried to sound nonchalant. "That is, if Rachel didn't fall in."

"Women, am I right?" said Bendy-dick.

"Uh," said Sam.

"What was that about women?" Rachel appeared from around the corner, wiping her hands on her jeans. Sam bit his bottom lip and tried not to laugh. She was smiling pleasantly, but her eyebrows were raised; it was the expression she reserved for shit-talking customers.

Benedict seemed to recognize it too. "No offense intended." He smiled, excused himself, and took the stairs quickly.

Yuri wouldn't look at Sam as they said their good-byes, and Sam hoped he wouldn't even remember in the morning. Sam waved casually from the curb and made a silent promise to forget about it too.

As soon as they were in the cab of Sam's truck, Rachel turned to him.

"So what was that all about?"

"That guy seems like a dick." A Bendy-dick.

"No, I mean you and Yuri—I come back and all of a sudden you two are like strangers. Did you get in a fight or something?"

Sam sighed. He should have known better than to question Rachel's powers of perception. He shifted into drive and pulled onto the street. "He kissed me."

"Shit. For real?"

"It's not a big thing, you know? Let it go, Rach."

"Let it go? Man, I thought he was over you," she said with a huff.

"He is. He was drunk, and it's not going to happen. He loves Michael."

"He wasn't *that* drunk."

They were paused at a red light, and Sam turned to her. "Don't tell him I told you, okay?"

"Are we still in high school?"

"Please?" Sam whined.

She bit her bottom lip. "Remember the time you spied on Josh Lawson jerking off in the locker-room shower? *Please Rach, don't tell anyone. Pleeeease. He'll kill meeeee.*"

"I do not sound like that." Sam stuck his tongue out.

"You really do."

"And don't tell Alex either. I don't want to make this into a drama."

"What? You can't tell me not to tell my girl a big piece of juicy gossip like this. There's a code."

Sam sighed and pressed the accelerator as the light changed to green. Since he'd made some repairs to his truck a couple of months back—thanks to a heavy discount from Nathan, who "knew a guy"—his junker looked like it might last another couple years.

"Are you going to tell Nathan?" Rachel's voice was hesitant.

"I don't know. It would only make things weird when we're all hanging out. He's already jealous of Yuri."

"You think?"

Nathan never said it in so many words, but Sam could tell he hadn't been particularly thrilled to learn about Sam and Yuri's former sexual relationship. "I think we should all forget this ever happened. It was only a little kiss."

"Hmm." Rachel crossed her arms over her chest. She seemed content to let the matter rest, for the time being.

When he dropped her off at her apartment complex, she squeezed his arm. "Be nice to him. Okay?"

He nodded, knowing she meant Yuri. "Of course. And say hey to Alex for me."

"I knew you'd fall for her eventually," she said with a grin. "Just like I did."

After the door slammed shut and Rachel disappeared into her building, Sam considered crashing at Nathan's, even though he wasn't home. The kitten needed company, according to Nathan. Sam wasn't worried about the little monster himself. In the end, he turned onto his own street, found a spot, and cut the engine.

Months before, he would have walked down to the Lucky Star, his favorite local and the bar where Rachel worked. Instead, he yawned as the exhaustion he felt all day caught up with him. He shut the door to the cab and glanced around, wondering at the vigilant silence, as though the city were watching and waiting. The street was deserted.

Pocketing his keys, Sam walked the block to his building. He considered whether it was too late to call Nathan. They hadn't really had a chance to talk earlier. He wanted to hear all about the case in New York and about the stupid, annoying, and interesting parts of Nathan's day.

He heard something. Pausing midstride, he waited, and then, convinced he'd been imagining things, started to walk again.

Footfalls.

Hairs pricked the back of his neck, and he froze. He glanced over his shoulder and saw nothing but shadow-darkened doorways, a few early jack-o'-lanterns, lifeless without their flickering candles. He'd almost forgotten Halloween was only a couple weeks away. Stonebridge always threw a giant street party downtown. He hadn't gone the previous year, and he wondered if they'd have the party at all that year, with the arsonist still on the loose. It was a shame. It would be fun to see his usually serious boyfriend dress up.

A movement in the alley next to his building caught his eye.

"Who's there?" Sam called out. His heart started a rapid tattoo as adrenaline spiked his blood.

A young man wearing a hoodie stepped out of the shadows and into the flickering streetlight. When he took off his hood, Sam recognized him immediately. Damon Blake.

Chapter 6

"DO YOU remember me?" Damon asked.

Sam didn't know how to respond. He glanced around, not wanting to take his eyes off Damon for too long. They were alone on the street. Damon's hands were empty and in plain sight. He didn't seem to have a weapon, but a shiver of fear traveled up Sam's spine, all the same. Damon could be concealing anything in his oversized sweatshirt.

"Yeah, I remember you. How'd you find my apartment?"

Damon put his hood back on and retreated into the shadows. It was risky for him to be out in public, and he obviously knew it, though Sam wasn't sure if he was aware of the extent of the search underway.

"It was pretty easy," said Damon in quiet voice. "I read your blog, and then I searched for your address. I wanted to see what you wrote about me."

Since Damon was named the main arson suspect, Sam's piece about the Y program had gotten a lot of negative attention from people upset about the way he'd portrayed Damon. He wasn't the main focus of the article, but Sam mentioned he seemed invested in the program and in his relationship with the little kid, Patrick. Most people seemed to think Damon was using the program to paint himself in a positive light, so he'd be a less-likely suspect when he committed the crimes. Sam wasn't sure anymore. He wondered if he should delete the damn thing altogether.

He realized he should probably get the hell out of there and call the police—he still hadn't reported the sighting like he promised Nathan—but something stopped him. Maybe morbid curiosity. If Damon was responsible for the Shady Brook fire, Sam wanted to know why.

"The whole city's crawling with cops looking for you."

"I didn't do it," Damon said.

"Who did?"

"Hell if I know."

"You expect me to take your word for it?"

"Nah. I don't expect anything. Never do. But I didn't light that damn fire. I never would have done something that fucked up."

Before he realized what he was doing, Sam stepped into the shadows to get a better look at Damon. When they'd met the first time, Sam noticed he was lanky, but he hadn't realized the extent of his height. He was probably as tall as Nathan. He stood up straight, with his chest thrust forward—not nervous or fidgety—though Sam could see the fear in his eyes. Sam didn't want to get too close in case he did have a weapon and decided to use it. Nathan would kill him if he ever found out Sam was conversing with a wanted suspect.

"What about the other fires? Do you know my little brother's at Shady Brook? He could have been killed." Sam was raising his voice—and probably antagonizing Damon as well—but he couldn't stop himself. "He's all the family I have left."

"Huh?" Damon scoffed. "You're crazy. I didn't do it, man."

"The cops think you're responsible."

"The cops are full of shit. Are you gonna call them?"

Sam's hesitation must have been obvious. Damon sucked his teeth, then spat on the ground between their feet. "Damn. I thought I had the right guy. I read the thing you wrote… about the fires. And last year you were the one who helped put all those bad cops in jail, right?"

"Yeah," Sam admitted.

"Well, shit. I thought you might want to hear what I have to say. I should've known better."

"You said you didn't know who did it."

"I don't. But I sure as hell didn't. And if those cops get their hands on me, I'm dead. Either that, or they'll lock me up so fast, I'll never see the light of day again." He thrust his hands into his sweatshirt and stared at the ground. "I just wanted to tell someone my side. Aren't you a reporter?"

Sam's throat went dry, and he licked his lips. "Yes. But there's a warrant out for your arrest. I can't help you."

"I didn't ask for your help. I asked for you to listen."

Sam wasn't sure he knew the difference. He couldn't exactly take Damon inside, give him a hot meal, and let him spend the night. He didn't know the punishment for harboring a fugitive, and he didn't want to do jail time for a story. Ending up in the drunk tank down at the station once had been enough, and he wasn't about to go back again.

Even worse, could he let Damon go free? If he did, and Damon started another fire, the blood of any victims would be on Sam's hands too. Poised between action and inaction, Sam tensed. "Why don't you turn yourself in if you're not guilty?"

"Are you kidding me? You didn't mean a word you said on your blog, did you? *'The reactionary racism exhibited by anonymous, presumably white, commenters should be treated seriously and interrogated by everyone in the community.'* Then again, you wrote that before you thought I did it." Damon started to turn away.

Sam's stomach squirmed. Hearing his words parroted back at him made him feel like a hypocrite. "Wait. You can't go on running."

"I'm not," said Damon. "Would I have come here at all if I was guilty?" Damon shook his head. His voice was bitter. "Nah, man. You might talk the talk, but you're just like everyone else." He started to walk away.

"Wait. Where are you going?" Sam didn't expect him to stop, but he did.

Damon spoke softly. "When I was a kid, they taught us about the witch trials in Salem. I remember my teacher saying it was about scapegoats. I was nine, so I didn't know what that word meant. I know now." He turned away again, but Sam heard his final words. "If you're such a smart guy, figure it out."

He disappeared into the night. Sam wondered if he'd made a terrible mistake. He was almost shaking by the time he'd climbed the four stories to his apartment and unlocked the door.

His mind was a jumble. All of his anxiety about Tim clashed with the memory of his first meeting with Damon and his latest, and of course, Nathan's confidence in Rivera's detective work. But Damon made a good point—why would he have approached Sam if he were guilty?

He tried to make sense of Damon's parting comment. There was a clue there. If Damon were hiding out nearby, he would have to pick somewhere off the beaten path, where no one went. It would help if the place was also obvious, so it wouldn't seem a likely hiding spot. Where was the last place anyone would look for a seventeen-year-old?

Down by the docks there were many warehouses, some abandoned, some large and filled with products. Any of those might make a good hiding place, but it would be risky. Stonebridge was still a major port, and the docks could get busy, especially when a container ship arrived. And anyway, Sam couldn't come up with a credible connection to Damon's comment about scapegoats or witchcraft. It was a strange thing to say.

Damon could be staying with a friend. It seemed the most likely option, certainly the easiest to arrange on short notice. But the police would undoubtedly have contacted every person who had some known connection to Damon. It would be dangerous to take the chance.

He sat on his couch, kicked off his sneakers, turned on the TV, and started flicking through the channels. He wound up settling on *Dirty Dancing*, figuring it would be boring enough to quiet his racing thoughts.

Nathan seemed so certain of Rivera's evidence. A history of violence, dislike for his foster parents, setting school property on fire—all of those things sounded like red flags. But there were the other fires—the duplex on Pine, for instance. What would be the motivation there? And how would a teenager, even a resourceful one, get his hands on the amount of accelerant needed for a series of such large fires without arousing suspicion? How could he escape detection for so long? It didn't make much sense.

Sam scrubbed his face and yawned. He didn't know all the facts in the case, and Rivera could have such evidence in hand. Maybe Sam should call the police and get it over with. Still, after ten more minutes, he was no closer to a decision. He lay down and tried to focus his attention on the movie. It wasn't as bad as he remembered. During the sequence where the shirtless Patrick Swayze lifted Jennifer Grey in the air, he started to get horny.

He needed Nathan.

Not wasting another second, he turned off the TV and got ready for bed, then scrolled down his contacts for Nathan's number.

"Hello?" Nathan sounded sleepy.

"Hey, it's me."

"What's going on?" Instantly more alert. "Did something happen?"

Sam hesitated a beat. "Nothing's going on. How's the case?"

"You called me at 2:00 a.m. to ask about the case?" Rough with sleep and gentle amusement, Nathan's voice made Sam relax against the pillows. He took a deep breath and rubbed his hardening cock through his boxer briefs. Hearing Nathan talk was more than enough to get him going.

"Sorry, I know you're leaving for DC in the morning."

Nathan chuckled. "It's all right. I'm glad you called." The whispers made it almost feel like Nathan was there beside him, save for the lack of his comforting warmth on the other side of the bed.

Sam gripped his erection and squeezed. "I need you. I'm horny as hell."

"Ah, is that the real reason?" Nathan sounded pleased.

Sam tried phone sex with a boyfriend in college, and it hadn't done much for him. He felt too self-conscious and didn't even come. But his cock was definitely interested in trying again. "I need to get off so bad."

"Are you touching yourself?" Nathan asked.

Sam closed his eyes and sighed. "Maybe." He put the phone on speaker and rested it next to him on the pillow.

"You have your cock in your hand?"

Sam slipped his hand down the front of his boxer briefs and gripped his shaft. "Mmm-hmm," he murmured.

"Pretend it's me touching you," Nathan said. "Cup your balls. Give them a tug."

His sack got tighter as he followed Nathan's instructions. He used one hand to hold his nuts and ran the other over the hard length. Some rustling on the end of the line made Sam smile. It sounded like Nathan was taking his own advice.

"How does it feel? Good?"

"Really good," Sam said, gathering the precome at the tip to slick himself. He loved hearing the telltale sound of Nathan beating off on the end of the line and the aroused hitch of his breath. Sam wished he could get his hands on Nathan, or better yet, feel him deep inside. He felt like he was going to explode. "I'm so turned on, I'm leaking everywhere."

"Fuck," Nathan said with a sigh. "Taste yourself."

He didn't know why it sounded so damn hot, but it did. Sam brought his fingers to his lips and licked the mild salty sweetness. Too lazy to go for the lube in the side drawer, he spit in his hand and started working faster.

"I'm close." Nathan's voice was hoarse, and Sam could picture his face and the expression he wore before he shot his load.

Sam's cock throbbed in his grip as he stroked. "Me too. Want you to come on me."

"Goddamn." As Nathan grunted his release, Sam emptied his balls with a moan probably loud enough to wake the neighbors. His jizz went everywhere, in spite of his attempt to catch it with his cupped palm.

"Shit," he said, slumping back against the pillows. After wiping his sticky hand on his underwear, he tossed them over the side of the bed and laughed. "Well, I don't know about you, but I feel a hell of a lot better."

Nathan laughed too. "Yeah. Same. I guess I didn't know I needed that. Thanks for waking me up."

"Anytime. But I prefer waking you up in person."

"Me too. How was the movie?"

Sam thought fast. He didn't want to tell Nathan about the kiss over the phone. He still wasn't sure he should tell him at all. And anyway, there was a more pressing issue on his mind.

"I need to know more about why Rivera thinks Damon Blake is the arsonist, Sid." Sam reserved use of Nathan's middle name for serious moments. In the months Nathan was away on a case, before they were a couple, he'd corresponded with Sam on his blog under the alias "Sidney"—a breach of the promise they'd made to give each other space. Later Nathan confessed he'd missed Sam too much to resist contacting him, which gave the name a special significance for both of them.

Nathan was silent for a beat. "Why?"

"Because I'm interested. Does Rivera have anything beyond circumstantial evidence?"

"You're not getting caught up in this, are you?" Nathan sounded wary.

"I'm thinking of doing some more in-depth research on Damon for another article." Cold squeezed around his heart at the lie, but he still wasn't sure what to do. If he told Nathan he saw Damon, there was no way Nathan would let it slide. And if Sam insisted on keeping it quiet, he would be abusing their relationship and asking Nathan to risk his job.

"All right. I'll try to see what else Tony has, but no guarantees."

"Thanks," Sam said gratefully.

"You're nothing but trouble, Sam Flynn."

Sam's heart thumped at the softness in Nathan's voice. "Pot, kettle."

"I'll be home before you know it."

After they said their good-byes and hung up, Sam stayed awake, thinking. While the orgasm had temporarily distracted him, he had to deal with reality. He had lied to Nathan, and apparently he wasn't going to call the cops yet either. He wanted to talk to Damon again first.

But where was he?

Sam tossed and turned as he mulled over every possibility. He wasn't satisfied with any of them.

Witches. Scapegoats. *If you're such a smart guy, figure it out.*

It struck Sam like lightning, and he almost bolted out of bed. *Old Stonebridge.* On the other side of the Baptist Street Bridge, the remnants of the original settlement remained. According to local lore, the last witch to be hung in the colonies had been strung up in the old town square. Most of the ancient buildings were crumbling ruins, but the Old Covenant Church was preserved by virtue of its strong stone construction.

Sam had never been inside, but as a kid, he and his friends scared each other with stories of zombies and mummies rising from the catacombs beneath the church. Not only had the settlers buried their most illustrious dead there, the tunnels served as an escape route for nervous Englishmen who constantly feared attack by Native Americans. The tunnels were considered dangerous, and had since been shut down. The conservation of the entire site was on hold, due to lack of funds, and the last time Sam drove by, he noticed that the land around the church was overgrown.

It seemed to make sense, given what Damon said. But why would Damon hint at the location? Maybe he was giving Sam the runaround—creating an illusion of trust so Sam would let him escape. And if Sam did believe him, and went there to hear Damon out, he could be walking right into a trap. Then again, if Damon wanted to hurt Sam, he had ample opportunity in the alleyway. Maybe he did just want to tell his side of the story.

Sam decided he would check it out the next day. If he was wrong, he'd call the police. He only hoped Nathan would forgive him when he found out the truth.

Chapter 7

THE GRAY stone façade of the Old Covenant Church rose up from a low-lying area not far from the bay. It was a wooden meetinghouse when the town was founded in 1763, but it had burned soon after, and in the early nineteenth century, it had been refashioned into a two-story stone church. Surrounding the church and beyond, the graveyard was filled with crumbling stones and statuary, and grass grew almost to knee height. Gulls cawed and wheeled in the late afternoon sky. Sam wondered if he should return with his mower and clean up the place, gratis. It was a shame for such an important historical site to be so neglected. If the city put funds into restoration, it would be a great tourist destination. The other buildings were in worse shape—several houses had sagging, rotten roofs, and listed dangerously to the side. Others were almost entirely destroyed. They were too close to the sea to survive.

In the distance, cars buzzed across the Baptist Street Bridge on their way between Stonebridge and surrounding towns. Sam parked his truck far off and came on foot, not wanting to draw attention to himself. With the traffic audible, he felt safe enough and not so alone. He hoisted his backpack higher on his shoulders to relieve some of the weight. Filled with food and a woolen blanket, it had been an afterthought, as was the pocketknife he carried for self-defense. He hoped he wouldn't have to use it.

Clouds appeared on the horizon—heavy, black thunderheads rolling in from Long Island Sound. The quickening breeze made gooseflesh rise on his arms and the back of his neck. Sam inhaled the salt air deeply. He could hardly imagine what life was like so long ago, when the streetlights of the city didn't blot out the stars above and threats lurked around every corner—Native Americans, disease, natural disaster. He zipped up his jacket and shivered as he approached.

The front door of the church was bolted shut. He circled around the outside, finally found an unlocked side door, and shouldered it open. A heavy object dragged against the floor and impeded easy access—a wooden pew, he realized as he made his way into the chilly structure. A quick inspection of the tracks it left, which he could barely make out in the gloomy natural light, indicated someone had recently moved it into position. Maybe Damon had done it as a precautionary measure. At the very least, the loud noise would alert him to any intruder's presence.

Sam decided not to call out and glanced around to get his bearings. The place had atmosphere. The last time Sam stepped foot in a church had been for Emma Walker's funeral. As a kid, however, he went to Mass with his parents on holidays, as both of them were guilty, reprobate Catholics. In spite of being bored to tears by the incomprehensible sermons, Sam had always liked the stained glass. He liked the smell of incense and the trembling bass organ. In the Old Covenant Church, there were no saints, no trappings of grandeur. It was as bleak and quiet as the grave. With its high ceilings and two-story balcony, it had a certain melancholy beauty reminiscent of a Thomas Hardy novel.

Most of the interior was empty, aside from some moveable wooden pews like the one blocking the door. There was a simple altar, and beyond it, an alcove led to another small room, presumably used to prepare for services. Sam's footsteps echoed on the granite floor as he made his way to the front of the church. The doors were locked from the inside, held together by a thick metal chain strung between two handles. He was beginning to think he was alone, until he noticed a narrow hallway to the left and a set of stone stairs.

As he climbed them, he almost stepped on a dead rat and made a noise of disgust.

"You figured it out."

Sam froze. Sure enough, Damon Blake stood at the top of the stairs, frowning down at him.

Sam clutched his chest. "You almost gave me a heart attack."

"You didn't bring the cops with you?"

"No, I didn't."

"All right. Come on up."

Warily, Sam obeyed and soon found himself on the balcony, looking at the altar and pews below.

He set down the backpack. "But I did bring you whatever I had in my pantry. Oh, and a blanket."

Damon blinked with surprise and licked his lips, and Sam realized how hungry he must be. He no longer regretted bringing the food.

"Are you wearing a bug?" Damon asked.

Sam raised an eyebrow. "Are you questioning my integrity as a reporter?"

"So you won't mind if I pat you down?"

Sam sighed and held up his arms. Damon was diligent—almost like a pro. He tickled the inside of Sam's thigh, and Sam shifted uncomfortably on his feet when Damon found his pocketknife.

"Hmm," said Damon. He chucked it over the railing, and it clattered on the stone floor below.

"You happy now? That was a family heirloom."

"I bet." Damon smirked at him.

"What about you? Any weapons?"

Damon held out his arms. "Be my guest."

Sam did a cursory job and wondered if patting down a minor for weapons counted as a bad touch. He avoided the crotch area, just to be sure.

They stood staring awkwardly at each other. Damon wore the same outfit as the night before. He slipped his hands into his pockets, and his shoulders drooped.

"So what did you want to tell me?" Sam asked. A pigeon cooed and pecked near his feet, impudently looking for a handout.

"This way." Damon gestured with his shoulder, and for the first time, Sam noticed another room on the second floor. It was hidden from the rest of the balcony by a pillar, but inside it was almost cozy, despite smelling like teenaged boy. A battery-operated lamp lit the musty, windowless room. On the opposite side, Damon sat down on a makeshift bed. There was a small stash of food—a couple pieces of fruit and a granola bar—set neatly on an overturned crate. Unlike the granite walls of the main church, the walls of this room were wooden and appeared to have been constructed more recently.

"Here it is. Home sweet home." Damon grabbed a pack of menthol cigarettes from underneath his pillow. He lit one with a match and inhaled deeply, not asking if Sam minded. Sam sat beside his backpack on the ground and wished for more ventilation.

"Those things will kill you," Sam said as he stared at the matches cast casually to the side. He wondered if he should consider them another red flag.

"Not for a while."

"This doesn't seem like a good place to hide. One exit. Small room. Aren't you afraid the cops will find you?"

"No one else comes here," said Damon. "And if they do, I see them long before they see me. Heard you coming a mile away. Anyway, I've been hiding here since I was a kid. I'm probably the only one who knows the way out."

"You mean underground? Those tunnels aren't safe."

"Life isn't safe," said Damon with a shrug. "I figure I'm safer here than most places. And I happen to enjoy the irony of the setting."

Sam nodded. Damon was definitely smart. "Scapegoat. That was a good one."

"I try." Damon exhaled a puff of white smoke.

"Anyone else know you come here?"

A spark of fear appeared on Damon's face. "Just Lydia."

"Who's she?"

"Foster sister. One of them."

"You don't think she'll tell?"

"No."

"You seem pretty certain."

"Yeah, I am. I know her." Damon's confidence had returned. He took a final drag of his cigarette and then butted it out. Sam figured they should get down to business.

"Okay. So you want to talk. I'm listening."

"All right. How about this. I didn't light those fires. None of them."

"A source tells me you lit fires on school property."

"It was only kid stuff," Damon said. "Me and some other guys used to go out behind our middle school and make campfires. We didn't mean anything bad by it. One of them got a little out of control," he admitted. "That's how they caught us."

Sam held his gaze. "The cops think it shows prior history."

"What do you think?"

Sam shrugged. "I don't know. Tell me what happened the night of the fire at your house."

Damon took a deep breath and began. "I was sleeping in the basement—that's where my room was—and something woke me up. It sounded like glass breaking. I thought it was a dream and I fell back asleep, but then about twenty minutes later I heard a crash. I went upstairs and grabbed the door handle, but it was hot as shit, and I smelled smoke, so I went back down to the basement and smashed a window to climb out." He held up his hands. In the dim light, Sam noticed the tiny, scabbed-over cuts on his knuckles and palms. "By the time I got outside, the firefighters were there, and I saw her… I saw Mrs. Jones…." His eyes went wide, like he was seeing it again. "She was all covered up, but I knew it was her. I saw her arm sticking out from under the sheet. I'll never forget it." He glanced down at his hands. "The ambulance came and took her. Then I saw you, the reporter from the Y."

Sam remembered the moment clearly. He nodded for Damon to go on, noticing he made no mention of his foster father. "Then what?"

"I ran away."

"Why?"

"Because I knew they'd think I did it."

Sam swallowed and leaned forward, but Damon wouldn't meet his eyes. "Why would they think you did it?"

"Because I wanted Mr. Jones dead."

THERE WAS no trace of remorse in the words, and from the look of contempt on Damon's face, Sam knew he was serious.

"I mean, don't get me wrong, Mrs. Jones was a nice lady. I liked her a lot, and it sucks what happened, especially for the girls to lose their mom. But her husband was a real asshole."

"Will you tell me why?"

"I don't want to get into it."

Sam considered what to say next. From Damon's reaction, he suspected he had been abused. "If you want me to believe you, I need to understand the whole story."

"It's not my story to tell," said Damon.

Sam took a guess. "The girls?" When Damon was quiet, Sam realized he'd hit the nail on the head. "What was going on in the house?"

Damon leaned back against the wall and grabbed another cigarette. "All right. Here it is. Mr. Jones was messing with her, with Lydia, whenever Mrs. Jones worked the night shift. I guess it was about four, maybe five months ago, when I caught him coming out of her room in the middle of the night. I went in there and Lyd was crying. I told him if he ever laid another hand on her, I'd kill him myself. Lyd begged me not to tell anyone. She's only fourteen. She was trying to keep him away from her little sisters. They're nine.

"Afterward, I watched out for her. He was careful... a lot more careful. Then one night I got home late from a party, and I caught him trying to go into her room, but she'd locked it, thank the Lord. That was it. I told Mrs. Jones. At first, she said I was lying, but Lyd told her the truth. She freaked out and sent the kids to be with her parents."

Sam cleared his throat, still trying to process what he'd heard. "Why'd you stay behind?"

"Well, Mr. Jones didn't want me in the house anymore, but Mrs. Jones made sure I knew I could stay. I wanted to get my GED. I figured in three months, I'd be emancipated anyway. Why bother going back to a group home and dealing with that shit? Anyway, the week after the kids left, the Joneses were fighting all the time. Mrs. Jones wanted a divorce. They started sleeping in separate rooms. If you ask me, that pervert set the house on fire himself to stop her from leaving."

Sam didn't know what to say. The story sounded plausible, especially if Lydia would verify it. Of course, it didn't necessarily mean Damon hadn't set the fires. He still had motivation.

"Are you sure you don't want to tell the cops your side of the story?"

"You still don't get it, do you? Until they have someone else to blame, I'm it. I don't want to go to prison." Damon had obviously forgotten about his cigarette, and now the ash fell and scattered on the floor. As Damon absently wiped it away, Sam stretched out his legs, which were cramped in the crossed position.

"Let's say I'm willing to believe Jones was responsible. Why the cars? Why the duplex? What's the connection there?"

Damon looked away. "Dunno. Did you ever think it's more than one person?"

Sam nodded. "I suppose it could be."

"But you still don't believe me."

"I'm not saying I don't, but there's still too much information missing." He needed to talk to Nathan again to find out what he'd gotten from Rivera. If the investigators were being thorough, they'd probably already questioned Veronica Jones's parents and corroborated Damon's story about the abuse. Along with his presence at the house that night and his history of playing with fire, that would be enough to issue a warrant. But... if Damon had alibis for the other nights, it would make any circumstantial evidence irrelevant. Pursuing that line of thought, Sam leaned forward and asked.

"I was sleeping," said Damon.

"Can anyone verify that?" Sam couldn't help feeling disappointed.

"No. It was the middle of the night."

"Not even your foster sisters?"

"I doubt it. They went to bed earlier than me. Are you going to turn me in?"

Frustrated at the dead end, Sam closed his eyes and rubbed the bridge of his nose. *What the hell are you doing?* he heard Nathan's voice whispering.

"I'm going to see what else I can find out."

"And then turn me in?"

"Would you let me leave if I said yes?"

Damon rolled his eyes. "I'd disappear if you said yes. If you thought I was going to hurt you, would you have come here alone with a rusty little pocketknife? Oh, I'm sorry, family heirloom—or are you just dumb?"

Sam almost laughed. "Maybe I am."

"Think about it. If I did it, I'd be gone already. There's nothing keeping me here."

Sam didn't know if that was entirely true. Bunkering down in Old Stonebridge was certainly safer than going on the run with no possessions, no money, and your picture plastered all over the evening news.

"I can't promise you anything, but I'll do my best to get to the bottom of this. Are you going to be all right here?"

"Yeah, I'm fine. Why wouldn't I be?" For a seventeen-year-old in his situation, Damon was remarkably self-assured, but Sam thought he detected a tremor of fear in his voice.

Sam emptied his backpack of the food and blanket. Then he got up and brushed off his jeans. "Look. Now you have my fingerprints. Think of it as collateral."

Damon wrinkled his nose as he picked up a can of ravioli. "You really eat this junk? Talk about stuff that'll kill you."

"Touché," said Sam.

Chapter 8

"I'M ALMOST home," Nathan said. "Thought I'd swing by your place."

The intent behind the words made Sam flush with the memory of their sex talk several nights before. He couldn't wait to get his hands on Nathan for real. He needed a distraction from the case that had consumed his brain for the past forty-eight hours, ever since he left Damon at the Old Covenant Church.

"That sounds great, but I'm already at yours."

"Really?" Nathan sounded pleased.

"Yeah. The demon cat was getting lonely." In fact, the little critter was now attacking his shoelaces and generally being a pest. But Sam needed to get out of his apartment and away from his Corkboard of Evidence, which was beginning to look like the Corkboard of Wild and Crazy Theories.

"You're there for the cat?" Nathan chuckled.

"We bonded while you were gone."

"I guess I'll believe it when I see it."

"Did you talk to Rivera about Damon Blake?" Sam knew Nathan had been busy with his seminar in DC, but he was chomping at the bit to get more information.

"Yes. But this is strictly confidential, all right? You can't run this in any article."

"Understood."

"They've established a solid motivation for the fire at the Joneses. Minors are involved, so they're keeping it quiet for now, but looks like there might have been some abuse in the house." Sam held his breath. So they had contacted the grandparents after all.

"Oh?" he said, feigning ignorance. "What about the other fires?"

"They found a menthol cigarette wrapper near one of the cars that was torched. Word is they're Blake's preferred brand."

His stomach plummeted. "Any prints?"

"No prints unfortunately. How's the story coming otherwise?"

"Fine." Sam grimaced to himself. He hated lying to Nathan, and with the news about the menthols, he wasn't sure he was doing the right thing. Maybe Damon was simply a very skilled actor. Of course, it could be a coincidence, but Sam didn't like the odds.

"Just fine?" Nathan asked.

"Do you think it's possible there could be more than one perp?"

"Maybe. Blake could have been working with someone else."

"You're sure it's him," Sam said despondently.

"I trust Tony's evidence, yeah."

Sam hadn't had any luck getting to the bottom of things. He went to see Chief Howard, but she was busy. He visited St. Mary's to talk to Lisa, only to discover she'd taken a couple vacation days. He planned to visit the Y again the following day to see if he could get some info from Shelby.

"You better be naked when I get there," said Nathan.

"Uh. Yes. I can definitely arrange that." Sam unbuttoned his jeans.

SAM FELT a little stupid—and cold—lying on the couch in the buff, but when Nathan surged through the door, dropped his garment bag, and raked his dark eyes over Sam's body, his uncertainty evaporated.

"Welcome home, Professor. How did it go?"

"It went well, actually. But—do you really want to know?"

"Later?"

Nathan was wearing an expertly tailored suit—dark gray, the one he preferred for travel. He was already pulling at his brightly colored tie as he crossed the room. Sam's cock filled.

"Paint me like one of your French girls," Sam said. He fluttered his eyelashes and put his hands behind his head.

"I didn't think you'd really obey me." Nathan's deep voice was smooth and seductive. Sam watched his lover undress, feeling as though he were pinned to the couch, though Nathan hadn't touched him yet.

Near Nathan's feet, the kitten meowed.

"If you start playing with the cat right now, I'll kill you."

"Understood."

Fully nude, Nathan was glorious. Sam drank in the sight of his thick, uncut cock rising and arching proudly into the air. Sam's mouth watered, and he reached out to encircle Nathan's waist and draw him closer. Nathan had different ideas. He swiftly covered Sam's body with his own and kissed him hungrily, grinding their erections together.

Sam grunted and wrapped his arms around Nathan's back. His lips and chin felt raw—Nathan hadn't shaved, and his stubble raked against Sam's smooth skin as they kissed.

"You feel so good," said Nathan.

The sweet oblivion of lust crashed over Sam in a hazy fog, making his groin ache and tighten. He wanted to forget about everything but Nathan. He didn't want to worry about the arsons anymore or the fact that he'd been avoiding Yuri at work. He didn't want to worry about how Nathan would react when he found out Sam had been in contact with Damon Blake. Or when he found out about the kiss.

Those thoughts almost derailed him, but Nathan was like a storm, swiftly enveloping him again and dragging him back under, making it impossible for his mind to function in any mode other than *sex now*.

"Bed?" Nathan asked.

"Bed."

They almost made it there. Nathan stopped them along the way to push Sam against the bedroom door and shut out a certain scampering, fluffy intruder. He steadied Sam with one hand and dropped to his knees.

"I can't get enough of you." Nathan held Sam's erection by the base and licked slowly around the tip. Then he swallowed him down.

It wasn't unusual for Nathan to suck him off, but there was urgency to it that night. Normally Nathan liked to take his time, using his incredible self-control to drive Sam out of his mind, but instead of the customary slow tease, he worked quickly, like he couldn't wait for Sam to come. Sam groaned and tipped his head back against the door as his orgasm built.

"Fuck. Nathan." Nathan responded with a grunt and took him in again and again, encouraging Sam to move his hips. The wet heat of Nathan's mouth felt incredible, but Sam didn't want it to be over yet. He whimpered, unable to do anything but hope Nathan would stop before he reached the point of no return.

As quickly as he started, Nathan rose to his feet and hugged Sam, trapping their hard cocks between their bellies. "I've been waiting for that all day. But as much as I'd love to have you come in my mouth, there's something I'd rather do first."

"Please tell me it has something to do with fucking."

"You read my mind."

Sam ground against Nathan. "Or something."

Nathan's smile took on a wild edge when Sam's legs hit the back of the bed, and they both went over, limbs tangling. They laughed and kissed as they touched each other, exploring, but dark thoughts threatened Sam once again.

"What are you thinking?" Nathan smoothed his thumb along Sam's jaw and over his lips, and Sam nipped at him. His heart pounded. "This line, here," Nathan pressed between his eyes to smooth the crease. "What's it for?"

Words were on the tip of Sam's tongue, but he held them back. He wanted Nathan to do to him what he'd done undercover to anonymous men and women who knew the language of this particular desire. He wanted Nathan to take control, fuck him hard, and get rid of all the shit in his head. He wanted to be bound, tied, spanked—whatever Nathan wanted.

He preferred having more dominant partners in bed, but he'd never considered a more formal exploration of sexual control until he met Nathan. Maybe Nathan hadn't asked him because Sam wasn't experienced? Sam closed his eyes against the sickening jealousy that rose up when he imagined Nathan in the arms of someone else—a man or woman who could please Nathan in a way he couldn't. He'd never been possessive of a partner before. What the hell was happening to him?

Of course, with the way Nathan looked down at him, his face a mixture of arousal and confusion, all of those worries seemed foolish—the product of insecurity and nothing more. Still, when Nathan asked him, "What do you want?" Sam shook his head. He felt oppressed by the weight of everything he was holding back. Nathan was going to be furious with him.

"Just you." He swallowed thickly.

"I don't believe you. Why won't you talk to me?"

I want you to hold me down and fuck me until I scream. I want you to tell me what to do so I have to obey, so I don't have to think. Sam knew his face looked panicked. His eyes pricked at the corners. God, he had to get ahold of himself. He didn't know what any of it meant.

He loved Nathan, and love had never brought him anything but pain.

Nathan was talking, stroking Sam's hair. "We don't have to have sex," he said, tenderness strangling the disappointment in his voice. "Do you mind if I…?" Nathan gestured to his lap and a rather fierce-looking erection.

It was enough to break Sam out of his headspace. The realization he was in love—which in some ways he'd always known—wasn't forgotten. He merely put it in a place to deal with later. He forced his lips into a smile, which became real when Nathan smiled back at him.

"I'm sorry. I missed you."

"I missed you too. Are you sure that's all?"

He wanted to tell Nathan everything, but he couldn't. "I want you."

"Glad to hear it."

Nathan kissed him again, slow and deep, and Sam's arousal shifted from simmer to boil. Sam spit into his palm and reached for Nathan's cock, savoring its hardness and length. Nathan's hips surged against his hand, and Sam watched his thick cock appear and disappear in his grasp. The hood of the foreskin slid over the head on each thrust.

Not wanting to lose momentum again, Sam brought Nathan's cock to the crack of his ass and rubbed it against his hole. Wet with precome, it slipped, but didn't quite penetrate. Nathan grunted and tried to push in.

"I want your come inside me." Sam whispered the words into Nathan's ear.

Nathan grabbed the lube from his bedside drawer and slathered himself with a generous amount. He bit his lip in concentration. Heart tugging, Sam positioned himself with his legs held back and open so Nathan could get between them and aim. He stroked his own cock to keep it hard as Nathan started to enter him.

The stretch and burn made Sam want to close his eyes, but he forced them open until Nathan was fully inside.

"Fuck," he said.

"Trying." Nathan worked his hips slowly, dragging his cock over Sam's prostate with every inward thrust. Sam couldn't help the noises he made as Nathan fucked him. He remembered the first time he fucked Nathan, how he arched and cried out in pleasure. His guttural sounds. Being the first man to do it was one of the most intense moments of Sam's life—but he couldn't deny having Nathan inside him was even better.

Nathan held Sam's feet by the ankles and leaned over him, his heated eyes glazed with pleasure. His balls slapped against Sam's ass, and the sound mingled with their heavy breathing and grunts of desire.

"Tell me what you want." Nathan swiveled his hips and drove deeper.

"Fuck me harder," Sam said.

"You little brat." Nathan gave him a full, long stroke, and Sam groaned. Nathan's hair, which had grown in the past several months, hung in his face. Sam liked it. "Spread it for me. Spread your hole."

Sam let go of his erection and did, face flaming as Nathan watched and licked his lips approvingly. His cock slid in and out slowly, in defiance of Sam's order.

"Like this?" Nathan smirked.

"I... ungh." What Nathan was doing felt so damn good that Sam lost the ability to object.

"Damn, that looks hot." Nathan stilled his hips and teased Sam's rim, pushing the head of his cock in and then pulling out again. Maddened by the sensation, Sam tried to drive it deep, but Nathan shook his head. His sweat dripped onto Sam's lips, and Sam tasted salt.

"I'm going to find out what's bothering you."

"By torturing me?" Sam wriggled his ass, but Nathan held back.

"This is hardly torture. You don't want to see torture."

Sam sucked in a breath. "Maybe I do."

"What are you talking about?" Nathan frowned.

"Never mind. Just fuck me."

"Jesus, Sam, this *is* torture." Nathan slid inside and let out a gusting sigh of relief. He closed his eyes.

"Yes." Sam hissed as Nathan pounded him harder, his cock hitting the most intimate spaces within. Sam's balls tightened as the orgasm built, fiery in the pit of his stomach, and he reached to stroke himself. Nathan grabbed his hand before he could.

"I need to come."

"You think you get to decide when you come?" The seriousness in Nathan's words coupled with the firm grip made Sam instinctively want to rebel. He tried to pull his hand free.

"No," Nathan growled.

Sam made a noise of frustration, and Nathan gave him a sharp look, the same look he wore, Sam imagined, when he was interrogating a suspect. He stilled his hips. "Do you want me to keep fucking you?"

"Yes."

"Yes what?"

Sam's heart pounded as blood raced through his veins, firing every nerve ending. Nathan wanted him to beg. "Yes, please. Please."

"No. You say, 'Yes, Sir.'"

Sam's mouth dropped open. Nathan was deadly serious, with no hint of their usual play. This was what Sam wanted, what he needed.

Nathan withdrew again and teased a finger over Sam's swollen rim. "Put your hands by your sides and don't move them, no matter what." Sam did as he was told.

"Yes, Sir." It was a whisper, but Nathan smiled. He leaned down and kissed Sam full on the mouth, rubbing their cocks together, both of them beyond hard. Though he felt a strong impulse to throw his arms around Nathan and hold on, Sam resisted it. He wanted to prove to Nathan he could obey.

"Can you come like this?" Nathan held them both in one hand and started jacking them off.

"Yes, Sir."

"Kiss me," Nathan whispered.

Sam did, opening his mouth and sliding his tongue alongside Nathan's. Their mouths sealed together messily while Sam's hands clenched into fists at his sides. He worried he'd orgasm with the urgent way Nathan was working them, and he wasn't sure if he was allowed to come without Nathan's permission. White-hot pleasure radiated from his spine to his groin and down his legs, so he tensed and whined against Nathan's mouth in warning.

Nathan broke the kiss. His eyes were tender. "You can come."

All it took was one look down at their erections slipping together and Sam let go, come spurting up his abdomen and nearly hitting his chin. He grunted, not knowing if it was okay to talk. Nathan was still rubbing Sam's extrasensitive cock with his own.

"You asked me to come inside you before. Do you still want that?"

"Yes. Fuck yes."

Nathan released Sam's softening cock and aimed his own for entrance. The penetration was swift and punched Sam's breath from his lungs. He dug his nails into his palms to stop himself from gripping Nathan's shoulders. It didn't take long. Nathan's movements grew erratic and his body tensed. He shuddered after only a couple of thrusts, the strength of the orgasm written all over his face.

He sagged against Sam and whispered something Sam couldn't quite make out.

"What?"

"Did I hurt you? Was it too much?"

Still trying to recover from the best sex he ever had, Sam wasn't sure he could speak. "No. Of course not. Can I… uh… move my hands?"

Nathan chuckled, and his belly rumbled and tickled Sam's. "Of course."

With his hands his own again, Sam squeezed Nathan tight. He buried his head against Nathan's shoulder and breathed in the smell of his sweat. "That was amazing."

Nathan kissed his forehead. "I know how hard it is to keep your hands still when all you want to do is grab on." The praise made Sam smile like a complete idiot. They stayed entangled for a minute, until the uncomfortable sensation of come cooling on their stomachs got the better of them.

"Shower?" Nathan offered.

"Mmm. Okay."

Later, while they lay in bed talking, their lazy touches and offhand comments gave way to a sleepier arousal. They sucked each other—a soft, languid buildup—until Nathan spilled against Sam's tongue, and Sam followed soon after. As they drifted off to sleep, Sam spooned Nathan from behind and kissed his neck.

Their bodies fit together so perfectly, he wondered again about love.

Chapter 9

DURING BREAKFAST, Sam noticed Nathan wasn't wearing his wedding ring. He'd worn it on his index finger as a fashion ring, due to the demands of his undercover work, but he'd never taken it off before. Sam stared at the hand resting on the table next to a glass of orange juice. There was a faint line of white where the metal had covered the skin.

It left him with a slightly elated, queasy feeling in his gut, whether from nerves or surprise, he didn't know.

As they ate, Nathan told Sam about the trafficking seminar in DC. It went so well that Nathan's boss wanted him to lead another, in Boston, the following month. It sounded like Nathan wanted to go.

"Maybe you can come with me," he suggested. "We can make it a long-weekend trip."

Sam took a bite of toast and washed it down with a swig of coffee. "That would be great. I could use a vacation, if we don't make it up north."

Then there was the case in Queens. Apparently the suspect easily cracked when Nathan presented him with a deal—less time in exchange for names—and they arrested three others in connection with domestic trafficking in two boroughs. Nathan and his team discovered a dilapidated apartment filled with homeless teenagers who were little more than sex slaves. It sounded like something out of a dystopian novel—or a nightmare.

The work weighed on him, though he'd never admit it. He had dark circles under his eyes. Sam vaguely remembered being awoken by tossing and turning, and he knew Nathan had risen before sunrise.

"Enough about all of that," Nathan said, pushing away his plate. The ringless finger begged a question Sam didn't feel comfortable asking. He distracted himself by reaching down and swooping up the kitten, which was launching an attack on his feet under the table.

"See? Best friends," said Sam as the beast tried to get at his food, sniffing the air like a tiny dog. "Or maybe she's just using me."

Nathan smiled and shook his head. "So what's on the agenda today?"

Sam had taken time off to follow up his leads on the arson case. He sent Yuri a text explaining, but he wasn't sure his friend bought the excuse.

Fuck. He needed to tell Nathan about the kiss. Was it a kiss if only one person participated? Had he let it go on too long?

"I'm heading down to the Y to ask some questions, and then I'm going to visit Tim. You want to come along?" He also knew Lisa was supposed to be back at work, and he wanted to ask her what she knew about Veronica Jones.

"I've got some stuff to take care of this morning, but I'll meet you at St. Mary's later?"

"Sounds good."

"Are you in a rush?" Nathan slipped a hand under the table and squeezed Sam's thigh.

Sam raised an eyebrow. The man was insatiable. "I think I have a few minutes to spare."

SHELBY NEWTON was a little less perky than she'd been on Sam's previous visit. He found her in her office sorting through a huge filing cabinet marked "Volunteer Files." Might be something interesting in there, Sam thought.

"Oh, hi," she said. She seemed surprised to see him. "Back so soon?"

Sam gave her his most winning smile. "I couldn't stay away."

Her pale, freckled face turned a mottled pink. "We love having you here. Everyone was so excited about your article," she said. "Did you want to talk to some of the kids again? I'm sorry, but except for the preschoolers, they're all at school."

"Actually I came to talk to you." He figured a little flirting never hurt anyone. It might help loosen Shelby's tongue.

"Really?" she said. "All right."

She cleared off a seat for him and pulled up another chair instead of sitting behind her desk, like he expected.

"I have to say, you were very helpful on my last visit. I got some great material."

"Oh, good." Shelby got even pinker. "We're so excited someone's taking an interest in the program."

"You make it easy. Your enthusiasm is contagious." Maybe he was laying it on a little thick.

She beamed at the praise, and Sam leaned forward and looked her directly in the eye. "I wanted to say I'm sorry to hear about Damon Blake's alleged involvement in the recent arsons."

"It's been so awful. What a shock."

"How well do you know him?"

She hesitated and bit her bottom lip. "A detective was here yesterday. He told me not to talk to anyone about Damon, especially not reporters."

"Do you remember his name?"

She nodded. "Antonio Rivera. He was from the FBI."

So Rivera wasn't leaving any stone unturned. Sam was irritated with himself for delaying his visit. He tried to hide his disappointment. "I see."

"I'm really sorry." She wrinkled her nose. "But I feel like I should listen."

"Of course," he said, plastering on a fake smile. "I completely understand. Open investigation and all."

She nodded vigorously. "Can I get you anything? Tea, coffee, water?"

He almost demurred, but then he remembered the filing cabinet. This would be the perfect opportunity to do a little snooping. "Coffee would be great, thanks."

"Great," she repeated, blushing again. "I'll be back in a minute."

When she left, Sam kept his eye on the open door and got up quietly. The cabinet wasn't locked, and he held his breath as he opened the top drawer and quickly skimmed through the A's to B.

Damon Blake.

Inside, there was a standard volunteer application filled out, presumably in Damon's hand.

Birthday: December 14.

Age: 17.

Reason for volunteering: I want to help kids who don't have a lot of opportunities.

Sam smiled to himself. He had a feeling Damon's foster parents hadn't entirely strong-armed him into the program, but he had no time to dwell on those thoughts. Behind the application, he found a staff evaluation form.

Damon is sometimes combative with authority figures, but good with the younger kids. He does best when he is allowed to work independently and is treated like an adult. Caught smoking on YMCA property on 9/13 and issued warning, but hasn't had a problem since.

In other words, he was a typical teenager, Sam thought with an eye roll. He skimmed the rest of the page but didn't see anything out of the ordinary. He barely managed to get the file into the drawer and sit down before Shelby returned with two cups of steaming coffee.

"I didn't know if you wanted cream and sugar, so I brought some."

"That's perfect. Thanks," said Sam, taking a cup.

He left about twenty minutes later with not much more information than he had before. The trip wasn't a total loss. At least he hadn't found anything to incriminate Damon. He didn't want Rivera to be right.

In the parking lot, he skirted around a group of children holding hands and following several adults on their way back from the playground across the street. One of the kids caught his eye. It was Patrick, the little boy Damon was working with on Sam's previous visit.

"Hi there," Sam said. Patrick looked up at him. "Do you remember me?"

"You're D's friend," said Patrick, though with his lisp, he pronounced the word more like "fwend."

Sam nodded. "That's right."

"Do you know if he's coming back? I miss him."

"I don't know, buddy."

"I hope he comes back soon. I drew a new picture for him. It's a horse." *Howse.* Sam smiled. He could only imagine what the horse looked like. The rest of the children passed, and then another teacher approached, bringing up the rear. Sam blinked twice as he came face-to-face with Michael's sister.

"Katherine?"

"Hi," she said with a shy smile. "I didn't expect to see you here."

"Me neither. You're a volunteer?"

She nodded quickly and reached for Patrick's hand. He took it and started twirling around, obviously impatient to get going. The rest of the kids filed into the building.

"That's great," said Sam. "It's a wonderful program."

"And you wrote such a nice article."

It was more than she'd said to him when they met at the party. Maybe working at the Y was good for her too. "Thanks. Well, I've got to run. Good to see you."

"You too. Let's catch up, Patrick."

The little boy realized Sam was leaving. "Bye D's friend," he yelled as Katherine led him away. "See you later, alligator."

SAM PARKED in the lot at St. Mary's at a little before one, but he wanted to speak to Lisa before he met Nathan. He hoped to catch her on her lunch break.

The hospital cafeteria smelled familiarly of canned green beans and fake mashed potatoes. Sam had spent a lot of time there after his parents' accident. It was where he'd bonded with Yuri, who was dealing with his father's death. The memories flooded back as he scanned the large room for any sign of Lisa.

He saw her trademark bright scrubs and made his way toward the table where she sat across from a nurse he didn't know.

"Hey," said Sam. "Lisa?"

She turned and smiled when she recognized him. Her straight bangs hung almost in her eyes. "Hey there, Sam. Come to sample the local delicacies?" She gestured to her tray, where a half-eaten Caesar salad wilted forlornly.

"Nah. I'm full on pizza," he said and patted his stomach.

"I wish I could eat like you. Unfortunately it goes right to my hips."

"Do you mind if I sit?" Sam nodded at the empty seat beside her.

"Of course not. What's up?"

Her friend got up and excused herself, leaving the two of them to talk.

Sam decided to be direct. "I'm working on a story about the arsons, and I'm hoping you can help me."

"Oh?" she asked cautiously. "What do you want to know?"

"I was wondering how well you knew Veronica Jones. Can you think of anyone who might have wanted to kill her?"

A flicker of unease passed across her face, and Sam knew Rivera had questioned her and probably warned her to stay quiet.

"Lisa," he said. "I'm asking as a friend. This case… I have a feeling it's a more complex situation than we're being led to believe. I want to get to the bottom of it. I promise you'll be left out of any article I write. I don't give my sources away." Sam tried to tamp down the frustration building inside him. It wasn't Lisa's fault. "Just a couple of questions. Please."

Still nothing. Then she covered his hand with her own. "I want to help you. I do. I didn't know Veronica extremely well, but we were always friendly. She usually worked the night shift, so I didn't see her much, except on staff meeting days, retreats, those types of things."

"Did you ever talk to her about her kids?"

Lisa glanced upward, like she was trying to remember. "Not personally. She had a picture of them in the break room. Three girls. About a year ago, I heard they were going to foster a boy, a sixteen-year-old."

"Damon Blake."

"Yes. A few other nurses thought she was crazy bringing a boy that age—a stranger—into her home with a teenage daughter."

"And did you ever hear any rumors later on? Did she ever regret it?"

"No. But again, we weren't close."

Sam mulled over what she'd said about Damon's age. He wondered about Damon's relationship with Lydia. He seemed very protective of her, but Sam hadn't picked up anything but brotherly affection. Still, it was something to consider. "Do you know if Veronica knew the nurse who died in the Shady Brook fire?"

"John? They both worked in the rehabilitation ward. But if you're asking if they were more than colleagues, I wouldn't know."

"I'm looking for motivation," said Sam. "If they were having an affair, for instance, it might have given Robert Jones a reason to kill them both."

"You don't think it was her foster son?"

"I have my doubts. What about you?"

She cleared her throat. "Well, there is one thing. I told this to the agent, but I got a feeling he didn't take it very seriously. You see, a few weeks ago, I overheard my supervisor talking on the phone. Honestly I wasn't trying to spy, but I was right outside his office and, well, I guess I don't have an excuse." She gave him a wry smile. "He sounded agitated, and I—to be honest, I've never liked him much."

"Go on."

"He was talking to his lawyer. It seemed like one of the nurses had filed a sexual-harassment complaint against him. I think it might have been Veronica."

"What gave you that idea? Did he say her name?"

"No. He… called her something I don't want to repeat. There are only a few African American women on staff, and the others are older, in their early sixties. Veronica was quite beautiful. Maybe I'm making assumptions."

Filling in the blanks left a bad taste in Sam's mouth. The guy sounded like a real piece of work. "I see. What's your supervisor's name?"

"He isn't anymore. My supervisor, I mean. He's been fired. But his name is Nick Granger."

Good riddance, Sam thought. Still, it was a promising lead. He was surprised Rivera hadn't taken it seriously—or perhaps he'd only feigned indifference, playing it close to the vest to investigate the lead later on. Sam's head was starting to hurt thinking about people's motivations.

And he was late to see Tim. Nathan was probably there, wondering what was taking him so long.

"Oh, and Sam? One more thing. Veronica was scheduled to work the night of the fire. John was called in as a substitute at the last minute."

Sam paused. "And Granger, was he let go before or after the fire?"

"Before," she said. "But he always did the schedules months in advance."

Her words stuck in Sam's head as he made his way to Tim's room, mulling over possible culprits for the Jones' house fire. He paused halfway, pulled out his cell phone, and jotted down a few notes for the Corkboard of Doom.

Nick Granger, nurse supervisor. Motivation: retribution for losing his job.

Robert Jones, husband. Motivation: anger at wife and foster son, desire to cover up alleged abuse. Suicidal?

Damon Blake, foster son. Motivation: anger at foster parents, protection of foster siblings.

Granger was easy to connect to the Shady Brook fire. He stood out as the top suspect. If Lisa was correct and he had completed the nurses' schedules before being canned, he would have thought Veronica was on duty, and he would have known the exact location to start the fire—near the place where on-duty nurses rested until they got paged.

Then there were the missing surveillance videos—the system had been down, according to Chief Howard. Sam didn't know if it was an equipment malfunction, but if not, only an insider could have disabled it without detection.

Meanwhile the new evidence seemed to exonerate Damon and Robert Jones of the Shady Brook fire, since they presumably would have known Veronica had called off work. They had no reason to target her there.

The duplex fire on Pine stood out, and the car fires weren't definitively explained. None of the three men had an obvious connection, at least as far as Sam knew. Perhaps Damon was right about multiple perpetrators. It was possible Granger was responsible for the Shady Brook and Jones' house fires, and someone else started the fire on Pine. Or Sam could still be missing some key piece of evidence.

He wanted to find Nick Granger immediately. But doing so might be dangerous, and Sam was pretty sure he would need backup.

"Hey," someone said from behind him. He whirled around and saw Nathan sticking his head out from Tim's door. He'd been so lost in thought he'd missed the room entirely. Nathan smiled, but his expression was confused. "Where're you going?"

"Uh, whoops," Sam said. He retraced his steps and pocketed his phone. "Guess I wasn't paying attention."

Sam entered and saw his brother resting peacefully under a pristine white sheet. He cursed silently when he realized he'd forgotten *Moby Dick*. He hated doing that. Nathan put his arm around Sam's shoulders. "Who were you texting?"

"No one. Just writing down some notes for my story."

"You're late."

It was nearly one thirty. Sam's mouth felt dry and cottony as he considered his explanation. He didn't want to keep lying. Still, he couldn't tell Nathan about Damon. If he did, Nathan would have no choice but to either turn Damon in or break the law. And with a new lead to follow up, Sam felt compelled to keep Damon's whereabouts secret.

But he could tell Nathan about his talk with Lisa and about Nick Granger. He hoped that, when the truth finally came out, Nathan would forgive him for the omissions.

Fat chance. He'll never forgive you.

"I wanted to ask Lisa about the fires."

"Oh? Did she have anything to say?"

"Yeah, actually. Some pretty interesting stuff."

Sam shut the door, and they pulled up a couple of chairs to the left of Tim's bed. After greeting Tim and giving him a kiss, Sam sat and watched the slow rise and fall of his brother's chest. He took strength in it as he filled Nathan in on Nick Granger.

Nathan frowned.

"What?" Sam asked.

"She said he wasn't interested in the lead?"

"That's what she said. He never mentioned this to you?"

Nathan shook his head. "This doesn't sound like Tony at all. He's an extremely thorough agent."

"I can't think of any reason Lisa would lie."

"Except she told you she'd never liked her supervisor." Nathan arched an eyebrow.

"True," Sam admitted, feeling a little foolish. He'd been so caught up in the story, he'd overlooked personal bias.

"Listen. I like Lisa a lot, and I'm sure she means well. It's very possible there's something to this, but I think I should talk to Tony again."

"I want to be there."

Nathan seemed like he might object, but then he nodded slowly. "All right. Let's see what he has to say."

Chapter 10

RIVERA MET them for a drink at the Lucky Star later in the evening. At first, Sam wanted to go directly to the station, but Nathan convinced him that a social approach might be more effective, and Sam deferred to his experience.

He hadn't been to the Star in months. The familiar, welcoming smell of stale beer and fried food made his stomach rumble. He'd had some good times in the place. Rachel was tending bar and gave him a wave, noting his company with a look of curiosity. He gave Nathan a "don't you dare start anything without me" look and went up to the bar to order for them.

"Hey, stranger, what're you doing here?" Rachel leaned over the bar for a quick peck on the cheek. "I'm not serving you, remember?"

"Don't worry. I'm having a Coke. Give me your best twelve-year for the others."

Rachel nodded. "You got it. Threesome?"

"Ha. No. Rivera's a friend of Nathan's. He's an FBI agent helping with the arson case."

"I see. You guys trying to pick his brain?"

"Exactly."

"Yuri's staying at our place, by the way." Rachel turned away to reach for a bottle from the top shelf. "He had a fight with Michael."

"Crap," said Sam. "About the kiss?" Which he *still* hadn't told Nathan about. Dammit. He was going to be in some deep shit.

"I assume so. He doesn't know you told me what happened, so I have to pretend like I have no idea what's going on. It's the worst."

"I'm so sorry, Rach."

"You've got to talk to him."

"I know. I know." He hoped to catch up with Yuri the following day at work. Now it seemed even more imperative, and he dreaded it. He threw down a couple twenties as another customer approached and distracted Rachel.

Gathering the drinks and bracing them against his chest, he maneuvered through the dimly lit room toward one of the tables near the back. It was the same one he and Nathan occupied the fateful night they first had sex, almost a year before, on Thanksgiving. It wouldn't do to get a hard-on now, but as he filled the vacant seat and slid Nathan his whiskey, he realized his lover had selected the table on purpose. He obviously remembered too, and his dark eyes sparkled with mischief. Sam kicked him under the table.

"Here you go," he said, giving Rivera his drink. "It's Lagavulin, one of my old favorites."

"Not anymore?" Rivera asked. Aside from the thin scar running down his cheek from his left eye to just below his ear, Rivera was a handsome man of around fifty. The few times Sam met him, he always seemed the quintessential cop, straight out of a crime novel. He spoke in a gruff, sandpaper voice and seemed to take in everything with his sharp brown eyes, which he focused on Sam's soda.

"Let's just say I'm the permanent designated driver."

"I gave sobriety a go when I was your age." He laughed and raised his glass. "It disagreed with me."

Nathan chuckled and shook his head. His expression warmed when he looked at Rivera. A frisson of jealousy stopped Sam cold. He took a sip of his drink to wet his throat. No. It wasn't possible that Nathan was attracted to Rivera. Was it?

As the two men entered into familiar conversation, it gradually dawned on Sam how little he knew of the professional side of Nathan's life. While they often socialized with Sam's friends, Nathan rarely went out with work colleagues.

All of them had known Nathan's wife. Was Nathan ashamed of being in a relationship with a man?

Sam's insecurities, which he mostly managed to repress, rose up and strangled him silent. He morosely sipped his Coke as Nathan and Rivera finished their drinks and ordered a second round. Nathan hardly looked at him. He directed all of his attention to Rivera, and Sam had never felt like more of a third wheel. He almost forgot why they made this appointment, until Rivera mentioned it.

"So why do I get the feeling this isn't just a social visit?" He aimed the question at both of them.

Sam couldn't interpret the expression on his face. Did he suspect that Sam had seen Damon? Did he know Sam had been snooping around the case?

Hoping it was the latter and determined not to be intimidated, Sam spoke up. "I talked to my brother's nurse today. She's a friend of mine. She mentioned a Nick Granger who used to work at Shady Brook."

Rivera sighed and gave Nathan a look of commiseration. "I suppose it's too much to ask witnesses to keep their mouths shut."

"But you did speak with Lisa," said Nathan. Under the table, Nathan rested his leg against Sam's and rubbed gently. The silent gesture of support made Sam evaluate the evening in a new light. Maybe Nathan was simply trying to put Rivera at ease and encourage him to open up. "I know you're keeping your hand close, Tony, and we're not asking for details, but can you at least tell us if Granger's a suspect?"

"I can't afford to have all my evidence plastered across the Internet." He aimed a pointed look at Sam. "This is an open investigation."

Sam couldn't help noticing how proprietary Rivera sounded, almost as though he had entirely taken over the investigation from the local PD. Sam wondered how Chief Howard felt about having him around. Probably furious.

"My lips are sealed," said Sam.

"You know you can trust me," Nathan added.

Rivera sipped his whiskey and ran a thumb along his bottom lip. "The fact is, Granger has a watertight alibi. He's been out of town, visiting his sister in Tennessee, ever since he got fired. We've got tickets and confirmation from the airline, as well as multiple sightings around the sister's place. Sorry, but he's not our guy."

"But is it true Veronica Jones filed a complaint against him?" Sam asked.

"Yes. But it doesn't discount the alibi."

"Maybe he hired someone else to do his dirty work."

"Unlikely." Rivera shook his head. "Granger's a gambling addict. He's in massive debt. He'd never be able to cover those kinds of expenses."

Sam wasn't so sure. "It might give him even more reason for resentment, if he lost his only means of income."

"But there's nothing to link him to the Pine duplex."

"There's nothing linking Damon Blake either," Sam said. He wondered if he'd given his hand away.

"Yes. There is."

All the sound went out of the room. "What do you mean?"

"Damon Blake knew Lindsey Krause. They used to go to the same school, until he dropped out. I've got a friend of hers who claims Damon pursued her, but she rejected him."

"Shit," said Sam.

"Do you want me to come up?" Nathan asked as they approached Sam's building. After the conversation with Rivera, Sam wanted to be alone. He needed to reevaluate his entire position and consider that he might have been duped.

He should tell Nathan the truth, turn Damon in, and face the consequences. All of those cans of food with his damn fingerprints. He'd grievously overstepped the bounds of any shield law.

"What's wrong? Why are you letting this get to you?"

Sam glanced away. He needed to talk to Damon again and find out if there was anything to Rivera's claims about Lindsey Krause. Although Sam couldn't imagine why her friends would lie, a part of him hoped for a compelling explanation.

"I'm sorry. I guess I'm not in the mood for company." And he still couldn't shake the insecurity their talk with Rivera elicited. Showing it would only drive Nathan away.

"All right. I understand."

Sam caught him by the hand, torn. Nathan waited expectantly.

"Good night," Sam finally said.

"Good night, Sam." Nathan leaned forward. His lips were warm and soft. Sam wanted to give in, but he held back. It felt slimy and dishonest kissing Nathan with so many lies of omission between them.

And he was about to do something really, really stupid.

Chapter 11

WITH HALLOWEEN a week away, the Old Covenant Church had an even more eerie, abandoned feel than it had on his first visit. Sam walked carefully through the crunchy fallen leaves toward the open door, imagining zombies rising up out of the moldering graves, or perhaps the ghost woman who'd been hanged as a witch. The Baptist Street Bridge glowed in the distance, casting bluish phosphorescence on the bay and extending its reach as far as the church. Sam's mind skipped back to the night when he, along with the rest of the town, had believed a mourning woman jumped from the bridge to her death. Although it turned out Patricia Feldman faked her suicide to unravel the mystery of her husband's murder, many other people had indeed plunged to oblivion in the icy waters underneath. He stopped in front of one sunken grave and squinted at the headstone, barely able to make out the name and date. *Sarah Ryder, 1759-1777.* Only eighteen years old.

Glad he was born in the twentieth century and sure he'd watched too many eighties horror movies, Sam focused on his task. The door was cracked open. Sam placed his hand on the coarse wood, pushed gently, and met with resistance. A harder push, and the pew dragged noisily across the floor. Damon had set up his intruder-detection system again, which suggested he might still be there. Sam turned on his flashlight and investigated the expansive interior of the church. He found only cobwebs waving gently with the influx of fresh air. Something scurried to the left, and Sam reeled around, heart hammering, but it was only a small animal.

He didn't want to waste any more time, so he found the stairs and ascended to the second floor.

"Damon?" Sam whispered.

Damon was not in his repurposed room, but something caught Sam's eye. One of the wooden panels opened into the interior of the wall, leaving a gaping entry about the height of a small child, but big enough for a crouching adult to fit through. Sam held his breath and examined the hole in the stone. He discovered a claustrophobic set of stairs leading down, probably to the catacombs and tunnels under the church. No wonder Damon had been so confident that he could escape from the police if necessary. This room was built to conceal the stone passageway.

Sam sat and waited. The little room was neatly laid out. A half-smoked pack of cigarettes and a lighter were set on the crate near the makeshift bed. Next to them, a few cans of food still remained, stacked one on top of the other. One of the blankets on the bed had a Sox logo.

At a little after midnight, he heard movement coming from beyond the wall.

Damon suddenly struggled through the narrow entrance. He wore different clothes—a warm coat and track pants—and carried a shopping bag filled with food.

He startled when he noticed he wasn't alone. "Shit."

"Sorry," said Sam. He sat with his flashlight on his lap. "Didn't mean to scare you."

"How long have you been here?" said Damon, his voice trembling slightly.

"Oh, not too long," Sam lied. "I wanted to see how you were doing. That's an interesting way of getting around." He gestured toward the passage.

"So, now you know about it." Damon sighed.

"How does it work?"

It was simple enough. Near the bottom of the door, an imperceptible wooden latch fit into the floor and controlled its opening and closing. Once sealed, the panel virtually disappeared. Unless you knew there was a passage beyond, it would be easily overlooked.

"You weren't supposed to find out about this." Damon's shoulders hunched as he unpacked the bag of food, placing new cans next to the ones on the crate.

"Where'd you get the grub?" Sam asked.

Damon glared. "I didn't steal it."

"All right," Sam said. He didn't want to provoke Damon. It was obvious Damon didn't trust him, which he supposed was fair. Still, it made broaching the topic of Lindsey Krause and the Pine Street fire seem impossible.

"So, did you find anything out?" Damon asked. His voice was neutral, like he was bracing himself for the worst.

Sam nodded. "A few things."

Damon removed his coat, settled on his bed, and lit a cigarette. He folded his long legs and hugged them with one arm. It reminded Sam of the way Tim used to sit when he played video games. The ember glowed bright orange in the dimly lit room. "Are you going to tell me, or do you get off on leaving people in suspense?"

"Why didn't you tell me you knew Lindsey Krause?" Sam blurted. Almost immediately he wished he could take the question back. Damon stiffened and pinned him with a stare.

"Because."

"Because why?"

"Because it's too crazy some girl who used to like me is one of the victims, that's why. I knew you wouldn't believe me if I told you. Hell, I don't even know what to believe…." He trailed off and shrugged. "She was all right, but I wasn't into her. There's no reason I'd want her *dead*."

"You weren't into her?" Without prompting, Damon had contradicted what Rivera had said—it made Sam curious.

"Nah," Damon said, shaking his head. He took a drag of his cigarette. "We used to be in the same English class. We hung out for a while after school, but when she started wanting to hook up, I told her no. She got all pissed off, and we stopped being friends. And then, once I dropped out, I didn't see her again."

"Why didn't you like her?" Sam had seen pictures of Lindsey Krause. She was very pretty.

"She only wanted me to get back at her dad. He would've flipped out if she dated a black guy." Damon snorted.

"So you felt like she was using you?"

"Eh." Damon shrugged. "I guess. I mean, she was hot. Don't get me wrong. I probably would have tapped that anyway if I… if I liked girls."

Sam raised an eyebrow. He almost couldn't believe it, but Damon was deadly serious. And shy. He glanced down at his hands.

"So we have something in common," Sam said.

Damon laughed. "I thought so."

Sam smiled back. Something eased in his chest as a narrative of what might have happened started to take shape, even as it worried him.

A popular girl like Lindsey would have been humiliated by rejection. She could very well have told her friends Damon pursued her, rather than the other way around, to avoid losing face. And now it would be those friends' word against Damon's.

"Did Lindsey know you were gay?"

"No one knows," said Damon. "I don't like to broadcast it. Shit was hard enough in the system, especially in the boys' homes, without adding being queer to the list. I figure it's no one's business but mine anyway. Mine and my man's." A secret smile lit up his face. Sam had seen the expression before and knew it was impossible to fake.

"You've got a boyfriend?" Sam felt like they were playing twenty questions.

"Who do you think got me all this?" He gestured toward the food. "I told you I didn't steal it."

Sam frowned. He made that assumption at first. He had made a lot of assumptions. "He knows you're here? What's his name?"

"No way, man. I don't want the cops thinking he had anything to do with it." Damon's voice softened. "We're gonna live together, once I turn eighteen. He's got his own place. I'd be there now if I could, but I don't want to get him in trouble."

"No one else knows?"

"No. He's a few years older. Don't worry—he's not taking advantage of me or whatever."

Sam ran his hands through his hair. Rivera seemed confident Damon was the right suspect. All of the evidence to the contrary pitted Damon's word against other people. And there was the menthol cigarette wrapper of the same brand at the scene of one of the car arsons.

What about this boyfriend character? How much older was he?

"Did he get you smoking?" Sam asked casually.

"Nah. He doesn't like it. He's a health nut." Damon gestured to the fruit he'd pulled out of his sack.

Sam wasn't entirely convinced. Without a name, it would be almost impossible to figure out the boyfriend's identity, unless he and Damon hadn't been as discreet as Damon believed. Getting the name from Damon seemed unlikely. But it was late, and Sam needed to get home and sleep if he was ever going to make it to work on time in the morning.

"Listen," Damon said. "I wanted to ask you a favor."

"What is it?"

"I want to know if Lydia's okay—and the twins. They're up with their grandparents now. Lyd must be so upset about her mom. I'm worried about her."

Sam blew out a breath. He wasn't exactly keen on contacting grieving people he didn't know. Then again, it wouldn't hurt to talk to them, maybe find out if they had any suspicions about who did it.

"All right. What's the name?"

"Chancellor," said Damon. "Met 'em a couple times at family gatherings. They're really old—like maybe seventy—but they seem nice."

"Chancellor?" The name was immediately familiar, and Sam cocked his head. "Not Frank and Beth Chancellor?" *Couldn't be.*

Damon's eyes brightened. "Yeah. That's them. You know them?"

"What a small fucking world," said Sam. "Frank used to work with my father. Opposite him, actually. My dad was the state's attorney, and Frank was a defense lawyer." He shook his head. Frank had given his dad a run for his money on more than one occasion, but his father respected him even when they disagreed. He once told Sam that Frank was the best trial lawyer he ever knew.

"Are they still in touch?"

Sam toed the floor. "My parents died a while back. Car accident."

"Shit, man. Sorry to hear it." Damon sounded sincere. "That's how my folks died too."

Sam nodded at him. "Thanks. It sucks, doesn't it?"

"Yeah. It really does."

"Here," said Sam, wondering if he was going to regret it. He pulled out his wallet and found one of his business cards. "Your boyfriend has a phone, right? This is my number. Call me in a few days, and hopefully I'll have word."

Damon took the card without a glance.

SOMETHING HAD been percolating in the back of Sam's mind ever since he first saw Damon's photograph on TV after the Jones arson. He couldn't quite articulate it to himself, but as he drove home, his thoughts were full of his interaction with Damon. He was still a kid in many ways, despite his brave face. Sam saw some of his vulnerability that night.

Weeks before, he'd written passionately about the racist response that many in the online community had to the arsons. He was angered by it. Even enraged. And he felt like he was above it.

How far removed from it was he, really? He weighed evidence to convince himself of Damon's guilt or innocence, and for what? If Damon was innocent, did it make Sam a hero for believing in him? He wanted to get to the bottom of the arsons, not for Damon, but to prove something to himself. If they were caught, Sam might face a few years in prison. He might even be acquitted. But Damon would be put on trial for arson and murder. He wouldn't stand a chance.

Sam still wasn't sure who the culprit was, but he seriously doubted Damon was guilty. In any case, it wasn't a game or a puzzle to solve. It wasn't about what Sam wanted to be true. It was about someone else's life, and Sam was in deep.

The realization shook him. When he entered his apartment and toed off his sneakers, exhausted, he almost didn't see Nathan sitting on his couch.

"Where have you been?"

Sam clutched his chest. "Jesus fucking Christ. You scared the shit out of me. I thought you went home."

"I did, but I came back and you weren't here. I was worried."

Sam turned on the light. Nathan looked as drawn as Sam felt, with dark circles under his eyes.

"I called you," Nathan said. Sam checked his phone, which showed two missed calls.

"Sorry. I went out for a drive to clear my head. Turned off my ringer."

"Oh? Where to?" The suspicion in Nathan's voice raised Sam's hackles—even more so because it was warranted.

"Just around—out to West Stonebridge and back. What are you trying to say?"

"I'm not trying to say anything. I'm curious about where you went." He smiled tightly.

"You're doing that thing," said Sam.

"What thing?" Nathan stood up. He was wearing jeans and a form-fitting Henley—a combination guaranteed to make Sam horny if he weren't so scared of fucking everything up.

"That passive-aggressive thing when you pretend everything's okay, but you're really pissed off. I wrote the book, so I should know. Honestly I only went out for a drive." The words came out almost unintentionally. He realized it was his last chance to tell Nathan the truth, and yet....

He couldn't. He couldn't ask Nathan to break the law and not report Damon. He would never be able to live with himself if Nathan lost his job.

What if he leaves you? How will you live with that?

Sam's stomach rolled.

"All right." Nathan threw up his hands. "I'm sorry."

"Don't *do* that," Sam said. Maybe he was spoiling for a fight.

"I'm trying to apologize. I told you I was worried when I got here, and you were gone and wouldn't answer my calls. I didn't like the way we left things earlier."

"Me either," Sam admitted.

"I'm sorry we didn't get better news about Nick Granger. I thought he might have something to do with it, given what Lisa told you, but Tony—"

Sam cut Nathan off. "I still don't think Rivera's right about this. How would a teenager get his hands on the materials needed for these kind of attacks?"

"He does have a history of arson—"

"Lighting fires in the schoolyard isn't the same thing as torching a damn house."

"I hate to break it to you, but kids in foster care often have problems. If this abuse allegation is true, it would give him pretty solid motivation. Not saying I don't sympathize—"

"But you are saying that." Sam advanced on him. He wanted Nathan to believe him, no questions asked, and he knew he wasn't being entirely fair. Maybe he was angrier with himself than with Nathan. "If you wanna talk evidence, how about the fact the surveillance cameras were down the night of the Shady Brook fire. It had to be someone who was familiar with the system, not someone from the outside. You yourself said it had to be a patient or staff."

Nathan nodded, but he still didn't seem convinced. "There was no evidence they'd been tampered with, though, according to Tony. The cameras had been down for a few days. It could just be a coincidence."

"I thought you didn't believe in coincidences," Sam snapped. How many times had he heard Nathan talk about trusting gut feelings? More than he could count.

Nathan responded gently. "I know it's hard to accept, but there's a real possibility this is the guy. And he's still out there."

Sam felt something squeeze under his solar plexus. Guilt. He couldn't look at Nathan.

"Innocent people don't normally run away from the police," Nathan added.

Sam winced. He'd thought that as well. He was still ashamed he hadn't known better. "They do when they're already condemned. I think you took one look at this kid and decided he's the one. Just like Rivera and most of this town."

"Are you accusing me of being racist?"

"Maybe I am. Or maybe you've got the hots for Rivera." Shit, he couldn't stop himself.

Nathan seemed amused. "You think I want to fuck Tony?"

"You obviously think the sun shines out of his ass. He can do no wrong, as far as you're concerned," Sam continued, feeling flustered and more than a little foolish. Nathan was being so calm. It was infuriating. "Tonight you hardly looked at me."

Nathan let out an exasperated sigh. "I was trying to help you."

"Did you ever think maybe Rivera's pursuing this lead to make Donna Howard look bad? He couldn't wait to get his hands on this case."

Nathan stood a foot away, but he'd never seemed so distant. Sam wanted to hold him and apologize for everything he said, but it was too late. Nathan was looking at him like he'd never seen Sam before.

"Tony would never do that. And if he wants a quick resolution, he's obviously not getting one." A pause, and then Nathan's expression changed. His lips parted slightly before he spoke. "What's really going on here? Do you know where Damon Blake is?"

Sam swallowed and met Nathan's gaze. "Of course not."

"You're lying to me." The words were laced with hurt. Sam could deal with disgust, even disappointment. He knew how to combat those things, how to defend himself. But this? Nathan was reaching for his coat. "Because I care about you, I'm going to leave now."

More than anything else, Sam didn't want him to go.

"Wait. I'm sorry. Nathan—" *I love you. Don't go.*

"Don't." Nathan shook his head. "Don't say another word. I've heard all I care to hear from you tonight."

The door shutting behind him wrenched Sam behind the rib cage. It seemed to tear his heart out at the root.

Chapter 12

SAM DUSTED off his hands, sat back on his haunches, and surveyed the new brick he'd laid on the twisting garden walkway of a client's home. Yuri was at the other end of the yard, talking to some of their workers about plans for the afternoon. They'd be cutting back the roses and readying the rest of the perennials on the two-acre property for the upcoming winter.

He and Yuri had acknowledged each other cursorily that morning but hadn't spoken since. Sam knew it was far past time. He fucked things up with Nathan, and he didn't want to lose one of his best friends too.

It had been a hard night. Sam went to bed after Nathan left. He tried to sleep but couldn't. He kept playing their conversation over in his head and wondering what the hell he'd been thinking. Nathan hadn't answered his texts, but Sam couldn't blame Nathan for ignoring him. He'd let his mouth run away from him—something he used to do when he was drinking. It was tempting to slip into those old patterns. Go out, get drunk, and find a guy to hook up with and take his mind off everything else.

Yuri came over, distracting Sam from his brooding thoughts. "Looking good," he said with a yawn. His hair was messy, and he had five o'clock shadow so dark and thick it looked like it might become a beard at any moment.

"Thanks." Sam stood and crossed his arms over his chest. The intricate spiraling brick probably should have been done in the spring, instead of the fall, but the homeowners were having a party and wanted everything perfect.

"You want to eat?"

"Yeah, I'm starving."

Both of them were quiet over lunch. They talked about trivial things like the weather, though Sam noticed Yuri gave him a few furtive glances. He wondered which one of them would crack first. Usually Yuri was the adult, but today he was playing the role of Sam—silent and stubborn. Sam was tired of pretending everything was okay.

"So, how're you doing?" he asked.

"I figured you heard. Rachel told you, right?"

Sam nodded. "She said you guys had a fight, and you were crashing at her place."

"I told Michael about what happened." Yuri blew out a sigh. "And then there was some other shit. It was pretty ugly."

"Sounds like there's something in the water."

"You too?" Yuri gave him a curious look.

"Yeah. Relationships are a pain in the ass, aren't they?"

"Yet they always seem so appealing when you're single."

"Who needs them?" Sam nudged Yuri with his shoulder, and the two of them laughed mirthlessly. "Is there anything I can do to help?"

Yuri shook his head. "Sorry again by the way. I never should have kissed you, but I was drunk and feeling alone, and you were there. It doesn't mean I'm still in love with you."

Sam stared straight ahead. "I never thought it did."

"Is that why you and Nathan…?"

"No. It isn't. We had some other issues. I'm sure it will work out." He wasn't so sure, really, but it seemed like the only thing to say. He didn't want to make it about him, as usual. "So, what do you think we should do?"

"Move on and forget it ever happened. If you think we can."

"Of course. Sounds good to me," Sam said.

Yuri set down his sandwich. "Do you want out of the business?"

Not expecting the turn of conversation, Sam felt his stomach squirm with unease. He hadn't prepared himself to broach that topic. "I was going to talk to you about it. I've been making some connections and getting some offers, mostly freelancing for websites so far, but I think if I had more time to write, I could make a name for myself. Maybe."

"That's great," Yuri said without much emotion.

"I'm not going to leave you hanging, buddy. I swear. And I'm not ready—"

"Juan wants to buy you out as partner. He's already approached me about it."

Sam's eyebrows shot up in surprise, and he glanced at Juan, who was sitting with some of the other guys. Juan raised his hand in acknowledgment. Sam nodded, and the guy went back to his conversation and laughed at something one of the other workers said. It made sense, Sam supposed.

Juan had the dependability and experience to make a good partner. A better partner than Sam could ever be.

"I told him to wait, so I could talk to you first. Of course, you can say no."

"What do you want me to do?"

Yuri shrugged. "It's your decision. But if you want out, this seems like as good a time as any. And Juan's been with us for a long time. I trust him. Let's face it, Sam. This was never what you wanted."

Sam didn't know how to respond. Yuri still didn't seem like himself. Maybe he was thinking about Michael.

"Maybe you should take a little time off," Yuri said. "Think about it. The season's slowing down until winter anyway."

Sam couldn't tell if it was an order or a request. "Okay, yeah." His throat was dry as he stood up. "Hey man, we good?"

"We're fine," said Yuri. He smiled, but the expression didn't reach his eyes.

"I hope things work out with Michael," Sam said.

"Me too."

Sam still felt uneasy as he got back to work after lunch. He couldn't shake the feeling that Yuri wasn't being entirely honest. And then there was the kicker—*it doesn't mean I'm still in love with you.*

Maybe Juan buying Sam out would be a good thing for their friendship, at least. Sam could still work on contract, whenever he was needed. It certainly seemed like Yuri wanted him to accept the offer.

Those thoughts occupied him until he started the drive home. He hadn't forgotten his promise to Damon to check in on his foster siblings.

Finding the number was easy enough, but Sam ran into complications right away when a home nurse answered the phone. The woman insisted Mr. Chancellor couldn't speak, since he was on strict bed rest with emphysema, and Mrs. Chancellor and the children weren't at home. Sam thought he detected bullshit when the screech of a child came through the line, but the nurse rushed him off the phone and hung up before he could protest, or even leave his name. When he called back, no one answered.

Sam lay down on his bed and closed his eyes. He burrowed his head into the pillow Nathan used whenever he stayed over and fell asleep.

HE WOKE to his phone ringing. With his heart in his throat, he checked the call screen and swallowed his disappointment.

"Hey, Rach," he said.

"Don't sound so happy to hear from me."

"Sorry. I've had the worst day ever. Actually make that days, plural."

"You and me both. It's like the *Dawn of the Dead* at my place, I swear. Yuri keeps making these weird groaning noises on the couch."

Sam let out a frustrated sigh. "Remember when we used to have fun?"

"Yeah. I miss fun. Meet you for coffee? It's not exactly fun, but at least we'll be together."

"You're on."

The coffee shop was a local place near Sam's with weak brew but awesome doughnuts. He and Rachel both got a jelly filled and a small cup and sat near the window, away from the other customers. Sam started to relax as he caught up with Rachel on all the latest gossip from the bar.

"Are you kidding me?"

"No. I'm not. They were red lace, with a little heart in front." She smirked and dunked the last piece of her donut in her coffee.

"I never knew he had it in him." Sam was suitably impressed.

"Me either, but I have a whole new level of respect."

"Do you think his wife likes it?"

She wrinkled her nose. "Gross. I don't want to think about my boss's sex life, thank you very much."

"You're the one who brought it up."

Rachel ate the soppy donut with a flourish and then fixed him with a level stare. "All right. Out with it. I know you're dying to tell me all your problems."

"You're my only emotionally stable friend."

"You're whining. Save your flattery."

Sam rubbed a hand over his face. He'd been friends with Rachel for so many years, sometimes he worried that he was taking advantage of her.

"I had a fight with Nathan."

"Figured as much. About what?"

"The arsons." Sam wondered how much he should tell her. He trusted Rachel completely, but he wasn't sure how she'd react when she heard about Damon. Deciding to compromise, he gave her the basic details of his encounter with Damon at the after-school program and outlined his gradual involvement in the case and his fight with Nathan. He made sure to include all of the potential suspects, including Nick Granger, but left out any information he'd received from Damon personally.

A server came around with fresh coffee, looking a little too interested in their conversation for Sam's comfort. He waited until she'd gone.

"I doubt he did it," he said.

"What about Lindsey's friends?"

"Maybe they didn't like him. Kids can lie. Who knows what Lindsey told them?" And Damon could have lied about being gay. But he didn't. Sam knew it.

"You think it's racial profiling?"

"Yes, partly. What do you think?"

Rachel reached for a packet of sugar. "I can't help agreeing with you. Whether it's conscious or not, it happens a lot."

"When we argued, I basically accused Nathan of being a bigot."

"You could have been a little more tactful." She pursed her lips and sipped her coffee. Sam's stomach twisted around his donut. "He probably doesn't even realize. And it seems like he trusts the agent on the case."

Sam nodded. "I wanted him to see things my way, you know? Maybe it's selfish. But his response made me think a lot about my own internalized prejudices too. I assumed a lot about Damon from the way he acted toward me when we met and the way he carried himself. And then I put myself in this position of trying to figure out if he did it—because I felt guilty for doubting him—but isn't that even more fucked up? I want to think of myself as above all that entitlement, but I'm not. I feel like a hypocrite."

"Hmm." She bit her lower lip, like she was weighing her reply. "This is heavier shit than I was prepared to deal with today."

"Tell me what you think anyway. Please?"

"I don't think any person is immune from prejudice. The important thing is to recognize it and do better. I've known you a long time, and I know you feel uncomfortable about your privilege. Maybe you do overcompensate a little. Like on your blog, when you write about oppression. I think it's important to listen to other people's experiences too. Just because you sympathize doesn't mean you understand what someone else has been through, you know? You can't always lead the charge."

Sam thought back over the last couple of weeks. He rubbed his temples to soothe the beginnings of a tension headache.

"Listen. You're one of my best friends, Sam, and you wouldn't be if I didn't think you were a good person. In a case like this, I think it's probably impossible to be impartial. My dad always says justice is never blind. As a black woman, I don't want to believe Damon did it—for my own reasons. But let's try to look at the facts."

In that moment, Sam was tempted to lighten his burden. If he told Rachel about Damon.... No, it wouldn't be fair. Making his friend complicit would be utterly selfish.

"Who else would have had the motivation?" Rachel asked.

"Someone connected to all the victims."

"Right."

"Someone experienced, who could avoid detection. Someone who could light fires without even being seen or suspected. We're looking for a fucking ghost."

Sam stared into his cup of coffee.

"I can't help coming back to the fact that two of the victims were nurses at Shady Brook. If Veronica Jones was supposed to be working the night of the fire, it seems like the arsonist made a mistake at Shady Brook and corrected it later. If we see it like that, the first nurse was an unintentional victim. That's why Nick Granger made so much sense. But maybe it *is* only a coincidence." The other link was Damon. He had connections with all of the burned buildings. But discounting Damon for a moment, who? The clear answer was his older boyfriend. Maybe Sam should go back and try to get a name.

"Or maybe it's not a coincidence at all," Rachel said. "Let's agree Veronica was the intended victim of two of the fires. Leaving out the main suspects so far, maybe there's someone else who might have had motivation—someone with a connection to the Krause family and to Veronica Jones."

Sam frowned. He had overlooked the duplex on Pine. He should definitely do some more digging on Scott and Lindsey Krause. "You know, I think you might be a genius."

"Remember what I said about flattery? Anyway, there's another possibility."

"What?"

"The cops are right, and Damon Blake is the arsonist."

Sam nodded slowly. He knew he had to keep the option open, but Rachel didn't know all the facts. "Right," he said simply.

She drained her coffee and glanced at her phone. "Now let's get out of here. I have about an hour before Yuri gets home from his talk with Michael, and I want to make the most out of it. Our walls are way too thin for sex, with him crashing on the couch."

Rachel's one-bedroom, which she now shared with Alex, had incredibly thin walls. Sam knew, because he'd had the unfortunate experience of hearing his friend in the throes of ecstasy on more than one occasion, back in the days when they used to party.

"So what they say about lesbian bed death isn't true?"

"Not even a little bit." She made an obscene gesture with fingers and tongue, and the server gave them both a dirty look from behind the counter. Sam laughed, glad for the lightening mood.

He finished his cup and grimaced at the lukewarm liquid.

"Oh, and I think you should talk to Nathan," said Rachel. "Don't self-sabotage this."

"Self-sabotage? Me?" Sam gave her a shocked look. "Why, I'd never."

"You gays and your drama, I swear to God."

"Where would you be without us?"

She raised an eyebrow, and Sam could tell she was holding back a retort.

They left the coffee shop, and Sam walked Rachel to her car. He figured he should head over to Nathan's to apologize in person, but the prospect gave him the jitters. There was a very real possibility Nathan would tell him to fuck off.

Well, then, so be it. Sam wouldn't give up without a fight. He wanted Nathan too much.

Chapter 13

NATHAN WASN'T home. Sam let himself into the apartment—wryly thankful that Nathan hadn't changed the locks—to find a very vocal kitten crying for her supper and twining between his legs with an eager, blue-eyed stare.

"No wonder he brought you home." He picked her up. Immediately, she began rumbling like a motorboat and closed her eyes as he scratched her under the chin. "I guess you are pretty cute."

She mewed again, and Sam carried her into the kitchen, fished out the half-empty can of wet food from the fridge, and scraped the gray, gelatinous mess into her bowl. He leaned against the counter with his arms crossed and watched the still-nameless kitten eat.

He hoped Nathan simply stepped out for a quick errand and would be back soon. But with each passing minute, the knot of worry in his throat got harder and harder to swallow. An irrational part of him said that maybe Nathan left on another case without telling him.

Came by but u aren't here. Demon wanted dinner so I fed her. I'm sorry. Can we talk?

When he hadn't received an answer to his text in a half hour, he gave up and left the building. The late October evening was chilly. Sam drew his leather jacket tighter and thought about going home. An early night probably would do him good.

But then he changed trajectory, walked in the opposite direction, and passed a bar on his left. The beast in his stomach woke and started clawing its way up his throat. *Just one drink,* it whispered. *You don't have a problem. You can stop whenever you want to. You've proven it. A couple drinks won't hurt.* The thoughts were too loud to ignore, and Sam found his hand on the knob, opening the door to a rush of warm, booze-scented air.

97

It wasn't a bar he'd ever been particularly fond of—too straight to cruise, and too overpriced, compared to the Lucky Star down the road. He couldn't go back to the Star and risk Rachel finding out, though he knew she was off for the night.

He took a seat at the end of the bar and ordered a single malt. The bartender, a tall man with a deep divot in his stubbly chin, gave him an affirmative nod, filled the glass, and slid it over.

Sam looked at the amber-colored liquid and brought it close to sniff. Sharp smells of malt and peat seared his nostrils, and his mouth watered in anticipation. He set the glass down. The place was crowded for a Sunday. People were getting a last taste of the weekend before real life set in again. No one seemed to notice him sitting with his fists clenched on the bar, but for some reason he felt observed, like a naughty dog caught tearing up the rug. He couldn't get Rachel's words out of his head. He wanted to be a better journalist, but he wasn't sure he knew how. He was pretty sure drinking Scotch wasn't the answer.

But it would taste damn good.

After almost an hour passed, the bartender approached.

"Something wrong with it, bud?" Sam hadn't touched his drink. If he sipped the whiskey, he would have a second, and a third. He probably wouldn't stop.

"It's fine. I've got a drinking problem." He didn't know why he said it out lout. The bartender didn't seem fazed. He nodded and reached for something under the bar. Sam flinched instinctively, like the guy was pulling a gun on him—persecution complex, check—but then he blinked in surprise when the bartender handed him a piece of paper. It was a list of AA meetings in the area, along with dates and times.

"They're meeting tonight at the Episcopal Church," said the bartender.

"I can read, thanks," Sam snapped. He stared from the bartender down to the drink he'd ordered. "I guess I'll get going. I don't need any meeting," he muttered, hopefully loud enough for the guy to hear. He fished out his wallet and threw down a twenty.

The bartender shook his head. "No charge."

Sam stood and left the bar.

He supposed he should have felt proud for resisting temptation, but dcsire still pulled him back in the opposite direction, reminding him how little control he had over himself.

SOMETHING ABOUT the Old Covenant Church felt different. As soon as Sam pushed open the door, he noticed the pew wasn't in place. With a sinking feeling, he made his way up the familiar stairs to Damon's room.

Damon was gone. Sam shined his flashlight around, but there was no trace of him save the disturbance of dust on the floor and some cigarette ash. Panic building, Sam went to the paneled wall and opened it.

"Damon?" he whispered into the darkness.

He realized he was breathing quickly, like he'd run a mile, and he hadn't even entered the corridor. He'd never been afraid of enclosed spaces, yet the idea of squeezing his way down the narrow passage, not knowing all the places it led or what lurked beyond, scared the ever-loving crap out of him.

There's no such thing as zombies. There's no such thing as zombies.

"Sam" came a familiar voice from behind.

Sam dropped his flashlight. The impact made the light go out, and he bent down to fumble for it in the darkness.

He finally managed to get it switched back on, stood, and discovered Nathan in the main doorway.

"You followed me."

Nathan wore a dark wool coat and jeans. He raised a hand to block the bright light. "Can you aim that thing somewhere else, please?"

Sam did. Able to see properly, Nathan glared back at him. "What the hell do you think you're playing at?" he seethed. "Where's Blake?"

"Gone," said Sam.

"I see. Gone where?"

"I don't know."

"And you wouldn't tell me, even if you did," Nathan gritted through his teeth. Standing in the small room, Nathan looked even larger and more imposing than usual. A shiver tingled up Sam's spine.

"Probably not."

"I can't believe this." Nathan stalked toward Sam and grabbed the arm holding the flashlight. Lurid shadows danced on the wall. "I mean, I know you like to stick your nose where it doesn't belong, but you lied to me—right to my face. You could go to prison for obstruction. Don't you know that? Or accessory, which would be worse. This isn't a game. Dammit. How could you be so careless?"

"I don't think he did it." The explanation sounded weak, even to his own ears. Nathan didn't seem very fond of it either.

"What does your opinion have to do with it? And how am I supposed to keep you safe if you run around helping wanted suspects?"

"There was a time when you didn't think that was such a bad thing," Sam shot back. The previous year, when Nathan was a main suspect in his wife's death, Sam refused to believe it, though his growing feelings for Nathan had gotten in the way of clear thought.

"You infuriate me, Sam Flynn." Nathan was close now, pushing Sam up against the wall. It hurt a little where Nathan squeezed his arm, but excitement warmed Sam's groin. He vastly preferred this passionate Nathan to the calm, controlled man he'd been the night before. Nathan nudged against Sam's temple.

The magnetism of the proximity derailed Sam's train of thought. He knew he should be irritated—Nathan had practically stalked him—and scared—where the hell *had* Damon gone—but Nathan's lips were so close, and he was breathing warmly against his face. Sam wanted to kiss him, the sexy bastard.

He might have whimpered. "I'm sorry."

"Don't try to distract me," said Nathan. "I'm angry as hell."

"I'm angry too. You followed me like a creeper."

"Do you really want to get into an argument about who's more guilty of lying and sneaking around?"

"Maybe not."

"There's something I'd much rather do," Nathan nearly growled.

Nathan's whole body caged Sam against the wall. For a minute, he wondered if Nathan would fuck him there. Probably highly inappropriate for church. But hot. Would it count as a sin if the church wasn't currently in use? Did Sam even care? Then he realized what Nathan was doing.

"You're smelling my breath." Sam wrested his arm away. He pushed Nathan—hard—and his lover staggered backward.

Nathan recovered quickly. "I saw you go into the bar."

"I didn't drink," said Sam. "But next time you're curious, why don't you ask me?" At least Nathan had the decency to look ashamed. Sam rubbed the place where Nathan had held his arm. Of course, Nathan's eyes tracked right to the spot. "Are you going to tell me why you followed me?"

"I got your text on my way home, and I saw you leaving my apartment. I meant to call out sooner, but when you went into the bar, I couldn't."

Sam nodded. Humiliation first muted his anger, and then increased it tenfold. He was struggling with the urge to drink, and Nathan saw it.

"Then you hailed a taxi, so I did too. You've been acting so strangely these last few weeks," Nathan continued. "At first I thought you might be seeing someone, and then I worried you might be drinking again, in secret. After yesterday, I started to wonder if it was something else."

"You still shouldn't have followed me."

"You're right." Nathan nodded. Sam noticed he hadn't exactly apologized.

"I guess you have the right to be skeptical. I did get pretty wasted while you were out of town, about five months ago."

"You never told me." Most of the anger had gone out of Nathan's voice. He was concerned, but not judgmental. If he had been, Sam might not have answered.

"I didn't want you to think I was weak. That I couldn't handle this." He gestured between them. "Or myself."

"I don't think you're weak. I must be doing something wrong if you don't know that by now."

"It's not you, it's me?" Sam indicated the joke with a fake drumbeat/symbol combo, and Nathan frowned.

"I think we need to talk, Sam. You might as well tell me everything."

Sam swallowed. He'd been dreading the conversation, and he couldn't have it in a creepy, possibly haunted, church. "Can we go home first? This place is freaking me out."

"Let's go."

RATHER THAN calling for a ride, they went on foot over the Baptist Street Bridge and took a moment to pause and look down into the inky water. Sam was transported back a year to the night he and Nathan took a similar trajectory to discuss potential suspects in Emma's murder. He wondered if Nathan remembered too.

Nathan listened as Sam relayed how Damon tracked him down, and why Sam decided to stay quiet about it, despite his misgivings. By the time they turned onto Sam's street, he'd gotten to the latest meeting and repeated what Damon told him about his friendship with Lindsey Krause going sour—and why.

"And you have no idea where he might have gone?" Nathan didn't seem pleased.

Sam frowned and unlocked the front door of his building. "Maybe to his boyfriend's?" It didn't mesh with what Damon told him, though. He wanted to keep the guy a secret to avoid implicating him.

"And the last time you saw him, he didn't give any indication he might be getting ready to run?"

"No. Nothing like that. In fact he asked me to get in touch with the Chancellors to check on his foster sisters. He seemed pretty worried about them. I still can't believe they're Frank Chancellor's grandkids," he mused, more to himself than to Nathan.

"Could he have gone to find them?"

"I guess anything's possible."

Once they entered Sam's apartment, Sam realized how late it was. He was starting to feel like a zombie as he kicked off his shoes and flung his jacket over a chair.

Nathan removed his coat. Instead of sitting, he paced the length of the room, doing a damn good impression of an irritated tiger.

Sam sat on the couch and put his head in his hands. He had actively pursued this self-fulfilling prophecy, and now he had to face the consequences. Nathan wasn't going to forgive him.

"I'm sorry," he said again, and his voice sounded pitiful to his own ears. *You're a selfish, cowardly bastard, Sam Flynn.* "Are you going to call Rivera?"

Nathan sat down on the couch too, but not close enough to touch. Sam's gut clenched at the pointed separation. He tried to steel himself for the inevitable rejection, but it was useless. Losing Nathan would be one of the worst things that had ever happened to him, and nothing he could do would change it. It was too late for self-protection—far too late. He'd been a fool to even imagine his heart stood a chance.

"I'm angry with you," said Nathan.

"I know."

"You've put me in a terrible position. I could lose my job."

The weight on Sam's shoulders reached crushing proportions. "I know."

"You know how much it means to me."

Sam nodded. He did. Nathan's job was the most important thing in his life.

Nathan sighed loudly and rubbed his fingers over his temples.

"I'll tell them the truth," said Sam. "I won't let you lose your job." He would likely face charges, but he would do it, even though the idea of betraying Damon made him miserable.

"I don't know what I'm going to do yet."

"What?" He turned to Nathan and flinched when he saw the conflict on his face.

"What you've said tonight makes me think it's possible Blake isn't responsible—more than possible. But that's not the reason. Dammit. Tony's a friend of mine, but he's not one to let something like this slide. Do you think I want to see you in prison? Even for a short time?"

"No. But your job—"

Nathan's stormy expression stopped Sam in his tracks. "My job means a lot to me. But you—"

Sam's stomach churned with nervous anticipation and fear.

"I don't want to say this when I'm angry. I'm very angry."

"I know."

"You're more important to me than anything else." Nathan watched him carefully. "Even though you lied right to my face. Even though I feel like I can't trust you now. God. So help me, I love you." He said it with force, but his vulnerability took Sam's breath away. In that moment, Sam saw his foolishness, and it made him flush with shame. He was so wrapped up in a selfish perspective of their relationship, he'd lost sight of what it meant for Nathan—for both of them, together.

Sam took Nathan's hand. Instead of the rejection he almost expected, Nathan grasped him tightly and threaded their fingers together. He held Sam's hand as though it were a lifeline.

"I'm in love with you, and I have been since the night you came over and found me in the backyard, after Emma died. You took me in when no one else would. You gave me hope. You believed in me. It didn't feel right to say it before, because of her." Sam saw the pain the admission cost him. Letting go of a loved one to love someone else—Sam understood the conflicting emotions of the journey all too well.

Without any more thought, Sam leaned forward and kissed Nathan firmly on the mouth. He tried to convey everything he hadn't said, all the things he wished he'd done differently over the past few weeks. When they finally parted, he looked at Nathan seriously. "You have no idea how happy you make me. It scares me, to be honest, and maybe it makes me insecure. What I'm trying to say—badly—is I'm in love with you too."

Nathan's smile softened. He wrapped one hand around the back of Sam's neck and drew him closer. They kissed like they were new to it, with exploratory mouths, and Sam marveled at the care Nathan took with him, how tender he could be when he wanted. He grasped Nathan's left hand and pressed an open-mouthed kiss to the naked finger where he used to wear his ring, silently letting Nathan know he had seen and understood the significance of the step.

"Do you want to talk about it?"

"It didn't seem right to wear it anymore. And I hoped you'd notice. I worried… not knowing what you were up to. Like when I asked who you were texting on the day we visited Tim. You looked so guilty. I thought for sure you were seeing someone else." The hurt on Nathan's face was unmistakable. Sam felt it like a knife to his gut. All this time, Nathan had worried Sam was drinking or fucking another guy, and yet he hadn't pushed. He hadn't rejected Sam. He waited patiently for Sam to tell him the truth. Sam never had that kind of loyalty—that kind of love—not even from his closest friends.

"I'm sorry. I've been so selfish—worried you were going to hate me, worrying about this case. I didn't think about what you might be feeling. There's no one else for me." Emotion lodged in his throat. "There never has been. Until you came into my life, I never thought I could feel this way. I hate that you can't trust me now."

"I want to trust you."

Sam wondered what he could do to regain Nathan's confidence. Maybe he should start with complete honesty. "Well, there is something else. But please, before I tell you, know it didn't mean anything."

Nathan eyed him warily. "Go on."

"When you were out of town, I hung out with Yuri and Rachel at his place, remember? Well, he got pretty wasted, and he kissed me."

Nathan's jaw clenched, and he stiffened away from Sam. "I see," he said finally. "Was it reciprocal?"

"I stopped it as soon as I realized what was happening. He's been fighting with Michael, and he wasn't thinking straight."

"I'll say," Nathan said darkly. "Why didn't you tell me before?"

"I kept waiting for the right moment, but so much has been going on, it never seemed to come. I'm sorry." Sam felt like a broken record with all of the necessary apologies. Nathan remained quiet. Sam could deal with anger, jealousy, anything but coldness, especially given what they'd just said to each other. "Don't you believe me?"

"He's still not over you."

"Yes, he is," Sam said with more conviction than he felt. "But even if he wasn't, you know I'm not interested."

"Does Michael know?"

"Yeah. I guess they've been fighting over Michael's sister staying with them, and Yuri told me Michael's been distant since they moved in together. I'm hoping it'll all blow over in a couple of weeks."

Nathan seemed to be considering what he'd said, so Sam took the opportunity to move closer. He rubbed the base of Nathan's neck, and Nathan relaxed infinitesimally. "I had a chance with Yuri before, but he's only ever been a friend to me."

"You slept with him."

"Slept. Past tense. And anyway, I seem to recall you sleeping with lots of people you didn't want a relationship with." Sam tried—and failed—to control his snark. In fact, hearing about Nathan's experiences on the job had once gotten him extremely hot and bothered.

Nathan huffed an irritated laugh and raised an eyebrow. "Fair enough. But… this is a relationship, not a prison sentence. If you ever decide you want someone else—"

Sam shook his head and cut him off. "I don't. I told you."

"I'm not saying I'd be happy about it. I'd be jealous as hell. But I guess I'm saying I spent a long time not being honest with the person I loved—or myself. I couldn't live like that again." Sam winced and Nathan continued. "There's no denying I feel very possessive of you, and I have to remind myself you're not mine to control."

"I am yours, though."

"What if I really gave Yuri a piece of my mind? It might be exciting to think of someone jealous over you, but it's another thing to see it in action. I don't think you'd like me very much."

"You can't help how you feel," Sam said.

"But I can control my reactions."

Sam rested his head on Nathan's shoulder and gently traced Nathan's firm stomach over his shirt. He wanted the connection of touch. "It's funny, because this whole time, I've been jealous—thinking about you finding someone else. Worrying that this is a phase and you'll leave me."

"A phase. So you mean, leave you for a woman?" Nathan asked gently.

"When we met with Rivera the other night, I was wondering why you haven't introduced me to many of your work colleagues. I worried you were embarrassed to be with me. I know you've never had a relationship with a man. What if you decide it's not for you?" Sam stared straight ahead, even as he slipped his fingers under the hem of Nathan's shirt to feel his warm skin. Talking about his emotions wasn't easy, though he found it less painful than he feared it would be.

"I've known Tony for over ten years," Nathan said. "He's always been sort of a father figure to me—a mentor—though don't ever tell him about the father bit. He was there for me when Emma was killed too." Nathan closed his eyes as Sam ghosted his fingers higher and grazed a nipple with his thumb. "I think some of the other agents might have believed I was guilty, but not Tony. He helped me organize everything to catch Sheldon and Hoff."

Sam could have kicked himself for being so blind. No wonder Nathan trusted Rivera so completely. "I didn't realize."

"It's not your fault. I didn't tell you. As much as I want to talk to you about Emma sometimes, I don't want you to think of yourself as a replacement. I'm not ashamed of you. Though I did think it was pretty funny you were jealous of Tony. The man's as straight as an arrow. Even if I wanted to fuck him, I'd be out of luck—which I don't, by the way."

Sam moved closer to kiss Nathan's neck as he squeezed one nipple, then the other, and twisted them both into tight beads. "I promise I won't lie to you again. I'll be better."

"I want you to be yourself. But with more honesty." Nathan's cock tented his pants.

"Yeah. Definitely more honesty."

"That doesn't mean I don't resent the position you've put me in with this case. But I can't think tonight, especially with you doing that."

Sam drew Nathan's bottom lip into his mouth. Soon they were dry humping on the couch like teenagers.

"If we're doing confession time, there is… one more thing," Sam said, stilling his hips. Maybe he was emboldened by the declaration of love, but he suddenly felt like he could tell Nathan anything.

"What is it?" Nathan looked up at him.

"I love what we do in bed. But I was wondering if you wanted to… you know… do what you did… what you learned." He struggled to remember the name of the woman who trained Nathan for his undercover work. "From Ryan."

Nathan's dark eyes grew blacker still. "You want to sub for me? You want to be my slave?" He was teasing, but there was a rough edge to his voice.

"I thought you knew how much I… uh… like it."

"I never thought you wanted to pursue anything. I thought you got off on dirty talk."

"Well, yeah. I like that too. It's part of it." Sam's face flamed, but he held Nathan's gaze. "I guess I was wondering why you didn't want to do it with me. Sometimes you seem like you want to, but you never bring it up."

"This has been bothering you?"

"A little. Like maybe I'm not kinky enough for you or something. I don't know." His face got even hotter. He wasn't a goddamn virgin—he had an entire drawer filled with sex toys.

Nathan rubbed up and down Sam's back. "Don't be embarrassed. Look, I wouldn't ever ask for that if I wasn't completely sure you wanted the same thing. I could go the rest of my life without going down that road again, if it meant I got to keep you."

"But if I want it too?"

Nathan laughed and his dark eyes flashed brilliantly. "You're one of the least submissive people I've ever known. You never listen to me."

"I did the other night, remember?" Sam lowered his voice to a purr. "When you asked me not to move." He ground his hips down for emphasis. "And when we talked on the phone." The conversation had his cock harder than it had been when they started, and he wanted Nathan to feel it. "I wouldn't want it to affect how we are together, on a day-to-day basis. But I could be so good for you, if you let me."

Nathan kissed Sam again, and the need and heat were obvious in his roving mouth. "You have no idea how much I want you. The thought of playing with you is the sexiest thing I can imagine. But I have to know you don't want it only because I do."

Until then, Sam hadn't known for sure that Nathan did want it, but hearing all the dark promise in Nathan's voice nearly had him out of his mind. "I can't explain…. It's like, I get into this place in my head sometimes, where everything is so fucked up. Being with you takes it away."

Maybe it wasn't the right answer. Nathan's face shuttered. "You can't run away from your problems with this, Sam. It only creates more of them. Believe me, I should know." His suddenly bitter tone was self-directed, and Sam remembered what Nathan once told him—how sex became like a drug. As someone prone to addiction, Sam wondered if he should feel wary about such a comparison.

He shook his head. "But I like losing control to you in bed. I trust you." If he didn't get out of his jeans soon, he was going to have a very messy problem on his hands.

Nathan hummed. He still looked troubled, but less so, and Sam definitely wasn't misreading the excitement underneath. He could feel it every time he moved his hips. "Let's discuss it again, once all this dies down. In the meantime, you should probably do some research to find out what you really want, and what you don't."

"You mean hard limits and all? Yeah, I read up on it. I don't think I have any."

"Yes, you do. Everyone does," Nathan said in his best teacher voice.

"Well, I don't want to wind up black and blue, but you said you're not into sadism, so I think I'll be fine." Sam touched Nathan's arm and traced the outlines of his tattoo. "Spanking might be kind of hot, though."

Nathan nosed against his cheek and chased it with a playful kiss. "I'm not only talking about the physical side."

"You mean mental stuff?" Sam wasn't sure he liked the thought of Nathan delving too deep into his brain. He repressed things for a reason.

"Yes. It can bring up some pretty serious emotions." Nathan's eyes grew dark. "There's no telling how you'll react in a scene, and even though I'd look for signs, you need to be honest about what you're experiencing. For instance, some submissives enjoy humiliation, others don't. I would never want to hurt you."

"You wouldn't. I know you wouldn't."

Nathan hesitated, and Sam noticed something he hadn't before—not fear, exactly, but discomfort. "To be totally honest, I need more time to think about it too, for a variety of reasons. I'm glad you finally told me what you want, though. If we get into anything more serious, we need to be able to communicate honestly with each other."

"You're right." Sam hadn't exactly proven his worth in that regard. Hopefully, they were taking a step in the right direction.

Nathan kissed him again, softly. "I do want you to know that whatever we decide for the future, this—you—is enough for me."

"I love you," Sam said again, testing the words on his lips. He hadn't said it to another living soul, except for Tim, since his parents died. And it was so different, and scary, and fucking awesome. Once, when he'd been bewailing the sad state of his love life, Rachel called him a commitmentphobe. An accurate assessment, though he was pissed off at the time. *Love is a leap of faith, Sam. There are no guarantees. But once you have it, there's nothing that'll keep you from climbing up that cliff and jumping off. It's worth the risk.* Then they laughed it off and he accused her of working for Hallmark. But the words still rang true.

It was a leap of faith, Sam thought, as Nathan grabbed his ass and rocked them together. He ran his hands across Nathan's arms and down his sides, loving the feel of the solid muscle. How had he gotten so lucky? He sucked on Nathan's tongue, teasing him, and they unzipped themselves to get closer. Once their cocks were free, Sam took them in hand and stroked as Nathan groaned into his mouth.

They drifted off to sleep tangled in each other's arms, too tired to move. Sam thought he might need to get a longer couch. This one was too small for two grown-ass men.

Two grown-ass men *in love.*

Chapter 14

THE CAR was on fire. Bitter smoke made each inhale painful, filling his lungs with caustic burning rubber, metal, and gas. Sam blinked and tried to orient himself, but he was upside down, strapped to the backseat, while all around him a wall of fire blocked any chance of escape. It was so hot, he felt like he was trapped in a vise. The air squeezed around him like a living, malignant force.

A man groaned from the front seat.

"Dad?" Sam called as recognition hit him. "Dad!"

His father's silver-black hair seemed to dance in the hot, smoky air. Sam reached for the seatbelt buckle keeping him trapped, but the lever was jammed. He cursed. The windows were broken, but it was impossible to climb out. "Tim? Mom," Sam screamed. He blinked and tried to see with his burning eyes, but his mother and Tim were gone. Outside, a circle of onlookers stood around two lifeless bodies, making no move to help. His father groaned again. His head pressed awkwardly against the steering wheel. A trickle of blood dripped from his mouth, bright red even through the wall of smoke.

"Dad!"

Sam shuddered, heart thudding hard as he lurched awake, back in his apartment. He gulped huge breaths of air, but something was around his neck, and he couldn't move. Only then did he realize Nathan was holding him. Sam settled back against the familiar, comforting weight as his breathing slowed and the remnants of the nightmare began to dissipate, leaving space for sleep to claim him once again. He could still taste smoke at the back of his throat.

But he wasn't dreaming anymore.

"Nathan, wake up!" Now fully in panic mode, Sam sprang off the couch, and Nathan lurched up seconds after.

"What's going on?"

"Fire in my bedroom," said Sam. "Shit, shit, shit."

The building's alarm sounded, a brain-melting screech, loud enough to wake the dead. Sam ran to the kitchen for the extinguisher attached to the wall near the stove. He grabbed it and started toward the fire when he felt strong arms wrap around his waist from behind.

"No," Nathan yelled over the alarm. "It's too dangerous, and the extinguisher isn't going to do anything. We need to get out of here, quick."

"I can't just leave it." But Sam knew Nathan was right. The heat of the fire radiated into the living room, and tall orange flames engulfed his bed, licking toward the ceiling and bathing the rest of the room in a vivid glow. Black smoke poured out of the room and filled the air. In only a matter of seconds, it would be impossible to breathe.

"Sam, come on." Nathan coughed and held his shirt over his nose. He had his phone up to his ear, no doubt dialing 911.

"I can't believe this is happening," Sam said, more to himself than to Nathan.

"Let's go."

Sam tossed the extinguisher onto the couch and grabbed his laptop, wallet, phone, and keys from the coffee table. He didn't have time to search for anything else. The fire was spreading, curling out into the open space of the living room. Resigned to losing everything anyway, Sam turned and followed Nathan down the hall toward the emergency stairwell. People were hurrying down, some carrying pets, some hustling their inquisitive children. Sam and Nathan assisted an older man with a brass-knobbed cane who was having difficulty on the stairs, and he thanked them, his wrinkly face bewildered.

As soon they were outside, Nathan began ordering people away from the building, using his arms and authoritative voice to guide those who seemed confused. They listened, and Sam clutched his laptop to his chest. In the distance, the wail of sirens cut through the din of voices, but the relief would come too late. Sam's apartment glowed, brightly lit against the backdrop of the night sky, as the fire spread to the floor above.

The minutes ticked by with excruciating slowness, until finally the first responders arrived. It didn't take so long in the movies. Firemen dressed in protective gear swarmed from the trucks and ran toward the building. A couple without helmets paused to see if everyone was safe. Meanwhile the police arrived to set up a perimeter. In all of the commotion, Sam lost track of Nathan, and fear shot through him, until he caught a glimpse of his lover among the other emergency personnel.

"Nathan," he called. His voice sounded small. Nearby a young husband and wife were standing with their arms circled around each other, eyes wide as they observed the spectacle. The guy from 512 glared at Sam from the sidewalk, lighting one cigarette with the end of the other. He was wearing blue fuzzy slippers.

"Lost my sound system, thanks to you," he said. "It's gonna be one giant fucking cold shower now, jerk. You happy?"

"Yeah, thrilled."

Flames punctured the windows of his apartment, and smoke billowed up to cloud the night sky. Sam thanked his lucky stars he'd stored his family photos in a rental unit, along with some keepsakes he hadn't been able to sell or throw away. Not all was lost, he told himself. He still had all his writing saved on his computer. He could buy new clothes and furniture.

Nathan *loved* him. Not everything was lost.

"Sam?" A familiar voice made him turn. "They want to talk to you."

"They think it was Damon?"

Nathan's lips were set in a grim line. He looked worried. "The good news is the alarm got everyone out in time. Listen, I don't think we have a choice anymore."

Sam tasted bile. "Do you think they'll arrest me?"

Before he had time to answer, Chief Howard interrupted them. She seemed to have dressed hastily, and her hair was pulled back from her face. It was the first time he'd seen her anything but perfectly groomed. Rivera was there as well, and he greeted Sam with a too-firm handshake. He had dark circles under his eyes. No one was getting much sleep that night.

"I'm sorry about your apartment," Rivera said. "If you don't mind, we'd like to go over some of the events of the night."

Chief Howard frowned. "I'll be asking the questions," she said, stepping between them.

"Of course. Whatever you say." Rivera held his hands up in mock surrender, but the tension between them crackled. For the first time, Sam suspected it might be sexual.

"Now," said Chief Howard. "Sam, did you see or hear anything suspicious tonight in your apartment?"

He breathed deeply. "Nothing out of the ordinary. We... fell asleep on the couch." His heart pounded in his throat. It wasn't technically a lie.

"Is there any reason why you might have been targeted?"

Sam kept his gaze steady. "Well...."

Before he could continue, a short, balding man pushed his way through the crowd toward them, followed quickly by two uniformed officers. The officers had twin expressions of annoyance on their faces. One of them was the man who had arrested him the year before for a drunk and disorderly, Officer Jain. The other was a woman he didn't know.

The man evading the officers planted himself in front of Donna Howard. "Chief, I'm Jack Reed," he said. Sam recognized the bald guy from the building across the street. He was a renowned neighborhood busybody, and he carried a tiny rat terrier in his arms—a vicious thing with a Napoleon complex, just like its owner.

"Can I help you?" Chief Howard asked.

"Sorry for the interruption, Chief," said Officer Jain.

"It's all right," she told him. "What's the problem?"

Jack Reed smoothed his free hand over his pale, bald head. "I was up at around two this morning, taking my dog here to do his business, and I saw someone over there climbing down the fire escape." He gestured toward the alley next to the burning building, the same place where Sam had encountered Damon.

She perked up. "Can you describe them?"

"Yeah," said Jack Reed. "Short fella, probably a little over five foot. He was wearing a hat and a leather jacket. Walked real fast out of the alley and down to a car parked at the curb. Someone else was driving. They took off pretty quick."

"It was a man?"

"Pretty sure. My dog's got the runs terrible—what a mess—but I got a decent look."

The rat dog bared its pointy teeth. Sam took a step back.

"Could you make out any other distinguishing characteristics? Weight? Ethnicity?" asked Rivera.

"Thin. But the hat was shadowing his face."

So not exactly a decent look. Sam frowned, but he didn't dare interrupt the interrogation when it was directed at someone else.

"What about the car? Did you get the make? Color?" asked Chief Howard. She pulled out a small notebook and pen to take notes.

"Blue car, older model. Could've been a Toyota. Ralph here was shitting himself all over the damn place. So yeah, I went upstairs and fell asleep, and I woke up when I heard the sirens."

"What sort of hat did you say?"

"Oh, didn't I mention it? It was a baseball cap. Yankees."

Sam glanced at Nathan, who was listening intently to the man's statement.

"Thank you, Mr. Reed," said Chief Howard, giving Rivera a pointed look Sam couldn't decipher.

The short man preened. "You're welcome. And if you want, I'll come down to the station and give a formal statement, so long as you don't mind me bringing the dog. I can't leave him alone, you see, or he'll piss all over—"

"That's not necessary, Mr. Reed," said the female officer, ushering him away. "Why don't you come with me."

Once they were safe from imminent attack by the rat dog, Chief Howard turned to Officer Jain. "We need video surveillance from all the neighborhood street cameras. Try to get the plates on that car."

Officer Jain nodded. "Right away, Chief."

Sam wondered if they'd have much luck. This part of Stonebridge was notorious for civic neglect, and he'd be surprised if there were any working street cameras within a mile radius. Still, it was worth hoping—and it also opened up new possibilities. He glanced back helplessly at the flaming building behind him. It looked like the fourth and maybe the fifth floors would be total losses, but the fire was slowly diminishing, which suggested it wouldn't take the whole building.

Feeling strangely numb, he almost missed the terse exchange between Chief Howard and Rivera.

"—said it wasn't worth looking into." Rivera was on the defensive.

"If I recall, that's exactly what you said." Chief Howard crossed her arms.

"Well, let's pull the vid again and see if we can get an ID from the witness."

"Damn right we will."

They glared at each other. For a moment, Sam wondered if they were going to start throwing punches—or making out in the middle of the street.

Nathan cleared his throat. "I'm obviously missing something here."

"We uncovered a surveillance vid from the front of the junk shop down on Pine." Rivera sounded resigned.

"It was only a few blocks away from the Pine duplex fire," Chief Howard added.

"Jake's Junk?" Sam asked. He and Yuri always recommended Jake's to clients for junk removal services. The owner was hot.

The chief nodded. "There were two people in the video. One of them is wearing a Yankees hat."

"No ID?" Nathan asked.

"Footage is too grainy. But we haven't gotten the professional analysis back yet." Chief Howard gave Rivera another look.

"Right. Well, let's get on it."

"It's not him."

"What?" Donna Howard turned to Sam. His heart pounded as he stared her down.

"It can't be Blake. He's a Sox fan. And he's not a short guy."

"How do you know?" She raised a skeptical eyebrow.

"I interviewed him down at the Y for my article. He was wearing a Sox jersey."

And of course Sam remembered the Red Sox themed blanket he saw at the church, but it looked like maybe he should keep the secret a little longer. "Come on, Chief, you're from Brooklyn. You know how strong the rivalry is."

"I'm a Mets fan."

"Yeah, but you know a Red Sox fan would never wear a Yankees hat." Except, Sam had worn Yuri's hat once at work, when he'd been burning up in the sun....

A chill ran over his body, like someone had stepped on his grave. He shook off the feeling, even as his mind whispered *Yuri knows how to get into your bedroom window. He knows about the fire escape and the broken latch.* Now he was even suspecting his best friend? Yuri had been acting strange since the kiss, but still. It wasn't like there weren't any other Yankees fans in Stonebridge—the place was crawling with them—and lots of them were probably on the short side.

"Well, we'll certainly keep it in mind," said Chief Howard. "Let's go, Agent Rivera."

"You don't need to call me—"

Still bickering, their voices faded as they turned away and started heading for the chief's squad car. They seemed to have forgotten entirely about questioning Sam for the moment, which suited him fine. With this new evidence to consider, Sam wanted to talk to Nathan before making any decisions. Most of the onlookers had already dispersed, and the sun was rising.

"Come on," said Nathan, putting his hand on Sam's shoulder. "Let's go home."

NATHAN MADE Sam take off his clothes and shower. Then he tucked him into bed in spite of his protests. Almost instantly, Sam fell into a deep, dreamless sleep.

When he woke, the sun was low in the sky. He found Nathan in the living room typing on his laptop.

The reality of the situation, held at bay during the height of the crisis, crashed down around him. Aside from the possessions he'd managed to grab before they escaped and a few random items he'd left at Nathan's over the past few months, he had nothing. No clothes, no shoes, no fucking socks. He glanced down at his boxer briefs and the T-shirt he'd borrowed from Nathan. That was now the extent of his wardrobe.

"Goddammit. Fucking shit," Sam said.

Nathan looked up from his laptop and quirked an eyebrow. "Sleeping beauty awakes."

"Shut up," Sam said. "I think I need a hug."

"Well, come here, then."

Nathan held his arms open wide, and Sam padded to the sofa and climbed onto his lap. He sighed into the warm strength of Nathan's chest and arms and hugged back just as tightly. They were quiet for a while, holding each other, and Sam blinked away the wetness in his eyes.

"*Mew*." The kitten obviously objected to being left out. She pawed at Sam's bare leg.

"Go away. He's mine," Sam said. Nathan chuckled.

After a while, the pain in his chest abated, and Sam slid off Nathan onto the sofa beside him.

"You know you can stay here as long as you want. I want you to stay."

Sam stroked the kitten's soft fur as she settled down next to him. He wondered if it meant Nathan wanted him to move in on a permanent basis. He didn't know how he felt about the prospect, so he didn't ask. Anyway he was probably being presumptuous. "Thanks."

"I went out and got you a few things."

"You didn't have to do that." He noticed a large pile of bags on the other side of the room with a name written in fancy script. Of course Nathan would have gone to an expensive department store.

"I didn't mind."

A few more beats of silence passed—he wondered what Nathan was thinking, whether he was still angry from their conversation of the previous night. The fire hadn't fundamentally changed anything. Sam had the opportunity to tell the cops about Damon, and he hadn't taken it. And then there was the baseball hat.

Sam figured he might as well broach the topic, since the elephant in the room was getting bigger every minute. "What do you think about what Jack Reed saw?"

"I think he's a little too obsessed with his dog. Otherwise he's the kind of man who wants to be important. He was excited to have an audience. But in spite of that, he wasn't lying. I think he saw what he saw, or at least he believes he did. And it doesn't hurt he might corroborate this older video footage. It would make more sense if there were two arsonists working together instead of one."

Sam didn't even want to consider the possibility that the guy Reed saw had been hiding in his bedroom while he confessed his sexual desires to Nathan. They'd talked about being in love for the first time, too, and the idea of anyone listening in on those intimate moments made his skin crawl. Worse, if the arsonist had been inside, he'd heard them discussing Sam's doubts about Damon. Maybe it had given whoever it was more reason to act.

"What about the Yankees hat? I suppose it could have been a disguise," said Nathan. "But the rest of the description doesn't match Damon either."

"No, it doesn't," Sam admitted. He didn't like the insinuation in Nathan's tone, however. "I know what you're thinking, and I want you to stop."

"The thought crossed your mind too."

"Yuri would never hurt me. He's one of my best friends. He's got no connection to the Chancellors or Shady Brook."

"But if—"

"No. Nathan, this is not happening." Sam stuck his fingers in his ears. "I'm going to sing until you stop. " He refused to believe Yuri could be involved. The thought was unconscionable.

Nathan took his hand. "All right, all right. I'm just considering all options—and perhaps overreacting a little, given what you told me about the two of you. I'm curious about this boyfriend of Damon's, if he exists. And there's something I found today while you were sleeping. Not sure what it means, if anything." Nathan grabbed his laptop from the coffee table. "It's about Scott Krause."

"What about him?"

"Take a look at his obit."

Sam scanned the *Gazette* article. It was written by one of the other freelance journos, a former colleague. Sam hadn't written for the paper in months. He stopped getting softball assignments after his blog indicted the *Gazette* for sugarcoating the recent upheavals in the PD during the Sheldon-Hoff trial.

"Hmm," Sam said, when he got to the end. "A donation to his funeral costs was made by Chancellor and Regan, Attorneys at Law. That's Frank Chancellor's old firm."

"Yes, and I did a little digging. Scott Krause used to work as a janitor for the firm, years ago."

"Another Chancellor connection," Sam said. Could this be the link between the fires they'd been looking for? It didn't seem to account for his own apartment, but his skin prickled with excitement all the same. "So maybe whoever did this wasn't targeting Lindsey after all. But why Scott Krause? Doesn't sound like he was a threating guy. He was out of work on disability. I think we need to talk to the Chancellors."

But Sam had no better luck contacting Frank. The nurse said that no one from the family was able to speak. They were in mourning for their daughter. She hung up after a terse good-bye. Sam sighed in frustration and threw his cell phone on the couch. It was running low on battery, and he needed a new charger. Another fucking thing he'd have to buy.

He put his hands on his hips and stared out the apartment window. Damon was gone. The person Jack Reed had seen in the alley didn't fit his description, and now the police had footage that seemed to place the same person at another crime scene, along with an accomplice. And now the Scott Krause/Chancellor connection. There seemed only one option given the fact they couldn't get the Chancellors on the phone. "Remember when we were talking about taking a trip to the Adirondacks? How about a drive through them instead?"

The conflicted look was back on Nathan's face.

"Trust me, Nathan. Please. You know the law isn't always right. It's not always just. Sometimes, you have to go against your principles to do the right thing."

"All right," said Nathan with a slow nod. "Let's go."

Chapter 15

THEY WOKE early on the day before Halloween. Sam dressed in a new green sweater and jeans and hastily gathered a change of clothes in case they had to spend the night. Nathan had even bought him new socks and shoes. Miraculously, everything fit, aside from being slightly tighter than what he was used to wearing. He fidgeted with the waistband of the slim jeans, which were probably worth more than all the pairs he'd previously owned combined. They made his ass look pretty damn good too. The way Nathan was eyeing him as they packed made Sam regret they didn't have more time.

"This isn't exactly how I imagined our first trip together," Nathan remarked, steering his Mercedes onto the highway. He insisted on driving the six hours to Potsdam, the upstate New York town where Frank and Elizabeth Chancellor had moved after their retirement, ten years before.

Sam wondered what Frank would say when Sam showed up on his doorstep—whether Frank and Beth would even remember him. He hadn't known them well. Both were prominent Stonebridge citizens. Beth once worked in his elementary school as a second grade teacher, and Frank had been the first African-American man to hold a seat on the city council. But even though Sam last saw them years before the accident, Beth Chancellor wrote him a letter of condolence soon after, one of the most heartfelt he received. He wished he'd called or written to thank her.

And he wished he were visiting under other circumstances. Not only was the family dealing with the loss of their only daughter, they had the additional burden of caring for three grandchildren in mourning—one of whom had likely been abused. No wonder they were screening calls. Sam would probably be halfway through a case of whiskey by that point.

"What do you think Rivera will say when he finds out you took off on his case?" Sam asked.

Nathan shrugged, his hands firmly at ten and two on the wheel. "He'll probably be irritated I didn't give him the tip, but I think your connection with the Chancellors might help. And in any case, I think Donna and Tony are letting their personal feelings get in the way of the investigation."

"Yeah, they hate each other's guts." And they were obviously both set on being right to prove the other wrong.

"Something like that," said Nathan.

His voice was strange. Sam looked at his profile. "They're fucking, aren't they?"

"*Were* fucking. Past tense."

"How did you know?"

Nathan seemed surprised. "How didn't you know?"

"Good point." There had been enough tension the night of the fire to kindle another one.

"Plus, even with the new lead, Tony won't let a thing like obstruction slide. He's by the book, all the way—under normal circumstances. I don't know how Donna will react. Hopefully we won't ever have to find out."

Sam bit his lip at the reminder of the burden he'd placed on Nathan. No matter what they said the other night, he still wouldn't forgive himself if Nathan lost his job.

At around eight in the morning, they crossed the border from Connecticut into New York. The farmland changed into the kind of wilderness Sam remembered from family camping trips. Since it was still early morning, their car was one of the few on the highway, and Sam could almost imagine being twelve again, fighting with his little brother in the backseat while his father drove and his mother tried to placate them with cookies and games of "I Spy." Occasionally a farmhouse appeared, decorated with pumpkins and cornstalks and the odd faceless scarecrow. Late fall leaves painted the countryside in a wash of yellow, red, and orange, though many had already fallen.

The sight jogged his brain. He turned to Nathan. "Do you think they're still going ahead with the Halloween party tomorrow night?"

Only a few short weeks before, Sam had been planning to dress up and attend with the rest of their friends, but now he worried what would happen with the arsonist—or arsonists—still on the loose. For all the anxiety in the community, he hadn't heard anything about a cancellation.

"I assume so. But yeah, that's probably not a good idea."

"It's all about the money," Sam said with disgust. The annual tradition brought more tourist dollars into Stonebridge's languishing coffers than every other day of the year combined. "Mayor White's priorities make me sick."

"Agreed. We should still go, though, if we make it back in time," said Nathan. "Keep an eye out for trouble."

A band pressed tightly around Sam's chest. He wanted the entire gang to go together, but he hadn't talked to Yuri since the other day at work, and he had no idea what he would say to Michael the next time they hung out.

"What's up?" Nathan asked.

"I want things to go back to normal. And I'm glad you came with me."

"Well, someone has to keep you out of trouble." Sam had a feeling Nathan wasn't going to let him out of his sight until the arsonists were caught. He didn't particularly mind.

He thought back to their conversation from several nights before and Nathan's reluctance to explore the Dominant/submissive side of their relationship. It was good for them to take their time, but Sam wondered what, other than his own recent dishonesty, might have accounted for the wariness he'd seen on Nathan's face. Certainly he wanted Sam to be sure, to enter into any relationship willingly and out of desire.

There was more to it. He seemed concerned about his own dominating tendencies, even while he wanted to exert them on Sam. Maybe Nathan resisted those impulses because he didn't want to be like his father. Or maybe Sam was way off the mark. In any case, there was no reason he couldn't indulge in the bedroom if Sam wanted it too.

The countryside continued to roll by, the sky a brilliant blue interrupted occasionally by thin cirrus clouds. They were getting closer to Potsdam.

"Have you told your parents about me?" Sam asked casually.

"Not yet."

Sam didn't know why he should be disappointed. He'd expected nothing else. "Oh."

"But I was hoping you'd come home with me for Christmas to meet them. What do you think? Too soon?" The car swerved subtly to the left and then straightened again. "My father will probably disown me, and my mother will pretend everything is fine. It should be entertaining, if nothing else."

Sam didn't hesitate a second time. "I would love to."

"Really?" Nathan's honest, pleased smile made Sam's stomach swarm with butterflies. "What about Tim?"

For the last six years, Christmas meant the anniversary of Sam's parents' death and the de facto loss of his brother. He usually spent the holidays drunk off his ass. Looking back, he realized he'd never expected things to change—and he hadn't tried. Living was harder than being miserable. And as much as he didn't like to think of leaving Tim alone for the holidays, he didn't want to stop living once he started.

"I have to live my life," he said.

"Yeah," said Nathan. "You do."

IT WAS noon when they reached the downtown area, a main street lined with shops and businesses celebrating fall with window displays designed to lure leaf-peepers. A craft fair for local artisans bustled on the town green. One large sign strung over the street on billowing white canvas advertised the annual pumpkin-carving contest the following day. In total, it was a picturesque town, typical of the northeast.

"You hungry?" Sam asked. He rolled the window down, and some street vendors beckoned with tempting smells of grilled meat.

"We should probably go straight there."

Sam assented. "You're right. I almost thought we were on vacation, for a minute."

Nathan continued to drive, following the directions on his GPS. The Chancellors didn't live far from the downtown area.

"Now when we get there, let me do the talking," said Sam. "I don't want them to feel like this is an interrogation."

"I wasn't going to interrogate—"

Sam gave Nathan a look. "I know how you are when you're trying to get information out of someone."

"Are you saying I'm a bully?"

"I'm saying you can get… uh… intense in the moment."

Nathan frowned at him, his bottom lip pouting slightly, and Sam laughed.

"Fine," Nathan said. "But you can't tell them you've seen Damon. You never know what they'll do with the information."

"I'll make sure to be very covert."

"Let's see what you've got, Detective Flynn."

THE WHITE two-story house had black shutters and a fenced-in backyard. Next door, neighborhood children chased a boisterous golden retriever, shrieking as they kicked through a pile of yellow leaves. Sam stepped onto the pavement and shivered at the chill in the air. There were two cars in the driveway. He hoped they'd catch Beth at home, since the nurse seemed determined not to cooperate.

Letting Sam take the lead, Nathan trailed behind him up the natural stone walkway. Nicely laid out, Sam thought. They must have a good landscaper.

He rang the doorbell and waited. When no one answered, he rang it again.

"They must be home," he said. "They have to be."

The door cracked open, and a teenaged girl poked her head out. She had tight braids and wide, wary eyes. It must be Lydia.

"Hello," said Sam. "I'm Sam, and this is Nathan. We're looking for Beth and Frank Chancellor. Are they at home?"

"Are you guys reporters or cops?"

"Uh. No. I know Beth and Frank from Connecticut, and we thought we'd stop by and say hello, since we were in the area." Too much information? Sam smiled and tried to seem pleasant.

The girl considered them. Finally she turned her head and yelled over her shoulder. "Grandma, there're some white guys here saying they know you and Grandpa. They're not cops or reporters. Not sure I believe them."

Sam could feel Nathan's silent laughter behind him.

A few seconds later, an elderly woman appeared at the door. She shook her head and tsked at Lydia. "Child, run along," she said. Lydia kept her wary eyes on Sam and Nathan as she backed away.

"That's my granddaughter," said Beth, smiling at them. "She's yet to learn good manners."

"It's all right," said Sam. "Her manners are better than mine."

Beth cocked her head, a thoughtful smile growing on her face, which was lined with age and grief, though still beautiful. "You're familiar to me."

"Yes, ma'am," said Sam. "I'm Sam Flynn. You knew my parents, Laura and Seamus? My dad used to work with Frank—or against him… whatever."

Beth brought a trembling hand to her lips. "Sam Flynn. Last time I saw you, you were hardly grown. Now you're the spitting image of your mother. Come in, come in."

"Are you sure we're not intruding?"

"Not at all." She opened the door wider, letting Sam and Nathan into her home. It smelled of cooking and a recent cleaning. Lydia had disappeared. "What on earth are you doing up here?" Beth asked, leading them into the living room. "Not that I'm displeased to see a familiar face."

Sam figured he might as well ease into the whole thing. No need to start asking questions right off the bat. "We were passing through, and I thought I'd stop by and pay my respects. I never knew your daughter, but I was very sorry to hear about what happened."

"Thank you," said Beth. Her brown eyes were watery. "That's very kind of you. Please, sit down."

The room was spacious and neat, decorated in a country style with plenty of framed photographs on the side tables and mantle. Sam glanced at a few pictures of the children at various ages—a young Lydia holding a baby who was likely one of her sisters, two toddlers sitting on the lap of an elderly man who still retained a whisper of the handsomeness of his youth. One picture, taken at Christmas, showed Damon standing next to the woman who resembled an older Lydia, presumably Veronica. She had her arm around his shoulders in an inclusive gesture, while the smaller children stood in front of them and smiled for the camera. Robert Jones was noticeably absent. Perhaps he was the one taking the picture.

"I'm Nathan, by the way," Nathan said, extending his hand. "Sam's partner."

Beth's brows drew together in confusion, likely trying to tease out the meaning of the word.

"He's my boyfriend," said Sam.

She smiled, and the tension left her face. "Ah, yes. Sometimes us old folks don't know all the new terminology. Boyfriend, I understand. So you say you're passing through? Are you still living in Stonebridge, then?"

"Yes, ma'am," said Sam.

"Please, call me Beth," said Beth. "Ma'am makes me feel as old as I am."

"Thank you, Beth. Yes, we're up for a couple of days, doing a little sightseeing. Beautiful this time of year."

"It is. Absolutely. I assume you've been to the craft fair?"

"Not yet. But we'll definitely check it out," said Sam.

The three of them looked at each other, and an awkward silence settled over the room. "Well, you must stay for lunch. I have roast chicken in the oven, and I'm sure Frank will want to see you after he wakes up from his nap. He can't come downstairs easily, you see. Not with the emphysema acting up the way it's been."

"We'd love to," said Sam.

Chapter 16

THE TABLE was spread with an impressive home-cooked meal of roasted chicken, butternut squash, stuffing, and gravy. Sam swallowed another bite. "This is delicious, Beth. I haven't had a meal like this in years."

"Cooking gives me something to do," she said, passing over another side dish. Sam took it and spooned some peas onto his plate. "Keeps my mind busy."

"We really do appreciate the hospitality." Nathan made small talk with Beth while Sam ate and tried not to feel self-conscious under the gazes of the three children who stared at him from across the table, picking at their food.

Lydia had hardly spoken a word to anyone, her grandmother included, since she came to the table to eat. Sam wondered what she knew about Damon. Had her grandparents told her he was a suspect in the arson cases?

There was no sign of Frank, but his unpleasant nurse appeared briefly to give Beth a report. Since then, she'd disappeared with two plates of food, probably upstairs to her patient's room.

The twins Damon told Sam about, Leah and Angel, were nine. They seemed a little less skeptical of their visitors, and whispered to each other back and forth, stealing less-than-subtle glances. Sam smiled and sent one of them—they were dressed identically in long-sleeved plaid dresses and wore their hair in pigtails—into a fit of giggles.

"What's so funny?" he asked. Nathan and Beth were in the midst of conversation about the food and the recent cool weather. Safe, innocuous topics.

"Are you and him boyfriends?" asked one of the twins. She blinked at him slowly.

Realizing he was blushing, Sam nodded.

"That means you like him the way a boy likes a girl," said the other.

"Shut up, Leah," groaned the first, obviously Angel. Satisfied he'd finally figured out their names, Sam fought for an answer. Dealing with little kids was not his thing, but he appreciated their bluntness.

"Yeah," he said. "I guess it does."

"It's not like we don't know about stuff," said Angel. "There was a girl at school who had two moms. They even got married."

Leah nodded. "It doesn't seem very fair to have two moms when we don't even have one anymore."

Sam lost his appetite. He felt bad about the false pretenses. As soon as lunch was over, he'd tell Beth the truth. Sam glanced at her, but Beth seemed oblivious to the entire conversation, caught in the snare of Nathan's charm. Poor woman.

"Our mama is in heaven," said Angel. "Grandma said so."

"Your grandma is a smart woman."

"I miss her a lot. And Daddy."

"I'm so sorry about your mom and dad," Sam said. "My parents are in heaven too." He didn't really believe in heaven, but if it did exist, he was pretty sure they were there. His statement seemed to impress the twins.

"They are?" Leah's eyes widened.

"Yeah." Next to them, Lydia had begun stabbing her chicken with her fork, staring glumly at her plate. Ending the conversation was probably in everyone's best interest. He looked to Nathan for help, and Nathan raised a quizzical eyebrow.

"Shut up. Just shut the fuck up. All of you." Lydia slammed her fist down on the table.

"Lydia," Beth said calmly. "Watch your language."

"Who cares about my language?" Lydia said. "My mom is dead, and you expect me to sit here and smile?" She glared at her grandmother and pushed her chair back to stand. "I hate this stupid town and this stupid house, and I hate you." The twin's eyes went wide as they clutched each other.

Sam exchanged a glance with Nathan.

"You don't mean that," said Beth. "I know it's hard, baby. It's hard on all of us."

"But you're talking about the weather. Damon is somewhere out there, and you're talking about the goddamn weather."

"Lydia, go upstairs to your room." Beth's voice was quiet and calm, though it quavered underneath. "Now. You'll disturb your grandfather, carrying on like that." But Lydia had turned her attention to Sam and Nathan and seemed to have no intention of leaving.

"What are you really doing here?" she demanded. "What do you know about the fires back home? Do you know where Damon is?" She turned her hopeful eyes on him, and Sam was tempted to tell her yes, he had seen her foster brother. It was obvious she had no idea of his whereabouts, so they had been wrong about Damon possibly coming there to hide.

"Well?" Lydia asked. "You don't really expect me to believe you guys randomly dropped by, do you?"

"Angel, Leah." Beth spoke up. "Go upstairs and play."

"But we haven't finished yet," Leah protested.

Her grandmother shook her head. "Go on and play a game in your room, and I'll be up soon."

"Okay." Angel stood up and grabbed her sister's shoulder. "Grandma wants to talk to these guys without us listening."

Once the younger children had gone, Lydia frowned. "I'm not going." She crossed her arms over her chest. "I'm right, aren't I?"

Feeling it was far past time for honesty, Sam put down his fork and pushed his plate away. "You are. I was waiting for the right time to mention it. I apologize if we misled you, but yes, we're trying to figure out who's responsible for the fires in Stonebridge."

Nathan cleared his throat. "Apologies, Beth. We should have spoken up sooner."

"I called several times and tried to talk to you," Sam said. "But we couldn't get through."

"I see." Beth didn't seem angry, only a little shocked.

Sam gave Lydia a small smile. "You're pretty sharp."

"You guys are pretty obvious."

"Maybe we are."

"Not police or reporters, you said?" Lydia arched an eyebrow and pursed her lips, reminding Sam of Damon.

"Nathan is with the FBI, and I'm a reporter. But we're here in an unofficial capacity."

Nathan nudged Sam with an elbow, telling him to get on with it.

"Right, then. My apartment burned down the other night. We assume it was the work of the same arsonist—or arsonists—who've been active in Stonebridge these last few weeks."

"I didn't know," Beth said. "I'm so sorry to hear that."

"Thank you. In any case, we were lucky." Sam took Nathan's hand. "No one was hurt in the fire in my building. But we want to make sure we catch whoever did this before anyone else is."

"You don't think it was Damon?" asked Lydia, her voice cracking.

"At this point, we have no idea," said Sam. "But I do doubt he was responsible. In fact, some new evidence has come to light that suggests there might be two people working together. The police don't have an ID on them yet, though, which is why we're here. Beth, do you happen to remember a man named Scott Krause?"

She looked from Sam to Nathan. "Yes. He used to work for my husband's office. He was a janitor some years ago." She shook her head. "Terrible, terrible."

"Sam and I think there might be a connection between the fires."

"What connection?" Beth's face paled. She gripped the edge of the table.

"Your family, to put it bluntly."

"I'm not quite sure I understand," said Beth.

Sam put his elbows on the table and then, remembering his manners, drew them back. "To tell you the truth, we're not exactly sure either. But one of the victims is your daughter. Another victim died at the place your daughter was supposed to be working, and a third is a former employee of your husband's. We need to see if there might be a link between them. Did Veronica know Scott Krause?"

Beth frowned in thought. "I imagine she would have seen him around when she visited Frank at the office. But I don't know if they were further acquainted, no. He was a troubled man." Sam suspected Beth might have said more, but refrained for Lydia's sake. "Still, my husband always treated him kindly. When we heard he'd died, Frank made sure his partner—did you ever meet Albert? Yes. Well, Frank made sure Albert made a donation for funeral costs."

So far, everything she'd said matched what Sam and Nathan knew.

"Damon hasn't come here? He hasn't tried to initiate any sort of contact?"

"No," said Beth. Lydia's bottom lip trembled, and a tear dropped onto her cheek.

Sam hesitated. "And do you know of anyone who could be helping him? Someone we could contact so we could help him too?" Maybe Lydia had some knowledge of this boyfriend. Damon seemed to trust her.

"Damon didn't have many friends," said Lydia. "Do you... do you think he's all right?" Another tear fell, and she brushed it away with a flick of her wrist.

Sam didn't want to give her false assurances, but he nodded all the same. "I think he is."

Outside, the wind picked up. The afternoon forecast predicted rain and wet snow. Beth got up from her seat at the table, went to where Lydia stood, and put her hands on her granddaughter's shoulders. She leaned down and whispered something in Lydia's ear, but the girl shook her head vehemently. Sam figured Beth had asked her to go upstairs with the other children. She dabbed Lydia's face with her sleeve.

"I'm fine, Grandma," Lydia said, pushing her away, though her tone was affectionate.

"Beth, we're so sorry to bother your family during this terrible time," said Nathan. "But do you think we could talk to Frank?"

She cocked her head and looked up at the ceiling. "You'll need to keep him as calm as possible. His emphysema makes it difficult for him to talk."

"Of course. We won't disturb him any more than necessary," Nathan promised.

"All right." She motioned to them. "Follow me. He should be awake by now."

The second floor consisted of five rooms, and the door closest to the stairs was cracked open, showing the twins sitting on the floor working on a puzzle. Lydia went in to check on her sisters while Beth led Sam and Nathan down the hall toward the back of the house.

"Frank loves this room. He can see the lake outside, beyond our property," Beth explained. She knocked gently.

Frank's nurse was finishing up with him when they entered. It smelled faintly of antiseptic and something less pleasant. The nurse spoke quietly with Beth for a moment and then gathered her things to give them privacy. She nodded curtly at Nathan and Sam on the way out.

Frank Chancellor appeared to be dozing, but when he heard voices, his rheumy eyes opened, and he regarded the new visitors curiously. Tubes wound around the old man's ears and under his nose, connecting to his oxygen supply next to the bed. The scene brought back vague memories of Sam's paternal grandfather, who had an oxygen tank on wheels when Sam was little.

"Frank," Beth said, turning on the light at the side of the bed. "We have some visitors today from Stonebridge. Do you remember this boy?

He's all grown up now." She spoke loudly. Frank moved his wizened hand to the bed controls so he could sit upright.

"All right, woman. Don't talk at me like I'm deaf." Frank was weakened by illness, as Beth had warned, but his voice still held traces of booming authority. "Stonebridge, you say?" He squinted at them.

"He can be a little irritable," Beth whispered with a hint of mischief.

"Don't tell these gentlemen what I can and can't be. Mercy." Frank rolled his eyes, and Sam grinned. In the few times they'd met, he always liked Frank Chancellor.

"Wait a minute," Frank said, looking at Sam. "I know you. You're Sam Flynn, aren't you? Little Sammy?"

"I guess so, Sir."

Frank barked a laugh, which became a phlegmy cough. "I can't believe it. I used to give your daddy a run for his money back in the day." Frank smiled. "He was a good lawyer and a good man, your daddy. You look like him."

Sam smiled at the fact that each of the Chancellors thought he looked like one of his parents.

"It was a damn shame what happened to your folks. Suspicious too, if you ask me." Frank tutted and shook his head. "And your little brother. What a sweet boy he was. I swear I—"

"Frank, that's enough." Beth turned to Sam and Nathan with an apologetic expression. "Don't mind him. He's been up here so long by himself he forgets how to talk to people."

"Only 'cause you never let me out, woman."

Sam laughed at their banter. It was easy to see how fond they were of one another, even after so many years of marriage. He couldn't imagine being with someone for fifty years. At one point, not so long before, he would have scoffed at the idea. But with Nathan… it wasn't an unappealing prospect. He caught a glimpse of his boyfriend out of the corner of his eye, and was gratified to find Nathan watching him with a warm expression. It helped alleviate the queasy feeling in his gut caused by the mention of the accident.

"We're very sorry about what happened to your daughter," Nathan said. Frank immediately sobered.

"Thank you." His voice quavered when he spoke again. "At least we have the girls with us now, and they're safe."

As though she'd heard herself being summoned, Lydia appeared in the doorway. She took a step into the room and glanced around at the adults to see if she'd be welcomed or sent away. Frank wiped at his eyes. "Hi, Grandpa," she said cautiously.

"Hey, baby. You come here now." She approached and sat on the side of the bed. "You all right?" he asked her, patting her hand. She nodded.

"Sir," said Sam, tentatively interrupting the family moment.

"Call me Frank," Frank replied.

"Frank, at the risk of bringing up a difficult subject, we need to talk to you about the fires happening in Stonebridge. My apartment building was the most recent target."

"Damn. You don't say?"

Not wanting to waste any more time, Sam quickly filled Frank in on what he'd told Lydia and Beth downstairs. As he spoke, Frank's eyebrows drew together until they nearly formed one thick line of gray.

"And you think there might be some connection between Scotty Krause and Veronica?"

"That's what we're wondering, Si—Frank," said Sam. "As far as the link to my own building, I'm not sure yet." Unless the arsonists had discovered Sam was meeting with Damon and wanted to silence him.

"You don't think it was the kid, hmm? I don't either. I've been saying all along to Betty, this is racial profiling, like we used to see in the fifties and sixties. People want to say things have gotten better, but they haven't. Not when you read the statistics. You know a black man is six times more likely to be sent to prison than a white man? Sometimes I get so mad I want to get up out of this bed and march straight to Washington."

"Your marching days are over," said Beth.

"I'll march for you, Grandpa."

Frank smiled up at Lydia. "You'll change the world, baby."

Sam stood off to the side with Nathan while the family talked. At least Frank hadn't entirely rejected the idea of a connection.

"All right, all right, son," Frank said, calling Sam back. "I want to find the person responsible as much as any man. How can I help?"

"Can you think of anyone who might have known both Veronica and Scott Krause?"

It was an obviously shitty question. Frank gave him an exasperated look. "Many people might have, but I've been away for ten years."

"Did Veronica have any enemies?" Nathan asked. A look passed between Beth and Frank, who in turn both glanced at Lydia. Sam knew they were thinking about Lydia's father.

"No one who would explain what happened to your place," Frank replied cryptically.

Beth echoed his sentiment. "My daughter was a sweetheart. Everyone loved her."

The answer made it obvious Veronica had never told her parents about Nick Granger and the sexual harassment suit at work. It made sense, given their advanced ages. She probably hadn't wanted to worry them. Sam figured he might as well let sleeping dogs lie. Granger had an alibi, unfortunately.

"Did you ever defend a client who might want to get back at you?" Nathan asked. "Maybe someone who wasn't happy with a court ruling?"

"Lots of them," said Frank. "I worked as a lawyer for over forty years, and in that time, I lost a lot of cases. Won lots of 'em too, but the client relationship is almost always difficult."

"I understand." Nathan looked slightly disappointed, but he pushed on. "Did anyone ever threaten you or your family?"

As they spoke, Beth wrangled Lydia off the bed and into the hall. After a few protests from her granddaughter, she returned and shut the door quietly behind her. Sam had a feeling the conversation was going to take a dark turn.

Frank closed his eyes and leaned his head back against his pillow. "Hmm. Yes. A few people through the years. There was… what was that man's name? Betty, do you remember? Back in eighty-four? Charles?"

"Charles Wilkins."

"Ah, yes. Charles Wilkins. Second-degree murder. Killed his wife with a frying pan." Nathan jotted down the name. "I think he might have died in prison, though."

"Anyone else?" Nathan asked.

"Samantha Robard. Drowned her three children. Terrible case, and one of my last. I argued postpartum, but she got time."

"Anyone who was accused of arson?" Sam glanced at Nathan's notepad and noticed he had drawn question marks after each of the names.

"Hmm. Not arson, but there was a man I represented. God, must have been almost twenty years ago. He was building bombs to blow up his old high school. There were plans in his basement, explosive materials, the works. He was a sociopath. You couldn't tell at first. No. At first he was a very charismatic, very charming young man. Working on his PhD until he dropped out. Rich kid. Brilliant. That's why the conviction was so surprising."

"What was his name?" Nathan asked.

"Randall Palmer. He was a zealot, and I don't mean the religious kind. No. He was the type who only believed in himself. Thought the world had done him a terrible wrong." Frank shook his head.

"Where was this?" Sam asked. He couldn't remember ever hearing about such a case in Stonebridge. Then again, he'd only been a kid at the time.

"Up north, near the Massachusetts border. Used to travel on occasion. When I agreed to take the case, he told me he'd been set up. Eventually it became clear that wasn't true."

"And was Scott Krause working at your firm during this time?" Nathan grabbed his phone out of his pocket.

"Let's see. In '97? Yes. I believe he was."

"Hmm." Sam caught Nathan's eye. "You think there could be something to this?"

"Could be. What did Palmer look like? How tall was he?" Nathan asked.

"He was a white guy. Average height. Maybe five foot nine? Brown hair. You can probably find a picture online."

Nathan kept typing, scrolling, and typing. Finally he let out a sound. "Found one. It's not very good quality."

He showed it to Sam. Randall Palmer looked like many young men had looked in the late nineties, with lank brown hair and a scruffy, bearded face. He wore an orange prison jumpsuit and stared at the camera with defiance. *Former Enfield High Student Charged In Domestic Terror Plot.*

"Nothing more recent?" Sam asked. The guy gave him the creeps, but there was something oddly familiar about him.

"No. And there's not much on him at all—just old copy on his conviction."

Disappointing, but at least they had a few names to go on. Sam didn't want to get his hopes up yet, though.

Nathan excused himself to make some calls, and Sam thanked Frank for his time and promised to keep in touch with any new information. He left him to rest. By the time Sam got downstairs, Nathan was on the phone with the federal prison where Randall Palmer had spent seventeen years of his life.

"I see." Nathan's face was a storm cloud. "I see. Can you pull that information for me after you check out my ID? Thank you."

Fifteen minutes later, Nathan was back on the line with whomever had put him on hold. "Yes, of course. The address, please." He started jotting notes down on a pad on the coffee table. Curious, Sam leaned over to watch.

129 Beech Street, Cleveland, Ohio appeared in Nathan's neat script. "Thank you, you've been very helpful." Nathan hung up the phone.

"Ohio?" Sam asked.

Nathan glared down at the address. "He moved after he was released on good behavior two years ago."

"Still there?"

"That's what we're going to find out."

The news wasn't good. Not only had Randall Palmer disappeared from his Cleveland apartment a year before, he hadn't been seen by the few acquaintances Nathan managed to get ahold of—including an angry landlady who was owed three months of missed rent.

"He could be anywhere in the country by now." Sam shivered. "What about the others?"

"Tony will be able to run the names."

Sam nodded. Feeling the need to do something, he called Yuri and Rachel while Nathan did his detective shtick, but only Rachel answered.

After he filled her in, she sighed deeply. "Sounds like this guy really has a chip on his shoulder. It's freaky no one knows where he is."

"Yes. So please, Rach, be careful out there, okay? After what happened to my place, I want to make sure my friends are safe."

"Thanks for the update. Take care, all right? Hugs to Nathan?"

"If you can get ahold of Yuri, tell him too. I left a message."

"Will do."

Sam hung up feeling unsettled. He thought again of the Yankees cap on the surveillance vid. Even if it was impossible for Yuri to be involved, the fact that he couldn't get his friend on the phone continued to bother him.

In the evening, Sam joined the family for dinner as Nathan worked—though Beth sent him a plate of food to eat in the living room. Everyone was curious about what was going on, especially Lydia. Sam apologized for the continued intrusion, but Beth insisted they stay as long as necessary and said she hoped they were onto something. After dinner, Sam helped with the dishes. He wasn't about to accept hospitality without giving back.

Later, in the living room with Nathan, Sam glanced at the time and could hardly believe the entire day had passed. It was after ten, and the night was dark and rainy. The thought of heading back on a six-hour drive did not appeal in the slightest. He yawned and slumped against the couch.

Nathan, who had been on and off the phone with many people throughout the day, only pausing to give Sam sporadic reports, sat next to him.

"Well, looks like Wilkins is dead and Robard was released last year, but she lives in Florida. No luck on ID'ing Palmer in Stonebridge. If he's there, he's likely under another name. He'd be over forty by now. Looks like they've found the blue Toyota on a street camera too. Stolen car."

"I was afraid you'd say that."

Nathan was quiet for a moment, scrolling through his phone. Another picture of Randall Palmer, this one taken at his conviction, showed a somber, angry man in an orange jumpsuit. Just as Frank said, he looked like the type of person who thought the world was out to get him. Of course, given the fact he'd just been sentenced to twenty years, he had good reason to scowl.

"You know, this is going to sound crazy, but there's something familiar about him to me," said Nathan. "I can't put my finger on it."

"I had the same thought," said Sam. "I've seen him before. But where?"

They stared at the picture for another minute. Sam shook his head and stifled another yawn. "Maybe we should head home."

Nathan wrapped his arm around Sam's shoulders. "You're exhausted."

"I'm fine." But being hugged was nice, and Sam closed his eyes, glad for the moment alone.

"I think we should get some sleep and leave first thing in the morning. There's nothing else we can do tonight. In any case, it sounds like Tony and Donna are working together now, not against each other." Nathan kissed his temple. His breath ruffled Sam's hair.

"But what if something happens? What about Damon? We need—"

Nathan interrupted. "We're not going to be very useful if we're tired, okay? Let's sleep. Beth said she has an extra guest room, and I could use a shower."

"You smell good to me," Sam said, breathing deep. Nathan's scent relaxed him, and the tension in his body started to melt away. It was true they'd done all they could for the moment. Maybe a little sleep wouldn't hurt.

Nathan chuckled, and Sam raised his head for a lingering kiss. Even with his mouth tasting of stale coffee, Nathan was delicious.

"I think we make a pretty good team," Sam said.

"Even though you don't think my interrogation techniques are effective?" Nathan asked.

"I never said they weren't effective. They're too damn effective, if I remember correctly."

Nathan huffed. "I don't know what you're talking about."

"Oh, no? You don't remember a particular night back at your old house?" Nathan had tried to pick Sam's brain regarding the last time he'd seen Emma alive, and Sam hadn't known whether Nathan was going to strangle him or fuck him. Neither happened at that moment, but the encounter still stood out in Sam's mind as one of the most erotic of his life, in spite of the heavy context of the situation. Sam gave Nathan a chance to chase the memory, and then a flush of recognition colored Nathan's cheeks.

Sam leaned up for another kiss. "I remember feeling bad for the criminals. No one could resist you. Though somehow, I don't think those same techniques would have worked on Frank."

Nathan laughed and squeezed his arm tighter around Sam. "Yeah. Probably not."

"Then again, you never know."

A gentle throat clearing let them know they weren't alone anymore, and Sam pulled back from the embrace, giving Nathan a small smile. He turned to see Beth standing in the doorway with one hand braced on the frame. "Well? Do you want to take me up on the offer? The bed's small, but it's comfortable."

Sam nodded. "Thanks, we will."

"We appreciate it," said Nathan.

Beth shrugged off the thanks. "It's the least I can do. You're going to find the people who killed my daughter." Her face crumpled. "Oh God," she sobbed, clutching onto the doorframe.

Sam recognized the moment of the break, because he'd had one of those himself the day of his parents' funeral. Until then, he'd been operating on autopilot. Numb. During the funeral, he stood next to his parents' caskets as they were lowered into the winter earth and then returned home to a host of strangers and friends offering their condolences. Meaning well, they filled up his refrigerator with more lasagna and tuna casserole than one person could ever eat.

Once the guests were gone, he stared at the accumulation of food for at least ten minutes, holding the fridge door open and letting out all the cold air. Then he slammed it. And slammed it, and slammed it. He took the food his neighbors brought and, in a frenzy of tears and anger, stabbed it down the garbage disposal until the thing broke and left him with a sink full of soupy ricotta cheese.

He'd gone upstairs with a bottle of his father's prized eighteen-year single malt, reserved only for special occasions, and woken up with the worst hangover of his life. The next morning he packed and left the house, never to enter it again.

Without thinking, Sam crossed the room and put his arm around Beth's shoulders. She pressed the back of her hand to her face as though the gesture might hold back the accumulation of tears. "I'm sorry," she said. "I shouldn't be like this. I'm making a fool of myself."

"Hey. It's all right. Cry all you want."

Nathan watched from the couch, his handsome face drawn with tiredness.

"I keep thinking she'll call and tell me she's coming back for the children. But she's not coming back, is she? My baby." Her voice was thick. "My only baby." Yes, Sam understood his own personal sorrow, but he would probably never know the profound grief that came with the loss of a child.

"We're going to find them," Nathan said.

Sam blinked back the burning in his own eyes. "We'll do whatever we can," he told her. It was tempting to promise, but he didn't want to give false assurances, not even for the sake of comfort. He had no idea what would happen once they returned to Stonebridge.

Later, under the floral duvet of the small but comfortable bed, Sam twisted to face Nathan in the darkness. The gentle whisper of air against his cheek made Sam think Nathan had already fallen asleep.

"I love you," Sam said anyway.

"I love hearing you say that."

A warm feeling spread through Sam's limbs, and he snuggled closer, so they were chest-to-chest. The proximity was nice after the emotionally charged day and, in spite of his tiredness and the inconvenient circumstances, Sam's cock responded.

"I don't think we should risk it," Nathan whispered against his cheek. His lips caught on the skin there, and Sam turned his head to greet Nathan in a deep, opened-mouth kiss.

Sam let out a shaky sigh when they broke apart. His dick didn't seem to care they were in someone else's house, and if the erection nudging against his pelvis was any indication, neither did Nathan's. "Then you shouldn't kiss me like that."

"Then you shouldn't be so sexy." Nathan's voice was rough with arousal. Risking the tease, Sam reached between them and squeezed Nathan's cock. "Dammit," Nathan groaned into Sam's shoulder. "Quit it."

"Do you really want me to?"

"We can't. There are children down the hall." Nathan wasn't doing much to stop him, though. He reached for Sam's neck and drew him close to kiss again. Their tongues touched as they breathed together, and Sam continued rubbing Nathan's cock through his briefs.

"I'd do anything for you, anything you wanted. I'm yours." He licked into Nathan's mouth, and Nathan shuddered against him.

"Do you want to play, Sam?"

"Yes."

"If you want to stop at any time, just squeeze my right hand, okay? We don't want to wake anyone up."

"We won't." Arousal warmed Sam's belly, and his groin tightened. "And I won't stop."

"Then suck my cock. And you better swallow every drop." There was an edge to Nathan's voice. "Do it now, before I change my mind."

Sam shimmied down under the covers. Their mingled body heat made it stuffy as he crouched between Nathan's parted thighs. Heart pounding with excitement, Sam wasted no time working Nathan's briefs down over his ass and gripping his erection at the base. He couldn't see the swollen flesh, but he could feel how hard Nathan was when he licked at the head and tasted his salty precome. He lapped the retracted foreskin and felt the velvet shift under his tongue.

Nathan held his cock with one hand and swept the other through Sam's hair and held his head firmly. "Open up," he whispered hoarsely.

Sam did as he was told. Nathan snapped his hips up as he tugged Sam's head down, impaling him deeply. His thick erection hit the back of Sam's throat. Sam's muscles convulsed as he tried to swallow the intrusion and breathe through his nose, but Nathan wasn't kidding around. He forced Sam's head down into his lap and fucked up with his hips. Sam fought his gag reflex on each thrust, even as Nathan held him tighter, his cock seeming to grow harder and longer. It was humid under the sheets, and Sam's eyes watered, but he held on to Nathan's hips, letting Nathan use him, reveling in the forceful slide of Nathan's silky cock, his taste, his musky scent.

Sam's dick ached, but he didn't make any move to touch it. He wanted it to be perfect. He wanted to show Nathan how good he could be if only Nathan would let go.

And he did.

The bed creaked slightly with one, two more strokes, and Nathan's cock throbbed hotly with release. Sam coughed a little, but he did his best to clean every last drop of come until Nathan was too sensitive to touch. Nathan shuddered and tugged Sam's shoulders to bring him up from under the covers. They lay side by side as Sam gasped and filled his lungs with cool, fresh air. His throat felt raw and scratchy from use, and his hard cock craved attention. He reached down to touch himself.

"No." Nathan moved his hand away. "You don't get to come tonight."

"What?" Sam's mind was foggy with lust. "But I did what you asked."

"You did, but only after goading me in the first place." Nathan's tone was firm. He petted Sam's sweaty hair back from his face. "You think you're ready to obey, but I don't think you know what it means."

Clenching his hands into fists so he wouldn't be tempted to touch himself again, Sam let the words sink in. This was another one of Nathan's tests—and as horny as he was, he could do this. He wanted to. "Okay."

"I know you're hard." Nathan cupped Sam's hard length and gave it a gentle squeeze. "You liked that, didn't you?" His voice was husky, darkly pleased.

"Yeah," Sam admitted.

"You liked me using you?"

"Yeah. But only because I knew you'd never hurt me."

"You trust me?"

"Completely."

Nathan sighed. Even in the darkness, Sam could see Nathan studying him. He hoped his continued silence was evidence he was mulling over the possibilities, seeing how serious Sam was. His balls were sore, but still he made no move to relieve himself, and gradually, excruciatingly, he started to soften.

After a few minutes, Nathan kissed him. His fingers gentled over Sam's swollen lips. "You were so good," Nathan said. He slid his arms around Sam, and in the embrace, Sam could feel some of Nathan's resistance give way.

It wasn't quite as good as an orgasm, but hearing Nathan's praise was damn close.

Chapter 17

THE MORNING of October thirty-first dawned bright and crisp. Overnight, the clouds and rain gave way to sunshine. After thanking the Chancellors again and promising they'd call as soon as they had news, Nathan and Sam were on the road heading back to Stonebridge, driving at well over the legal limit. Nathan grinned as he floored the gas. He looked well rested and sated. And no surprise, Sam thought grouchily. *Someone* had gotten an awesome blow job.

Nathan's phone rang. "It's Tony," he said. He turned on the speakerphone so Sam could hear the conversation too. "Walker here."

"Hey, Nate," Rivera said. "Got some news you might find interesting."

"What's up?"

"Well, Palmer's mother died at Shady Brook three years ago—complications from an aggressive brain tumor. His father committed suicide soon after."

"Are you serious?" Sam asked.

"Hello, Sam. And yes, I'm always serious," said Rivera. "Then we did a little digging on Scott Krause's work history and disability claims. He had many of them, some fraudulent. And I found something in his bank records. About five months ago, he got a lump sum deposit. No paper trail."

"How much?" Sam asked.

"Twenty grand."

Nathan whistled. "A payoff?"

"Maybe. We have a warrant to pull his phone and e-mail records now. It's possible Krause recognized Palmer somewhere and tried to blackmail him. Then he blew through the money and wanted more. He only had five dollars in his account when he died."

"Hmm. Does sound suspicious."

"He worked at a bunch of places over the past year," Rivera continued. "The high school, a couple supermarkets, the college, as well as some private residences. We're looking at all fellow employees and customers, but it's quite a list. Oh, and another thing. The Toyota showed up last night in a swamp outside of town. Someone dumped it. We've got it in the lab now."

"Sounds like you've moved on from Damon Blake as a suspect," said Nathan.

"He could still be involved. But I think we're finally getting somewhere. All right. Gotta run. Don—the chief's here."

Nathan raised an eyebrow at Sam, and Sam grinned back. "Wait a sec, Tony," said Nathan. "What's going on with the party tonight?"

"It's still on. Mayor White says if we cancel, the terrorists win."

"Are you kidding me?" Sam could hardly believe what he was hearing. Thousands of people in costumes with killers on the loose. What could go wrong? Nathan sped by another car and passed on the dotted line just in time to avoid some oncoming traffic.

"There'll be a heavy police presence."

"We'll be there too," Sam assured him.

"Be careful. Stay out of the spotlight. You should still consider yourself a target."

When Nathan ended the call, he glanced over at Sam. "It's not his fault about the party."

Sam scoffed. "Talk about stupidity." A huge crowd of people would create an ideal situation for further escalation of violence. With everyone in disguise, how could the cops even track down the arsonist? Rivera had sounded so in control on the phone, but Sam knew the pitfalls of overconfidence. If he fucked it up, they were all screwed.

He stared out the window and thought over what they'd learned. The twenty grand sounded suspicious, but something about it didn't make sense.

"I don't get it. If Scott Krause recognized Palmer over five months ago, why didn't the guy just kill him then? Why pay him off?"

Nathan hummed. "Could be he wasn't ready. From what Frank said, Palmer was meticulous. He'd been planning the high school bombing for over a year when he was caught. Maybe he thought he'd buy some time. Or maybe he didn't want to kill him until he had no other choice."

"But he did in the end."

"Looks like it."

"And now he knows we're involved. Maybe he read my blog? He could have followed me and seen me talking to Damon. Do you think he tried to stop us from going to the Chancellors'?" Sam shifted uncomfortably in his seat.

"It's possible. And it makes me concerned for Damon, to tell you the truth."

Sam shook his head. Damon could be anywhere. He could be in danger. He could already be—no, Sam wouldn't even think it.

"What I want to know is who's the accomplice," said Nathan. "If it is Palmer, he's average height. That description doesn't match the man Jack Reed saw. And we already know Damon doesn't either."

Sam covertly cracked his knuckles, a habit Nathan hated, as he tried to sort out the details. He had a feeling they were missing something crucial. Worse, Yuri still hadn't returned his call or any of his messages. Maybe he was at work. Or maybe Michael didn't want Sam to talk to him now they'd reconciled. In any case, he was going to kick his friend's ass for making him worry. "Hopefully they'll find something in the car. Even if it was in the water, fingerprints and DNA can still survive, right?" he asked to distract himself.

Nathan passed another car on the left, crossing over the solid line, and the woman driving gave them the finger. "Yes. Especially since it was only for a short period. He might know the cops are onto him. And a desperate criminal is a dangerous criminal."

Sam checked his phone again. Nothing. Frustrated, Sam shut it off to conserve the low battery and watched browning cornfields speed past.

"YOU LOOK—"

"Like an idiot."

When they reached Stonebridge, they immediately headed to the picked-over costume shop to grab what they could, both agreeing it was a good idea to blend in at the street party and conceal their identities. Nathan found a Batman mask and cape amongst the rubble, and rounded out the outfit with tight black jeans and his old Doc Martens—not a terrible costume, given it had been thrown together in five minutes. He looked damnably sexy. Sam, however, wasn't so lucky. He stood in front of the mirror with his arms crossed.

"I'm not going anywhere in this."

"I was going to say," Nathan whispered in his ear from behind, "you look hot."

The label on the package read "Sexy Scotsman" and showed a picture of a man with a kilt down to his knees, but Sam figured his version must be child's size. The thing barely reached midthigh. It was a miniskirt. He tugged it down, but it didn't budge. He might as well be carrying a "TOP NEEDED" sign.

"I'm wearing jeans."

"That's not very traditional," Nathan said, running his hands up and down Sam's torso, which was bare except for a flimsy swath of plaid fabric wrapped from waist to opposite shoulder. His touch made gooseflesh pebble Sam's skin.

"I'm not wearing the hat, either." Sam pointed at the offending cap on the floor. It had a *feather*.

"Fine. Ruin the look." Nathan kissed his neck and chuckled. "But I might want to get the full effect another time." He squeezed Sam's ass to give his intent more visceral meaning.

Sam wrinkled his nose. "I look like Britney Spears circa 1997."

The doorbell rang. "Put on jeans. Don't put on jeans. We have to go."

Rachel and Alex were chatting with Nathan when Sam finally entered, his dignity restored with a pair of jeans and a long-sleeved shirt under the plaid debacle.

"What are you supposed to be?" Rachel asked. "Nineties grunge?"

"A Sexy Scotsman," Sam mumbled.

After the peals of laughter died down, Sam got a chance to check out his friends' costumes. They'd done the couple thing, both dressed in shapeless khaki, but he couldn't quite figure it out. "So you're prisoners?" Rachel wore a long black wig instead of her natural hair.

"We're Piper and Alex," Rachel said with exasperation.

"But I'm Piper, and she's Alex." Alex fluffed her blonde bob. "Prison lesbians. Isn't it so meta?"

"Ahh. *Orange is the New Black*. Very clever," Sam said.

"So, have you guys heard from Yuri and Michael yet?" Rachel asked, watching Nathan adjust his Glock with a slightly alarmed look on her face. Sam wasn't going to object to Nathan arming himself, though. They'd need the protection if they ran into the arsonist and his accomplice.

Sam shook his head. "No. I've called Yuri a few times, but no one's answered."

"He hasn't answered my calls either," said Rachel. "Do you think they're all right?"

"They're probably holed up in their love nest having make-up sex." Alex drew out the word love and fluttered her eyelashes.

"Honey, you are so romantic, it's adorable." Rachel nosed the side of Alex's face.

"That's why you love me."

"One of the reasons." They kissed and smiled at each other like lovesick puppies, and Sam might have barfed if he hadn't been guilty of looking at Nathan the same way. He whistled, and Alex and Rachel broke apart.

"Maybe we should swing by their place to check," said Sam. The uneasiness he'd felt for most of the day returned with a vengeance.

Nathan snapped his holster into place and pulled his black leather jacket over it, then tied the cape around his neck. The whole vigilante-out-for-justice look was a little on the nose, given what they planned, but it was perfect.

"Okay," Rachel said, still making gooey eyes at her girlfriend. "What's our strategy?" Sam had filled her in on the latest developments.

"Sam and I have been talking it over," Nathan said. "There's no guarantee anything will happen tonight, but it's best to be prepared." He handed Rachel and Alex a can of pepper spray. "We're going to keep our eyes and ears open for anything unusual. If something happens and we get split up, call the police immediately."

"Got it," said Alex.

"Let's take two cars in case," suggested Sam. "Maybe one pair of us should head over to Michael and Yuri's first?"

"Great idea. Rach and I will go. I know you've been worried, sweetie." Alex kissed Rachel's cheek.

"Maybe it would be better to divide guy-girl, guy-girl," said Sam. Nathan agreed.

Rachel rolled her eyes at them. "Oh, like Sam's going to protect us? With what, his smart-assed attitude?"

"Hey!" he exclaimed.

"Come on, enough sexist bullshit. I've had to kick guys bigger than Nathan out of the bar. I'm staying with my girl."

"It's a matter of training—"

"Save it, Nathan," said Sam. "She's got that look in her eye."

Rachel stuck her tongue out at him. "Listen. I'll call you when we get over there."

"Call Nathan. My phone's almost dead."

"Will do. Stay safe."

"You too."

Sam took Nathan's gloved hand and squeezed. "I think we're good to go."

BY THE time Sam and Nathan arrived at the party, hundreds of people filled the streets, wearing all manner of costumes from minimalist to the most extravagant cosplays Sam ever saw. He tried not to look suspicious by staring at anyone for too long.

"Do you think we should wander, or stay put?" Sam asked Nathan, who was getting quite a few appreciative looks from women. One, around Sam's age, stopped her friend on the street and whispered in her ear, and the two stood and gaped like they might want to have Nathan for breakfast, lunch, and dinner. Sam couldn't blame them. Nathan didn't seem to notice. He was in work mode.

"Let's wander a little."

Several streets were blocked off for the event, and the vendors lining them sold everything from candy apples to hot dogs to pumpkin pie. Sam took Nathan's hand, even though it earned them occasional dirty looks from some of Stonebridge's less-tolerant citizens. Sam ignored them and continued scanning the crowd.

They passed a band on the courthouse steps playing seventies cover rock with the occasional Halloween standard thrown in for good measure. There was a very visible police presence mixing in with the revelers, as Rivera had promised.

"So what do you think?" Sam asked Nathan. They'd been up and down the main drag and back alleys at least a dozen times, with no sign of trouble. The area was getting more and more congested, which made Sam nervous.

"Hang on a sec. My phone's buzzing." Nathan put one hand to his ear and answered. "Hi, Rachel. Really? Hmm. Well, maybe you should head back here, then." A pause. "Yes. I'm sure that's true."

Sam's stomach sank. "They're not home?" he asked when Nathan hung up.

"Rachel thinks they might have come to the party after all. Let's take another look."

They continued the search with renewed urgency, but after another fifteen minutes, Sam realized they were wasting time. He sighed with frustration and grabbed Nathan's arm.

"This isn't doing us any good."

"You're right," Nathan agreed. "Let's wait for Rachel and Alex over by the food vendors."

Sam's stomach was growling, so he availed himself of a burger and soda while they hung tight. As he ate, he kept scanning the crowd hopefully. Where were Yuri and Michael? They couldn't be involved. But Yuri said Michael had been acting strangely since they'd moved in together. Was it completely crazy to think Michael might be hiding something?

"What is it?" Nathan asked.

Sam quickly relayed his doubts to Nathan, who frowned.

"I suppose it's possible. He's got motivation." *That damn kiss.* "But what about the other fires?"

"I know, I know. It doesn't make much sense. And he's been having some family problems."

"With his sister, right?"

"Yeah, Katherine." Sam trailed off as he said the name.

"What is it?"

"Randall Palmer. Let me see his picture again."

Nathan brought up the image, and as Sam examined the defiant, bearded young man, the vague recognition he'd been trying to tease out ever since the Chancellor's house crashed over him with startling certainty. It had been staring them in the face all along.

"I know where we've seen him before." He flipped the phone back toward Nathan. "Add twenty years and put him in business casual. Give him glasses."

"Yes. The professor from Yuri and Michael's party." Nathan looked amazed as he glanced from the screen back to Sam. "I knew I recognized him. Nice work, detective."

Sam smiled mirthlessly. He might have preened over the praise if circumstances were different, but he had a feeling they shouldn't break out the champagne quite yet. Bendy-dick was the kind of man no one would look at twice, no one would ever suspect… Frank said he'd been a graduate student before his incarceration. He was obviously an accomplished actor as well. He'd looked Sam right in the eye and said he was happy Tim hadn't been injured in the Shady Brook fire. *The sonofabitch.* "I saw him again at Yuri and Michael's when you were away. He seems like kind of a d-bag, but I never got a dangerous vibe. Do you think he could have hurt Yuri and Michael?"

"I sure as hell hope not."

Sam turned his phone on again to check for messages. "Wait. I've got a missed call. Unknown number." It was difficult to hear with the boisterous crowd around them, so he plugged his free ear with his finger and turned up the volume. He was half expecting a message from Yuri, but another familiar voice caught him off guard.

"This is Damon Blake. I'm at the church. I found something in one of the tunnels. Looks like a lot of chemicals and stuff. Shit. Someone's coming. I'll call you back."

"There you are," Rachel yelled as the message ended. She and Alex held hands as they wove their way through a group of revelers. A drunk guy staggered out in front of Sam, stopped, and looked him up and down.

"What're you supposed to be, faggot?" he slurred.

Instead of saying "your worst nightmare" and punching him in the face, like he wanted to, Sam stared at his phone as the battery died. "Crap." The call had come almost an hour before.

"What's going on?" Nathan asked Sam, pushing the drunk away with a forearm to the chest. "Who was that on the phone?"

"Hey. I should've you 'rested for salt'n'battery," the guy protested.

"Get the hell out of here, you asshole," said Rachel, and the drunk's less inebriated friends came to collect him, muttering their apologies.

Sam yanked at his hair. "It was Damon." Tripping over his words, he relayed the rest of the message to the others as quickly as possible. "We've got to get over there."

"Damn right, we do," said Nathan. "I'll call for backup."

"Wait a second, you think this guy Benedict is the arsonist?" Alex asked. "The guy from the party?"

Sam nodded. "That's what we're going to find out."

"We're coming with you," said Rachel.

Sam started to protest.

A loud, rupturing sound roared through the air, mingling with the sound of glass breaking and the screech of torn metal. The ground rumbled as people screamed and ran.

Sam turned, his eyes widening with horror at the sight at the end of the street. The Episcopal Church was in flames. Half of its peaked roof was gone. A second explosion went off in the building and smoke billowed into the sky as bits of metal and wood rained down upon the crowd. While some people fled with shocked expressions, others ran toward the burning church to help. Police whistles sounded. Somewhere, a gun went off.

Nathan grabbed his arm, and Sam found himself manhandled into a huddle with Alex and Rachel at the mouth of a dark alleyway, away from the fleeing crowd. People ran into each other, some streaked with face paint, some wearing masks, some in cumbersome costumes—all trying to get to safety.

Alex's face was almost green in the glow of the streetlights. "We have to stay and help. There could be people hurt," she said. "I think I saw a woman get trampled."

Rachel nodded. "I know CPR. I'm going to go see what I can do."

Sam couldn't believe what he was hearing. "It's too dangerous, Rach. You've got to get out of here. Both of you." Before he could stop them, Rachel and Alex disappeared into the chaotic night.

Sam took Nathan by the shoulders and felt the tension in his muscles under the layers of fabric and leather. He knew every impulse in Nathan was screaming to go after their friends. "We've got to get to the Old Covenant."

Chapter 18

NATHAN SWERVED his Mercedes to avoid a pumpkin in the middle of the road. "Damn kids." He had his phone at his ear. Aside from emergency vehicles hurtling toward the site of the explosion downtown, the streets were almost empty. They were about five minutes from Old Stonebridge, but every passing moment was a moment too long. "I can't get Donna or Tony, not even 911. I've got to leave a message."

Sam half listened as Nathan finished his voice mail asking for backup. His heart was pounding in his ears. How many people had been injured? Killed? If something happened to Rachel or Alex…. If Nathan got hurt…. If Yuri was in trouble…. Fuck. He dug his short fingernails into his palms until they nearly bled. He needed to get his fear under control or he'd be a liability. "What are we going to do?"

"*We* aren't doing anything. You need to stay put in the car while I check it out."

"Are you listening to yourself? You can't go in there alone. You don't even know where the passage is." Sam figured there were probably several access points leading to the tunnels underground, but he'd only seen the one Damon used.

Nathan turned the car on a dime, and Sam's shoulder slammed against the side door. He rubbed at it, almost glad for the distraction of the pain.

"Sorry," Nathan said. He paused. "Okay. You're right."

"I am?"

"But you need a gun."

A wave of instinctual panic swept over Sam, even as he realized he did. Over the past year, he'd seen enough violence to understand that some situations required the use of force. He didn't have to like it, but he could accept it. And maybe he felt a little burst of pride at being treated like Nathan's work partner.

"All right."

"Check the glove compartment."

Sam opened the latch in front of him and drew out the pistol Nathan kept there. Despite its small size, it was a surprisingly heavy, cool weight in his hand. "I hate guns."

"I know you do. You said you've used one before?"

Sam stared at the sleek black metal. "At the shooting range, with my dad." Though he'd taught Sam to consider violence only as a last resort, his father insisted Sam learn how to handle a gun. Maybe it was all those years prosecuting violent offenders. Sam hadn't been terrible, but he hadn't been great at it either.

"You should know the basics, which is good. You see the little switch on the top right? That's the safety. Careful, it's loaded."

Sam nodded, sweating profusely.

"Don't take the safety off until we get out of the car. And when you do, keep the gun pointed away from your body. Don't aim at anything you're not prepared to shoot. The first thing we're going to do is check the periphery of the church. I need you to stay ten feet behind and cover me. If we engage, hold your fire unless someone else fires first. We have no idea who's down there."

Sam tried to stop his hands from trembling. "Here's hoping no one."

"Now, when you aim, aim for the torso. And remember, only shoot if someone is threatening to use deadly force. If someone is going to kill you, make sure you hit the fucker first. I don't care where."

"Okay." Sam licked the sweat from his top lip. He hated the idea of killing someone, but he'd do it to protect Nathan.

"Squeeze slowly. And there'll be kickback, okay? Make sure to keep your grip tight. Hold on with both hands, and keep your dominant arm straight. Flex your left arm a bit."

Sam modeled Nathan's instructions. It had been a long time, and he wanted to make sure he was doing it right.

Nathan glanced and nodded. They were about to cross the Baptist Street Bridge. "Yes. Keep both thumbs clear of the hammer."

Sam made the adjustment.

"Focus on the front sight and aim just below the target. Last thing, make sure your knees aren't locked, or you'll fall over. I don't have any earplugs, unfortunately."

Sam smiled. It was adorable of Nathan to worry about such a detail at a time like this. "It's okay. I don't need my hearing. Anything else?"

Nathan pulled the car to a silent halt as they reached the gravel driveway leading toward the church and the other ruined buildings. "Yes." Nathan leaned across the bucket seats and took Sam's face in his hands. "I love you. Whatever you do, don't get hurt."

"Same." Sam brushed his lips against Nathan's.

The phone rang again, interrupting the kiss. Nathan answered it swiftly. "Walker here."

In the following exchange, Sam surmised Rivera had his hands full downtown but was mobilizing backup.

"Are you sure you trust Rivera?" Sam asked.

"I'd trust Tony with my life. He'll be here."

Sam swallowed. The assurance was going to have to be enough, even if he didn't like it. "Okay. Let's go."

MOONLIGHT FILTERED through the mostly barren trees, bathing the crumbling stone walkway in front of the church in pale light. A cold breeze skimmed across the bay, making Sam glad he'd decided to wear the extra layers.

Nathan held his hand up and motioned for Sam to follow him along the periphery of the wall. They used the shadows to their advantage, keeping close to the building and moving as slowly as possible to avoid the crunchy fallen leaves.

The skeletal frame of the Baptist Street Bridge loomed behind them, a silent sentinel. Nathan clipped his badge to his belt, pressed his shoulder against the side of the church, and held his gun in both hands, as he'd shown Sam. Without the cape and the mask, which he'd left in the Mercedes, Nathan looked poised and in control. Sam might have gotten turned on if he hadn't been scared shitless.

They rounded the first corner with their guns ready.

There were two cars parked in the shadows to the right of the church. Sam froze when he recognized one of them as Michael's. Panic swept through his entire body, making him tremble. He closed his eyes, but when he opened them again, nothing had changed. Nathan was staring at the car with the same look of stricken disbelief on his face.

Nathan shined his small, powerful flashlight into the interior. No one was inside. He rested his hand on the hood for a second, testing its coolness. Then he gestured again. They rounded another corner to the back of the building where they found the door Sam used before—wide open.

Nathan went first and slipped into the darkness to the right of the open door. Sam did the same. The stone was damp and comfortingly solid against his back as he caught his breath, but his heart rate didn't slow. His friend was in danger. A new, cold urgency swept over him, and with it, the certainty he was going to kill anyone who laid a finger on Yuri.

They were alone in the main chamber of the church, with no sign of Damon or anyone else. The full moon illuminated the room through the leaded glass windows, giving them enough light to see—but it would be dark where they were going.

"This way," Sam whispered. As they approached the stairs at the front of the church, something on the floor caught Sam's eye. He bent down.

A Yankees hat.

It was unmistakable. Yuri had always insisted this old ugly hat was good luck. He'd been wearing it during the '09 series. Sam thought he might be sick, but almost immediately rage replaced fear. He left the hat where he'd found it and rose to his feet. Nathan nodded, conveying urgency with his eyes. No doubt he'd recognized the hat too.

Walking quickly, Sam led the way up the stairs toward the second-floor balcony, and then to the little room where he visited Damon. The paneled door was cracked open.

Inside, the passage was pitch black. Nathan turned the flashlight back on and started in, contorting his tall frame to fit. After a moment's hesitation, Sam did the same.

Groping awkwardly with one hand as he climbed through the narrow space, Sam found his footing and followed Nathan down the secret stairs into the inner sanctum of the church. The air was stale and smelled of earth and decaying organic matter. Nathan's flashlight bounced off the crumbling walls, which wasn't exactly a comfort. Sam wasn't a claustrophobic person, but the walls and ceiling of the passageway were far too close. His blood thrummed in his ears.

The stairs wound down in a tight spiral, and they seemed to go on forever. Sam avoided looking up, sure they had spiders and bats for company. It didn't matter. Nothing mattered except finding Yuri—and Damon—alive and well.

Once they finally reached the bottom, they spilled into a large, rectangular chamber, likely one of the catacombs that had previously held human remains. It was empty now, save for a few puddles of standing water. Sam clenched his gun and listened. Silence. Then a chilling sound—the faint echoes of human laughter.

Nathan tugged his hand toward the sound, and Sam trailed after him. After a little investigation, they discovered another passageway running flat underneath the church. A considerably taller man, Nathan had more difficulty maneuvering the corridor than Sam, and Sam heard more than one whispered curse. Sandbags filled the passageway in some places, making it even more narrow and treacherous to traverse, and at one point, Sam sloshed through an unexpected puddle and winced, hoping the sound hadn't traveled.

The voice they'd heard in the antechamber got louder, but it was speaking this time, and Sam started to sweat again. He was grateful Nathan was with him. If anyone could get them out of there, Nathan could.

After a while, they turned another corner and seemed to change direction. The grade rose ever so slightly, and another smell joined the musty, damp earth. Gasoline.

Sam sucked in a breath of surprise as the familiar chemical smell coated his throat and tongue. Once he'd spilled a can in his parent's garage—the stench had stung his nose and made his eyes water—but this was far more intense. Nathan pulled him up short. The voice—no, voices—were clearer now, and there was a flickering light coming from the end of the tunnel, where a stone archway marked another turn, probably into a larger chamber. Nathan pocketed his flashlight.

They slowed to a crawl. Sam was conscious of every sound he made. Their safety depended on the people in the next chamber remaining unaware of their approach.

When they were only a few feet from the entranceway, they stopped. A man with a nasal voice was speaking.

"You're getting too emotional. If we don't leave now, we're going to be caught. Is that what you want?"

Bendy-dick, or Randall Palmer. Sam grimaced at the words and tried to focus on what came next.

"You know I don't. I want to be with you." It was a woman's voice. Katherine. Sam could see the vague outline of Nathan's frowning profile as he made the connection too. The short man Jack Reed had seen fleeing from the alley near Sam's apartment building hadn't been a man at all.

But why the hell would Michael's sister be involved?

"Well, I'm going," said the man. "I've done what I came here to do. It's over. Now, I've got two tickets leaving from Montreal on the 6:00 a.m. flight. We've already delayed too long. The diversion won't keep them occupied forever." Referring to the explosion downtown as a distraction made Sam see red. He couldn't wait to get his hands on the bastard.

"But Benedict—"

The man cut her off. "I told you... that's not my name."

"I know. But... I still think of you as Professor Ben. I can't leave my brother down here. I can't."

Muffled grunting punctuated the statement. Sam clenched his gun tightly, and the glance he exchanged with Nathan confirmed they'd both reached the same conclusion. More panicked grunting echoed from the room beyond. It seemed Michael and Yuri were at the mercy of Katherine and her sociopath boyfriend. Was Damon in there too?

Palmer spoke again. "It's your fault they followed us here in the first place. You let them get concerned."

"But... no one will find them down here. They could starve."

"It's not my problem."

Another muffled sound, this one more like screaming. Sam had been gagged once as a prisoner, and saliva ran in his mouth at the memory. He hoped Yuri and Michael hadn't been badly injured.

"Now, you go on ahead. I'll finish up and meet you at the car," Palmer said.

"Finish what?" Katherine asked cautiously.

"Not so fast." A third person entered the conversation, and Sam instantly recognized the voice. Damon. He'd probably hidden when he'd heard the others arrive. Sam held his breath and listened.

"What the hell are you doing down here?" Palmer demanded.

"Damon?" Katherine asked. "But how—"

Damon scoffed. "I can't believe you. All the times you came down to help with the after-school program, acting like you were friends. You killed my foster parents and Lindsey. And you smiled at me and let me take the blame for it."

"I didn't try to frame you. Now put the gun down." Palmer sounded cautious.

Wait. Gun? The situation was rapidly spiraling out of control. They had to make a move. Nathan nodded at Sam and pushed off the wall, tucking his Glock to his chest.

Damon spoke again. "I heard you burned down Sam's apartment too. You didn't like him snooping around, right? Maybe he'd figure out I didn't do it."

Sweat dripped down Sam's nose as he listened. It was hot as hell in the close quarters of the tunnel. He knew Nathan wanted to avoid any sudden escalation by busting in—but Damon was in serious danger, even if he did have a gun.

"He was trying to steal my brother's boyfriend."

More grunts from Yuri and Michael.

"Damn, girl. Doesn't sound like your brother's a big fan of that kind of reasoning."

Damon was such a smartass. Sam could have hugged him.

"Are you even a professor?" Damon asked.

"I don't have to answer to some kid," said Palmer. "If you don't put the gun down, you'll regret it."

Nathan didn't delay any longer. "This is the FBI. Drop any weapons and put your hands up where I can see them. On three," he whispered to Sam.

Sam's heart skipped as Nathan counted. "Two… three."

He rounded the corner, and Sam followed immediately behind to cover him, as they'd planned.

His breath caught in his throat. A caged electric light dangled from the center of the ceiling, powered by an unknown source. Boxes were stacked up in various formations, filled with who knew what, and the smell of gasoline was strong enough to wake the dead.

Benedict—Randall Palmer—held a small object in his hands. He was watching them carefully. "I don't think you want me to drop this, do you?" His eyes were sharp, calculating. "If I do, everyone in this room is dead."

The bastard held a grenade in one upturned palm. He was dressed in jeans and a turtleneck, over which he wore a brown corduroy jacket. With his bad haircut and plain, doughy face, he looked the part of a middle-aged college professor. Sam had never seen anything more incongruous. He held his gun up at the ready, flanking Nathan.

"Well, well," said Palmer when he saw Sam. "Looks like the gang's all here."

Yuri and Michael sat back-to-back under the hanging light, bound together with bungee cords. Their mouths were sealed with masking tape. Their seated figures cast a short shadow on the dirt floor, and they stared at Sam with mingled expressions of hope and panic.

Damon stood close behind them, beyond a waist-high pile of boxes. He was holding a black gun around the same size as Sam's and aiming it at Palmer.

"Damon."

"Sam."

Though he'd sounded confident and even cocky when they'd been listening in the hall, Damon looked frightened. Sam wanted to give him a comforting nod, but he only managed to jerk his head on his neck like a puppet on a string. They were all Palmer's puppets now.

"It's live," said Palmer. "You shoot me, this hits the floor, and we're all dead."

"What do you want?" Nathan asked.

"Safe passage for me and Katherine. I assume you heard we have a flight to catch."

"Not gonna happen. Give yourself up." Nathan's voice was as cold as the steel in his hands.

"I guess you don't value the lives of your friends as much as I thought."

"Ben, don't do this," said Katherine. She moved to stand between her brother and Palmer. She wore black jeans and a leather jacket. Without her long hair to give her away, she could have been mistaken for a man.

"I haven't done anything people haven't made me do," Palmer said to her. "They took my life away from me. I thought you understood."

"I do. I do understand."

"And these people don't care about you. I do. I'm the only one you need."

She nodded slowly. The guy clearly had her brainwashed. Sam couldn't muster any sympathy for her, though.

"You were my best pupil," said Palmer.

Sam watched Nathan carefully while Palmer and Katherine were distracted. Nathan gestured with his eyes, indicating Sam should take up position on the other side of the room. They had to keep Palmer talking.

"What about Scott Krause?" Nathan asked. "His daughter was only eighteen."

Palmer rounded on Nathan. "The man was an idiot," he spat. "He tried to blackmail me. But no one can have that kind of power over me, not ever again. I already did my time." Palmer was shaking, livid with rage. His thin lips curled into a sneer. "I wish I'd killed more." There was no remorse in his voice.

Sam's blood boiled with fury. He wanted to shoot the guy right then and be done with it, and he probably would have, if not for the grenade. One false move, and all of them would end up wall décor.

"And you started with the cars to throw off the police," Nathan continued.

"They were amateurish. But I'm not an amateur." The pride in Palmer's voice was unmistakable. "We fooled this whole town."

"You're a real smart guy," said Nathan. "Yuri's hat was a nice touch."

"It was Katherine's idea."

Sam kept his gun trained on Palmer and slowly moved behind him.

"But it backfired in the end. We might never have connected the two crime scenes if not for the hat."

Palmer shook his head. "It doesn't matter anymore."

"I don't know. I don't think you want to die," continued Nathan. "If you did, you'd never have arranged for an escape plan. You would have thrown that grenade by now."

"Do you want to find out?"

"I don't want to live without you," said Katherine. "I love you, Ben."

For a second, there was a flicker of something other than hate in Palmer's eyes. Maybe Katherine was more than just a pawn after all. He faltered.

"Now, Sam," Nathan shouted.

Without thinking, Sam pulled the trigger, aiming for Palmer's upper thigh. Blood splattered in a grotesque arc as the gunshot ripped through the air. The man went down with a surprised howl. Nathan lunged for the grenade as it slipped out of Palmer's grasp, and caught it an instant before it hit the hard-packed floor.

"Jesus fucking Christ," screamed Palmer, holding his bloody wound with both hands, his face a twisted mask of pain. "You broke my leg."

"And just as I thought, the grenade wasn't live. It's just a shell. If the pin had been pulled, it would have exploded already." Nathan held it up. The relief on his face was obvious, and Sam's heart leapt with pride.

"You were right," said Sam. Yuri and Michael groaned and grunted from behind the masking tape.

"Let's not celebrate quite yet," said Nathan. "Sam, cuff Katherine." He tossed Sam a pair of handcuffs from his jacket pocket. Sam grabbed them and quickly went to where Katherine stood trembling in disbelief, watching her lover writhe on the floor. She didn't put up any resistance as he fastened her hands behind her back. "Good," said Nathan with a curt nod. "Now, Damon, why don't you come on over here and finish the job."

"What?" Damon's eyes widened. He took a step back, his gun slipping from his fingers. It hit the ground with a thump. Sam was equally shocked. He felt the blood drain from his face.

"Nathan, no." This wasn't right. Sure, Palmer had done terrible things, but to ask Damon to—only then did he realize his lover was smiling.

"You're joking?" he asked in disbelief. "How can you even—"

"It's a toy gun, Sam," said Nathan.

Damon bit his lip, looking sheepishly at his fallen weapon. "How did you know?"

Nathan kneeled on the floor and grabbed Palmer, forcing him to sit up so he could wrestle his hands behind him. "I have many talents. It's a decent replica, though. Had me going, for a second."

Sam turned on Damon. "You tried to confront these assholes with a toy gun? You could have gotten yourself killed."

Damon smiled wryly. "I'm black. I figured they'd be scared enough."

"And you." Sam turned to Yuri, who fastened his wide eyes on Sam. "You scared the hell out of me, you asshole. Answer your damn phone." He was quivering with more adrenaline as he bent to untie Yuri and Michael. Damon moved quickly to help him.

"Sorry," said Yuri, once his mouth was free. "I was a little tied up."

DAMON LED them upstairs via a route that didn't utilize the narrow passageway and windy stairs—lucky given Palmer couldn't walk, and Yuri and Michael were shaky on their feet. Sam was pretty shaky on his too, though he managed to handle Katherine while Nathan carried Palmer.

They met Antonio Rivera and a group of cops in the main chamber of the church. When Rivera saw the situation was under control, he straightened up and lowered his gun. "Looks like I missed the party."

"Took you long enough," Sam muttered.

"We saved you some cake." Nathan thrust an insensible Palmer forward, and a couple of cops dragged him away. Another cop led Katherine after him.

"I knew you could handle it," said Rivera. "Tried to get here sooner, but it's a bad scene downtown."

Sam frowned. "How many injuries?"

"Hard to say. At this point, we've got a death toll of seven. The remote detonation device was pretty sophisticated."

The number hit Sam square in the gut. A total of twelve people had been killed, and who knew how many injured—all because of one man's warped perception of what life owed him. He thought of Rachel and Alex downtown, at the sight of the blast, and hoped they were all right.

He was vaguely aware of Rivera on his radio giving the all clear to the agents outside. Nathan conferred with Rivera to fill him in on what had happened in the tunnels.

Yuri and Michael stood next to each other, talking quietly. Sam spied Yuri's hat and approached them.

"Hey," he said. "I think you lost this."

Yuri left off talking to Michael. He took the hat, and with another step forward, embraced him.

"Thank you," he whispered.

"It's only a hat." Sam hugged him back.

"You know what I mean, you asshole."

"Yeah. I'm… glad you're okay." Sam's throat felt tight as they separated. His reunion with Michael was a little more awkward.

"I can't thank you enough," said Michael. "I'm so sorry. My sister… I don't know what possessed her. I never thought she could be capable of something like this. I knew there was something going on with her and Benedict but…. Shit." His eyes filled with glossy tears.

Sam didn't know what to say. He could hardly imagine what he would do if he found out his brother had been involved in such a terrible crime.

Yuri turned back to Michael and hugged him while he sobbed, and with one last nod at his friend, Sam made his exit.

He wandered outside and found Damon smoking a cigarette under a tree. He was talking on the phone, but hung up when he noticed Sam's approach.

"Boyfriend?"

"Yeah. He's pissed at me because I was supposed to stay at home. He works nights. Probably shouldn't tell him I took his kid brother's toy gun. Or, you know, that I almost got killed tonight."

"You've been with him this whole time?"

"Ever since I saw you last."

"I guess you figured I was going to turn you in after all, huh?" Sam couldn't blame him.

"Not exactly. I heard someone drive up and park next to the church, so I snuck out through one of the tunnels. They must've been using this place for storage. Anyway, I started wondering, and tonight I came back to take another look around. Figured, since I thought it was a good place to hide out, other people might. Just my luck they showed up."

"And you confronted them. Weren't you scared?"

Damon shrugged, flicked his cigarette to the ground, and butted it out with his heel. "Yeah. I was scared. I don't think I knew what I was doing, to tell you the truth. It was like I was on autopilot or something. Then I recognized that girl, and I couldn't believe it. I was so damn angry for what they'd done."

Realizing Damon had no idea about what had happened with the Chancellors, Sam took the opportunity to fill him in, paying special attention to Lydia's concern over him and what Frank had told them about Randall Palmer.

"Wow. So he wanted to get back at Frank by killing his daughter? That's fucked up."

"I'll say."

"I'm glad Lyd's okay." Damon lit another cigarette and stuffed his lighter back in his pocket. His eyes shone. He swiped them with the pad of his thumb and looked away. "I wonder if I'll see her again."

"Of course you will."

"It'll be back to the youth home for me," said Damon. "Month and a half till my birthday."

"Maybe…. Do you want to stay with me and Nathan?" Sam asked hesitantly. They hardly had the room, but Sam hated the idea of Damon going back to a place he so obviously disliked. He didn't know what the laws were, but certainly something could be arranged, given the circumstances.

"Nah, it's okay. I'll be fine. It's not so bad when you're older. Curfew is later, and people don't mess with you. I'll be able to see Raph whenever I want. That is, if he doesn't kill me once I tell him what happened tonight."

"It's good you have someone like him." He fought for the words, but all of them sounded inadequate. "Listen. I'm sorry for doubting you. I'm sorry you had to go through this, and I'm sorry there are people out there like Palmer. But I'm not sorry I met you."

"Me neither." Damon smiled crookedly and raised his fist. "We're cool, Sam Flynn."

THE STATION was filled with cops, FBI agents, witnesses, and suspects. Sam relayed the night's events to Officer Jain in a small room that reeked of fresh paint. He wanted to get away from all chemical smells.

Once he was finally free to go, he ran into Chief Howard in the hallway. She looked as ragged around the edges as Sam probably did.

"I heard what you did tonight."

He thrust his hands into his pockets and shrugged. "I did what I had to do."

"Your friends all right?"

Sam nodded. He'd seen Yuri and Michael again briefly before they headed home to crash. "They're a little shaken up, but I think they'll be okay. Where's Nathan?"

"He's in the waiting room now, with Damon. I took his statement myself, by the way." She ran a hand through her hair. "That young man is quite a character."

"He sure is," Sam said.

"He spoke warmly of you."

Sam's stomach bottomed out. Shit. He'd never asked Damon to keep quiet about their acquaintance. Could Sam still be charged, even though Damon was innocent? He gave her a wan smile. "Oh yeah?"

"It's almost like you know him or something," Donna said with a wink.

IN THE waiting room, a raggedy group stood together. Damon, Nathan, and—Sam was surprised to see—Rachel and Alex. When Rachel saw him, she swore like a sailor and grabbed him in a bear hug before he could speak. "There you are, jerk."

They held each other at arm's length and inspected for injury. Apart from a few dirt smudges on her costume, Rachel was fine. She shook her head at him. "You shot a dude."

"Yeah. Well, he was a terrorist. And he'll live." He still hadn't quite allowed the experience to sink in.

Damon whispered something under his breath that sounded like "unfortunately."

While the others talked, Sam focused his gaze on Nathan. Aside from the tired circles under his eyes, Nathan was in one piece—and he was Sam's. They'd gotten out of that crazy mess unscathed.

Sam crossed the room to stand by Nathan. "I'm sorry I can't give you back your gun. They took it for evidence."

"Well, I have a couple more."

Sam rolled his eyes. Nathan had an arsenal in his closet safe.

"Let me feel you're okay," Nathan whispered. He ran his hands up and down Sam's arms.

"I'm okay." They embraced, hard, and Sam's cock stiffened. In spite of his fatigue, he was fired up, and if he didn't get a blow job tonight he'd probably explode.

"Aww," said Damon, making a kissy sound. "Aren't you two sweet?"

"Shut up," said Sam, flushing but not letting go.

"Can we get out of here, please?" asked Rachel. "My ass needs a bed."

"You read my mind." Sam squeezed Nathan tighter and raised an inquiring eyebrow.

They left the station without a second glance. The night was cool and calm, strangely at odds with the earlier chaos, but very welcome. They could see the remnants of the Episcopal Church, still smoldering.

"I could use a cigarette," Nathan said, patting his pockets absently as they descended the steps.

"Do you mind menthols?" Damon offered him his pack.

"Not at all." Nathan took one, stooped for a light, and cupped his hand around the flame Damon offered.

Sam supposed he could live with it the once.

And when they got home, he got his blow job too.

Chapter 19

SAM POUNDED the pavement, and his breath came in shallow bursts. He'd been running for an hour, longer than ever before, and the fresh air combined with adrenaline to get his blood pumping.

The previous week he'd signed the paperwork to sell his stake in Manella's to Juan. He would still occasionally work on larger projects with Yuri, but only as a contracted employee. As the three of them walked out of the lawyer's office and shook hands, Sam knew it was the right thing to do. His freelance work had nearly doubled in the past month and brought in enough money to pay his share of Nathan's rent and utilities, though of course, Nathan had refused to accept any cash from Sam at first. Sam insisted. Until he found a new affordable place, he was going to pay his way.

He slowed to a walk at the bottom of their street and lowered the volume of the music on his phone. Funny he should think of it as *their* street, even though he knew the situation wasn't permanent. They hadn't discussed their future plans much, and while Nathan might want him to stay put, Sam wasn't sure either of them was ready. Sure, Nathan might like the idea of playing house, but what about in six months when he got fed up with finding Sam's dirty socks on the floor? Sam had seen enough good relationships go bust over stupid little things. What they had was too good to ruin. But after losing everything in the fire, how could he move out? And did he want to?

He was distracted from his thoughts by someone calling his name. A cab pulled to the side of the street, and the back window rolled down to reveal a familiar face.

"Welcome home, Professor," Sam said, grinning. He jogged over and leaned down for a kiss. "How did Boston go?"

Nathan wore his gray suit and tie with the top two buttons of his white shirt undone. He gave Sam's sweaty torso an appreciative look. "Fine. But it reminded me of why I hate that city."

"Oh yeah? Why?"

Nathan paid the driver and shouldered his garment bag as he stepped onto the curb. "Because you're not there."

"YOU LIKE calling me that, don't you?" Nathan captured Sam's mouth in a kiss. They'd spent the afternoon in bed.

"Hmm?" Sam groaned around Nathan's tongue. They'd fucked once, and his hole was tender as Nathan's fingers slid into the open slickness. Still, if Nathan wanted to go again, he was game.

"Professor."

"I like to tease you." Sam bit his bottom lip and pushed back against Nathan's questing hand.

"I think it gets you hot." Nathan's dark eyes were all pupil. His fingers nudged deeper. Sam knew the feel of his come in Sam's ass turned Nathan on. Sam liked it too, knowing he'd been so intimately marked.

"I'm trying to reclaim the label." The thought of Randall Palmer almost made him lose his reemerging hard-on. "It's a good thing that asshole wasn't a real professor."

Nathan laughed. "I missed you last week. Did you miss me?"

"No, not at all." Sam rolled his eyes.

"Have you thought any more about staying?"

Sam's cock thickened and grew as Nathan continued slowly fingering him. "Yeah."

"And?"

"I can't think when you're doing that." Sam let his head fall back against the pillows. Nathan took the opportunity to kiss and bite at his exposed throat.

"Well," he whispered. "I guess I'll have to keep doing it until you say yes."

RACHEL FROWNED at Michael, who was flipping through the film offerings on iTunes. Nathan's living room was filled with the sounds of their chattering friends as the inevitable debate between Rachel and Michael raged on. Rachel crossed her arms and narrowed her eyes whenever Michael paused on a movie she disliked.

"What about *Captain America*?" He clicked on Title and read the blurb out loud.

Rachel snorted. "Stop trying to act like you're interested in the plot. You just want to ogle Chris Evans's ass."

"But Hayley Atwell is in it too." Michael raised an eyebrow.

Alex stifled a yawn. "Why do I get the feeling you two only pick movies based on who you find attractive?"

"I'm offended you think I'm so shallow," Rachel said, reaching for her drink. "And I'm not watching it if it doesn't pass the Bechdel test."

Michael frowned and continued flipping through movies. "Nothing on here does."

"What about *Jaws*?" Yuri asked. He popped a tortilla chip into his mouth and crunched loudly.

"No," both Michael and Rachel exclaimed.

"No one hot in it?" Sam joked.

"I'll watch anything, but I'm not watching *Batman* again," Alex said.

Nathan, who'd been paying the pizza-delivery person, reentered the living room with two boxes.

"Are you people still making fun of my Halloween costume?" he asked. "That was a month ago."

As the argument continued, Sam slid onto the couch next to Yuri, making sure to keep a respectable distance between them. He didn't want to make things weirder for Michael or Nathan, but neither of them seemed to notice. Nathan had joined the movie debate and was apparently siding with Michael. He was a closet Marvel fan—and probably also a fan of Evans's ass.

"You guys doing okay?" Sam asked Yuri. He'd noticed Yuri and Michael hadn't spoken much to each other since they'd arrived.

"We're taking a break."

"Really?"

"Yeah. I mean, I'm staying at the house for now, but I think… It was a lot, moving in together, then what happened with Katherine. Don't make a big deal out of it, though, okay? I'm fine. It was my decision."

Sam swallowed the lump in his throat. Only two months before, Yuri and Michael had been so happy. "All right, if it's what you want. You know I support you."

"Thanks, man."

He hesitated before asking the next question, not sure he wanted to know the answer. "Has he talked to her?"

"Yeah. I guess Benedict had her under his thumb. But as much as he wants to let her off the hook, I just... I can't. It's been hard on his parents too. What a mess."

Katherine Smith and Randall Palmer were being held, awaiting trial for countless felony charges. In the weeks since the church bombing and the discovery of the explosives cache under the Old Covenant, more information had come to light about their activities. Experts had identified both suspects in the junk shop surveillance video, and there was evidence in the blue Toyota that had been dragged out of the swamp. Scott Krause's phone records included several calls to Palmer at a number registered to Benedict Anderson, a real professor at another university who was currently on sabbatical doing research in Germany. He'd had no idea his identity had been stolen.

Then there were the victims. In total, twelve people had died, along with twenty more injured in the Halloween blast. A memorial fund had been set up to help the victims and to rebuild the Episcopal Church. Meanwhile the press was blasting Mayor White for failing to cancel the Halloween party in spite of the dangerous circumstances.

Sam squeezed Yuri's shoulder. "I'm so sorry. I wish there was something I could do to help."

"Thanks. Hey, by the way, I saw Damon on TV again the other night." Yuri was obviously eager for a change in subject.

"CNN?"

"PBS."

"That was a good one."

"It was sweet seeing him reunited with his foster sisters."

While several of Sam's articles on the subject had gotten substantial attention, Damon and his family fascinated the world. He was the real hero, and he was using his experience to raise awareness about unequal treatment under the law. There couldn't be a better spokesperson, as far as Sam was concerned. Damon had called him the previous day with more good news. Next year he'd be attending the University of Connecticut, courtesy of Beth and Frank Chancellor. He wanted to be an FBI agent.

Speaking of FBI agents, Sam watched as Nathan opened the box of pepperoni and distributed paper plates around. He had been so eager to invite the whole crew over for movie night, and Sam suspected that, as much as Nathan liked his friends, he'd done it to show Sam there was a space for him there.

He sighed. "Nathan wants me to move in."

"You're thinking about it, aren't you?" Yuri's voice held a trace of teasing. "How the mighty have fallen. Let me guess, you're scared shitless."

Sam let out a nervous laugh. "Obviously." If Michael and Yuri couldn't make it, why would he and Nathan be any different?

"Well, it's your decision. If it doesn't feel right, don't do it."

The problem wasn't that it didn't feel right, though. The problem was it felt *too* right. "What if he gets sick of me?"

"I know what you're doing. Don't base your decision on Michael and me. We're not the same people. Couples fight and get irritated with each other. Relationships aren't easy. You just have to decide if it's worth it." Yuri looked at Michael, who was throwing his hands up in the air, having obviously lost the Bechdel-test argument with Rachel. His face was thoughtful and a little sad.

Before Sam could answer, Alex stole the controller, stood up, and held it behind her back. "That's it. No more fighting, you guys. We're watching *Frozen*."

Everyone stayed silent.

"No objections?"

"I haven't seen it," Michael said casually. "I've heard it's okay."

"I guess that would be fine, if it's what you want, sweetie." Rachel tried to sound long-suffering.

Sam grinned at Nathan as they all attempted to mute their enthusiasm. Alex saved the day. Meanwhile Nathan looked to be doing his best not to watch Sam and Yuri too carefully. Sam patted the couch next to him, but the damn kitten jumped up instead. She mewed and settled down between him and Yuri. Sam shrugged at Nathan. Over the past few weeks, she'd become his little shadow. He liked her okay.

And the movie was actually pretty decent too.

Chapter 20

"I'M NOT sure you're listening." Nathan stood above him, his thick, hard cock thrusting between Sam's parted lips. Sam kneeled on the kitchen floor, naked except for one of Nathan's ties, which Nathan used to restrain his hands behind his back.

Nathan yanked Sam's head up by his chin, forcing him to meet his gaze. "I told you to take it all." Tears had formed at the edge of Sam's eyes, and Nathan sneered. "All the way, boy." Sam did his best to swallow the entire length without gagging. Nathan didn't like it when he gagged, and he was trying to be so good.

"Such a pretty little cocksucker, aren't you?"

Sam hummed around the intrusion in his throat. He loved being used like this, being forced to take Nathan's cock as deep as he could. His mind quieted as he focused on the task, feeling the glide of the hardness over his lips, the salty-sweet taste of Nathan's precome slicking his tongue. Nathan's thighs quivered, his eyes raptly focused. Knowing he could please Nathan always thrilled him, but that day was different. Something crackled in the air between them.

Sam had returned from an afternoon of writing at a coffee shop to find Nathan waiting with a stern expression on his face. At first, he didn't understand why Nathan was angry, but once Nathan ordered him to strip and kneel, his heart hammered with anticipation and arousal. He was the student who'd arrived late, and Nathan the irritated professor. Maybe he would have found the role play silly with another lover, but Nathan was so serious—he made it incredibly hot. Sam had been sucking Nathan's cock for at least ten minutes.

Over the past month, they had several more talks and compiled a list of things they did and didn't want. They'd both decided saying "halt" would work as a safeword. No need to be fancy about it. Sam wasn't planning on using it, anyway.

His erection throbbed and dripped onto the floor between his legs. He was desperate for friction, but Nathan wouldn't let him get off so easily. If there was any hope of coming, he had to be a very good boy.

Strange how easy it was for him to slip into that mentality, but as Nathan's dark eyes focused on his lips, Sam thought of himself as Nathan's boy. He smiled around the cock in his mouth.

While he might challenge Nathan or disobey him outside in the world, with just the two of them, he could let go. He could surrender up the part of him that wanted to be dominated. He didn't have to feel ashamed or embarrassed or like less of a man for those desires.

Maybe he was being too good. With a pained groan, Nathan pulled out of his mouth and ordered him to stand. "Lean against the counter. Spread your legs."

Sam did. With his back to Nathan and his hands tied, he could only bend against the cool marble, which pebbled his nipples into tight beads.

He listened, chest heaving, to the sounds behind him. Nathan had stayed almost fully dressed until then, but a faint rustle of clothing suggested he was getting naked. Sam's whole body shivered in anticipation. Maybe Nathan would put him out of his misery and fuck him after all.

Something too slick and cool to be a finger breached him—a toy of some sort. Not one of Sam's—they were all lost in the fire—but then he remembered seeing an unmarked bag a couple days before. He'd been curious at the time, but he forgot to ask about it. Clearly Nathan had gone on a shopping trip and hadn't invited him along.

Nathan pushed harder and Sam hissed as the slippery rubber went deeper, wider, expanding his hole until it finally bottomed out, filling him. Sam whined and squeezed his ass around the plug.

"You'll learn not to come to my class late, won't you?"

Sam nodded against the marble counter. "Yes."

"I can't hear you." As Nathan twisted the plug, it nudged against Sam's swollen prostate. His cock twitched in response, and he worried he'd come before he was allowed. He had to hold his breath and count backward from ten. But then Nathan yanked his head back by his hair. It hurt. "Answer me when I ask you a question."

"Yes, Sir. Yes." Sam gasped. Nathan's mouth was a vivid, beautiful red, and it was so close. Sam wanted to taste it.

"Hmm. I'm not sure you're learning your lesson. I think you might like this punishment too much." Even so, he kept fucking the plug in deeper until Sam wanted to scream. It fit him so perfectly. His balls ached with pent-up frustration.

"Isn't that right, boy? You're desperate for cock, aren't you? Well, I'm not going to give you mine, no matter how much you beg."

The word "please" had been on the tip of Sam's tongue, but he bit it back.

"Do you understand me?" Nathan asked.

"Yes, Professor."

"Today, you're going to fuck me, and you're going to keep this in your ass while you do it." Another vicious twist of the plug. "If you come before I do, I'll be angry. And don't come inside me."

Reeling at the unexpected change of pace, Sam nearly collapsed against the counter as Nathan untied his hands.

Nathan slapped Sam's rump as they traded places, and he braced his hands against the counter. His naked ass beckoned Sam like a fatal beacon. As turned-on as he was, there was no way he could fuck Nathan and not come.

"What are you waiting for, boy?"

"I don't know if I can." Sam held his cock at the base. He felt tentatively and found Nathan's hole slick and loose. The knowledge Nathan had prepared himself made Sam's insides melt with tenderness, and he realized this was about what Nathan needed just as much as it was about him. He didn't want to let him down.

"Do you want to stop?"

There it was—his out. Sam shook his head.

Nathan frowned over his shoulder. "Then fuck me now, or I'll change my mind, and you won't come at all."

Without another word, Sam lined himself up and pushed the head of his cock inside. God, Nathan was hot and tight around him. Sam had to pause to catch his breath. He slid in a little deeper, gasping at the sight of his cock disappearing into Nathan's ass.

"Is that the best you can do?" Nathan asked, breathy in spite of himself. Sam shuddered as he finally bottomed out. It was almost like being in the middle of a threesome, the plug fucking him from behind with each thrust into Nathan's tight heat. Slowly he moved, plunging balls deep as his sack tightened. He hadn't known sex could feel so good.

"Good boy. Harder." Sam's eyes rolled as he held on to Nathan's hips and obeyed. It was excruciating to hold back. Each movement nudged the plug inside him, bringing him closer to the edge. "Harder."

"I'm sorry—gonna come." Sam let out a breathless whine. He began to pound Nathan, and the plug was merciless, unspooling his last vestige of control. His belly clenched, and he pulled out—too late. His cock spurted helplessly all over Nathan's ass. It seemed to go on forever, full-body shudders that curled his toes and liquefied his spine. Nathan turned and held him with one arm and grabbed his dick to work the last of the come out. Sam moaned at the touch on his sensitive cock.

After his climax subsided, Nathan smirked at him. His deep-red erection bobbed between his legs. "We're going to have to work on your stamina, aren't we? I didn't give you permission to come."

"Yes, Sir." Sam could barely get the words out. He was exhausted and felt fuzzy-headed, almost like he was having an out-of-body experience. He hated letting Nathan down.

"Now kneel. Finish me off."

Sam did. He eagerly wrapped his lips around the tip of Nathan's impressive length. "That's it. That's a good boy. Open your throat for me." Sam groaned as Nathan fed his cock deeper. He loved it, loved it, loved it.

After a couple forceful thrusts, Nathan pulled out of Sam's mouth and painted his face with his orgasm. Sam clung to Nathan's thighs. Not getting to swallow was his punishment for coming too soon. "I'm sorry, Sir," he said. "I'm sorry."

Nathan kneeled down and gathered Sam in his arms. He pressed a kiss to Sam's temple and, without another word, reached behind to pull the plug out. The sensation, combined with his heightened state of emotion and arousal, was too much. Sam fought the sob welling in his throat.

"So beautiful." Nathan kissed him again, stroking his hair and holding him to his chest. At some point, Sam realized he was being cradled in Nathan's lap, petted and caressed. Nathan used a dishtowel to clean them off. "That was so good. Are you okay?"

Sam swallowed around the hoarseness in his throat and nodded. "I'm sorry I disappointed you." He tried to keep his voice neutral, but it wavered.

"You could never disappoint me," Nathan said. His brows drew together. "Not ever. You're wonderful."

Sam shook his head. "I couldn't hold back."

"I wasn't expecting you to."

"You knew I'd come?"

"I thought you were ready for a challenge." They'd played similar games earlier in the week, and Sam had been able to restrain himself every time. "But that's what you're afraid of, isn't it? Being a disappointment? Why didn't you safeword if you were upset?"

"I want to please you. I want you to like what we do. I'm afraid you'll realize I'm not worth the trouble."

Nathan's eyes were soft. "First off, you know that's not what a safeword is for—we talked about this. If you need to stop at any time, you use it. This isn't about ego. I'm going to spank you later, by the way." He grinned, but it didn't reach his eyes.

"I guess you were right about the emotions thing," Sam muttered. Nathan warned him, before they started, about their play triggering emotions—both good and bad. Sam hadn't understood until then. He buried his head into Nathan's neck, wanting to stay close. He'd never felt so vulnerable, so open to anyone before. He couldn't lose that.

"I don't know what else I can say to make you understand how I feel about you. Is that why you won't move in with me?"

Sam nodded, unable to speak as a few tears slipped out. He wiped them away, vaguely aware he was being ridiculous. Still, Nathan hugged him tightly.

"I love you, no matter what you decide," Nathan said. "If you think this is too much for you, that's okay too. But I want you to know I understand, and I feel the same way sometimes. I worry about not being good enough for you."

Sam snorted, but Nathan had his attention. He stroked Sam's back as he spoke.

"It's true. You're a better man than me in so many ways. Your idealism, your passion. You have so many friends who love you. I never had that. I gave myself to my work and didn't have time for anything else, even Emma. Sometimes I wonder what you see in me, but I have to trust you, trust us, or what we have is nothing."

When Sam felt he could finally talk again, he disengaged himself to look Nathan in the face. "I do trust you." He'd learned a lot about trust in the past few weeks, and a lot about himself—both alone and as part of a couple. He knew he would continue to stand up for what he believed in, even when he clashed with Nathan. But he also knew Nathan respected him for it, as long as he was honest. "I just got caught up in the moment. It took me by surprise, how much I could feel. It was…."

"Intense." Nathan's eyes stayed guarded. He always seemed to worry he'd gone too far.

Sam kissed him and tasted traces of their sweat and come on his lips. "Yeah. And I loved it. It was amazing. You were amazing. And don't think I don't want to do it again, because I do."

The relieved, flattered expression on Nathan's face lightened the pressure squeezing Sam's chest. His anxieties seemed less substantial, burned off by the catharsis of sex and talk. He knew they hadn't been eradicated completely, but they weren't as daunting. It was helpful to know Nathan didn't find him disappointing. Those fears were his, and his alone.

Nathan kept him close the rest of the night. They didn't talk much, but simply enjoyed each other's company, snuggling in bed and then making a lazy, impromptu dinner. Nathan didn't ask again about Sam moving in on a more permanent basis, and Sam refused to let his fears get the better of him. Gradually the intense emotions faded. When Nathan showed him the selection of very interesting toys he purchased at the adult store, they both got so turned on at all the possibilities they wound up making love again, face-to-face, with Nathan moving slowly into Sam from above.

It was perfect.

"I THINK I have an idea for the kitten's name," Sam said one morning several days later. The little beast in question was under his feet, as usual, attacking the laces of his running shoes. He scooped her up and plopped her on the couch next to Nathan, who was on his laptop.

"Oh yeah?" Nathan asked distractedly.

"How about Shadow?"

"Seems appropriate." Nathan smiled and shook his head at the pair of them, but then he looked back at his laptop and frowned. If he hadn't yet chastised Sam for his sweaty ass on the furniture, he must be preoccupied.

"What's wrong?"

"I got an e-mail from my mother."

Sam's stomach sank. With Christmas only a week away, he'd bought his companion ticket. As hard as it would be to leave his brother behind, he was getting excited about the trip. He told Lisa about it, and she was enthusiastic about Sam taking some time for himself, which helped lessen the guilt. Tim was back at Shady Brook, which helped too. He knew Nathan had told his parents he was bringing his boyfriend home for the holidays, and he was waiting for a response.

Well, he might as well rip off the Band-Aid quickly. "Bad news?"

"My mother is excited to meet you."

"But not your father?"

"She says he's 'getting used to the idea,' which could mean just about anything." Nathan made a face. "In any case, I don't care what he thinks. You're coming." The kitten—Shadow—wriggled out of Sam's grasp and pounced on Nathan's leg.

"Are you sure—?"

"Positive. End of story. Unless… you don't want to?"

"Of course I do." Sam figured he could handle an awkward Christmas with Nathan's father. It obviously meant a lot to Nathan. It meant a lot to him too.

But he wasn't done with their conversation.

"There was something else I wanted to talk to you about." For some reason, even broaching the subject made Sam nervous. He wiped his sweaty palms on his running pants. "Something important. I have a confession to make."

"Oh?" Nathan arched an eyebrow.

"I hate furniture shopping."

"It can be brutal."

"And the realtors in this city are crooks."

Nathan nodded, playing along. "Tell me about it. You know how much I paid in finder's fees for this place?"

Sam slid closer until their thighs were touching. "Not to mention how much it sucks to look at apartments, once you have some lined up."

"Good luck finding one that isn't cockroach infested."

"It's a dangerous prospect. Unsanitary."

Nathan tsked and shook his head. "I agree."

"And this one is nice." Sam looked around, feigning nonchalance. In truth, he'd come to love Nathan's apartment.

"I've always thought it was cozy."

"So… maybe it would be better for me to stay put. If you don't mind."

Nathan shrugged and set the kitten down on the floor. "It seems the most logical course of action." Sam didn't think he'd ever seen a bigger, more honest smile on Nathan's face. It lit him up from the inside.

"I'm glad you agree."

Even though he was still sweaty, Sam leaned over and kissed him. He wanted to tell Nathan it had started to snow while he was running, the first real snow of the season. It felt like the first real snow of his life.

Stay tuned for an exclusive excerpt from

Blind Spot

The Stonebridge Mysteries: Book Three

Living together is bliss for Sam Flynn and Nathan Walker, but things never stay quiet in Stonebridge for long. On the night of Sam's twenty-ninth birthday, the much-hated mayor of Stonebridge is found dead at his home. Sam suspects foul play, but just as he starts investigating the list of possible culprits, Nathan gets word of a new undercover assignment—one that includes a mysterious, sexy new partner. Though Sam struggles to trust Nathan and control his jealousy during Nathan's absence, the stress makes a return to the bottle seem not only tempting, but inevitable—especially when Nathan starts avoiding his calls.

Yet Nathan's fidelity isn't the only thing on Sam's mind. A visit from the mayor's ex-assistant puts Sam in the line of fire, and he's drawn into a complex web of duplicity spanning back to the night of his parents' accident. Sam's journey to uncover the truth about what really happened threatens to unravel long-held beliefs about his parents and puts his relationship with Nathan to the ultimate test.

www.dreamspinnerpress.com

Chapter 1

THE LUCKY Star resembled an eighties-movie prom set. Streamers hung from the ceiling, and a disco ball spun in the middle of the room, flashing tiny beams of light. In the corner, a DJ played "Born to Run" from bass-heavy speakers, but the small crowd was even louder, screaming and blowing noisemakers as Sam Flynn stood holding his boyfriend Nathan's hand. He blinked in surprise.

A banner reading *HAPPY 29TH BIRTHDAY, SAM* hung behind the bar, where everyone was hiding when Sam and Nathan entered.

"So this is why you wanted to hurry down here so fast," Sam yelled in Nathan's ear over the music.

Nathan chuckled and grabbed him around the waist. "Maybe."

"You sneaky bastard." Even though he'd stopped drinking, Sam loved the Star, not least because one of his best friends, Rachel Mayer, tended bar. She stood behind it, clapping and looking very self-satisfied. To her left, her girlfriend Alex wore a glittery birthday hat over her short white-blonde bob. Further guests included Sam's other best friend, Yuri Manella, and Damon Blake, whom Sam hadn't expected to see, since he'd recently moved from Stonebridge, Connecticut to Hartford. He gave Sam a smile and a nod.

"I wondered what you all were planning." Sam tried to hide his grin and mostly failed. Some guys from Manella's Landscaping whooped and raised beers to toast in the corner. Even Antonio Rivera, one of Nathan's FBI buddies, was there.

"Are you surprised?" Nathan leaned down and kissed Sam on the cheek. His new beard scratched lightly against Sam's skin.

"Hell yeah, but you shouldn't have done all this."

"Why not?" Nathan's dark eyes glinted in the flashing lights of the disco ball. Sam hadn't been sure about the beard at first, but it was growing on him—pun intended. Nathan looked hotter than ever. After six months of living together and over a year of dating, Sam still thought Nathan was the most attractive man he'd ever seen.

"Because you know I hate surprise parties."

"I know you say you do, but I also know when you're lying. Don't I?" Nathan arched an eyebrow, and Sam flushed all over. He wondered what Nathan had planned for them later, after the party. In fact, he'd been tingling with anticipation since Nathan mentioned it over breakfast.

"Yes, sir." He urged Nathan's head down and whispered into his ear, grateful for the loud music. If any of his friends overheard him addressing Nathan in that way, he'd never live it down. They had no idea what he and his boyfriend got up to in the bedroom, and they didn't need to know. Nathan responded with a devious smile.

After the song ended, the DJ leaned into the mic. "Welcome to the guest of honor, Sa-a-aaam Flynnnnn." He played some annoying sound effects—fart noises and whistles—and Sam wondered where the hell Rachel had picked him up.

Everyone erupted into an off-key rendition of "Happy Birthday." Sam rolled his eyes and leaned back into Nathan's embrace. He didn't mind being a year older, but for a long time he'd dreaded birthdays. They always reminded him of his parents, who had made a big deal over every milestone for both of their sons. This year he'd spent a quiet morning with Nathan and then gone to visit his little brother, Tim, at Shady Brook, the facility he'd lived in since a car accident had killed their parents and left him comatose over seven years before. Sam's throat tightened. He wished Tim could be here.

The singing fizzled out into more shouts and whistles, and then the music started up at a more conversational volume. Sam and Nathan crossed the room toward the bar and greeted their friends.

"Hey, you," said Rachel. "Happy birthday." She slid him a Coke sans rum. "You should have seen the look on your face when you walked through the door." She grinned and put both hands to her cheeks, making a silly "surprised" face.

"You're all conniving and can't be trusted," said Sam. "But thank you." He leaned over the bar and kissed her cheek. "You look great."

"You like it?" Ever since high school, Rachel had worn her hair Afro-style and liked to streak it with color. Instead of her usual purple, however, this time she used silver.

"Yeah. It's very dystopian future."

"That's what I was going for."

Alex took the opportunity of his distraction to wrangle a party hat onto him from behind. He grunted with protest and went to remove it, but Rachel shook her head at him. "Don't you dare. She's so excited about those damn hats."

They chatted for a while about the party, until Sam realized Nathan had disappeared to talk with Rivera on the opposite side of the room. His lover was smiling and laughing at something the older man said. Instead of the pang of jealousy Sam felt months before when he suspected Nathan might be attracted to Rivera, now he was simply pleased Nathan was enjoying himself. He only hoped Nathan wouldn't be disappointed when his friend headed back to New York.

A slap on his arm made him turn. "Hey, stranger." Yuri grinned at him, cheeks dimpling. "Happy birthday."

"Thanks. Great to see you, man." Sam hugged his friend. They'd been partners in Yuri's family landscaping business for years, but recently Sam had sold back his share in order to pursue his journalism career. He still worked part-time during the week, but it had been a while since he'd been on a project with Yuri. "How've you been? Had any hot dates?" Sam waggled his eyebrows.

"Oh, you know. A few here and there. Nothing serious."

"Good for you." Lord knows his friend deserved a little R&R after the breakup he'd gone through in December. Yuri had an amazing body, a sweet personality, and a sexy Greek accent to boot.

Yuri took a sip of beer and licked the foam off his top lip. "So, the big two-nine."

"Yep."

"Almost thirty."

"Shut up." Sam gave him a light punch. "And anyway, you'll be here soon, my friend."

"Attention." Rachel started dinging a spoon against a glass. "Thank you all for coming. We're here to celebrate Sam's birthday. I wanted to plan a roast, but Nathan talked me out of it." There were a couple of good-natured boos from the crowd and scattered laughter. Nathan shrugged sheepishly.

"It's a shame, because I have some really good material," Rachel continued. "Sam, you're a pain in the ass, but you're our pain in the ass. I've known you for fifteen years, and I love the hell out of you. We've been through a lot together. I know this last year hasn't been easy." People nodded and murmured. Stonebridge was still recovering from a spree of arsons that had culminated in a Halloween-night explosion at the Episcopal Church, leaving a total of twelve people dead and many more injured.

Sam met Damon's eyes from across the room. The teenager had been the lead suspect in the case until Sam and Nathan uncovered the real culprits, who were now safely behind bars. Damon gave him a half-smile of commiseration.

"But our city is strong," Rachel continued. "Our community is strong. We won't be defeated when we have people like Sam in our corner. Not when we have people like Damon Blake, who's here tonight and starting college in the fall. Let's raise our glasses to Sam and Damon, and to Nathan, Sam's sugar daddy, who you can thank for the open bar."

Another cheer erupted, and Sam laughed and clapped. He said goodbye to Yuri and made his way toward Damon.

"Hey man," said Sam. "I'm glad you could make it. Thanks for coming."

"I wouldn't have missed it." Damon thrust out a gift, looking slightly embarrassed. He ran his hand over his closely shaved head. "It's not much."

Sam was touched. He took the package, which felt decidedly like a paperback book, and then pulled Damon into a one-armed hug. "You didn't have to. Things are going well?"

"Yeah. It's weird to be out of town, but it's a nice change of pace."

Sam smiled. "Good to hear." They chatted for a couple of minutes, until other partygoers started to interrupt. Sam put them off to say goodbye to Damon, who was getting ready to leave. As a rule, the bar didn't allow minors after nine.

"Anyway, if you're ever in Hartford." Damon put out his hand.

"I've got your number."

Sam scanned the crowd to find Nathan. Well-wishers and friends stopped him for hugs along the way. By the time he managed to get to his boyfriend, the music had switched from rock to club music with a sultry beat.

"Dance with me?" Sam asked.

"Of course."

Nathan was a great dancer. He moved his hips in a seductive rhythm, staying close to Sam and guiding him onto the impromptu dance floor.

Though Nathan was five inches taller, Sam never felt dwarfed by his height, but rather complemented by it, just as Nathan's dark looks balanced his light. Sam wrapped his arms around Nathan's back and felt his strong muscles working as they moved.

All eyes were on them. Sam caught a glimpse of Rachel, who gave him the two thumbs-up signal. They were showing off a little, but Sam figured it was his right. He was the birthday boy, after all, and he was dancing with the hottest guy in the room. Nathan leaned down to whisper in his ear. "Do your friends really call me your sugar daddy?"

Sam laughed at the unexpected question. He'd almost forgotten what Rachel had called Nathan.

"Yup." After all, not only did Nathan pay for Tim's health care, he always objected whenever Sam reached for his wallet on other occasions. At least he allowed Sam to front his share of the rent for their apartment. It was one of the reasons he'd stayed on part-time at Manella's. While he preferred writing to the landscaping work, it didn't quite pay the bills.

Nathan frowned. "I'm not old enough to be a daddy." His recent birthday—thirty-seven—had given him a taste of midlife crisis. Sam kept expecting him to show up at home with a new sports car and a babe in the passenger seat.

It made him consider his answer. "You're so smoking hot, they have to call you something when they describe you, or they'll embarrass themselves."

"Nice save, but you're lying. Your pulse picks up. Here." Nathan put his hand to Sam's racing jugular, sweeping his fingertip down the arch of Sam's exposed neck.

"That's not the only thing that makes my pulse race." In fact, the dirty dancing was creating a problematic situation for polite company. At least others had joined them on the dance floor. Rachel and Alex were swaying together a few feet away, staring at each other with grins on their faces.

"I've got plans for later. Can you wait?"

"I don't know…. I might need a reminder in self-control."

"Hmm. Just wait till you open your present." Nathan leaned down to give Sam a brief, opened-mouth kiss. Sam didn't detect any booze, which meant Nathan was abstaining—he usually did as moral support for Sam when they went out, but it also meant they'd be playing later. Early on, Nathan had made it clear each of them had to be sober when they scened.

No booze, no drugs—which was fine with Sam. Being with Nathan was enough.

"So, what are we doing later?" Sam asked.

"You'll have to be patient."

They continued dancing for a couple more songs and then grabbed a few snacks from one of the side tables. Rachel announced it was time for presents.

"I told you guys, no presents," he protested.

"Sit down and shut up."

Most of them were inexpensive, which was fine with Sam—a few books and Blu-rays he'd been wanting, a couple gag gifts from his work friends—but when it came time for Nathan's gift, Sam paused and weighed the small package in his hands.

On Christmas, Nathan had given him a new laptop computer, an ultrathin silver model he'd secretly drooled over for months. He hadn't exactly been able to reject the gift sitting in Nathan's parents' living room, but it was an extravagance he felt a little ridiculous accepting, seeing as his own gifts to Nathan—the new Murakami novel and a sweater Rachel had helped him pick out in a desperate dash to the mall—were worth barely a fraction of what Nathan had paid. Of course Nathan hadn't seen the problem, but later, after Sam explained his embarrassment, he promised no more expensive gifts unless they agreed beforehand. He hoped Nathan had taken their talk seriously and that, when he opened this present, he wouldn't be confronted with a gold watch or something equally lavish.

When he opened the package, he frowned down at a simple silver keychain. It gleamed in his fingers. The initials on it read S+N.

A few guests muttered things like "oh how nice," but Sam could tell they weren't impressed.

"Do you like it?" Nathan asked. He was fighting a smile. There was obviously more to this present than met the eye.

Sam nodded. "I love it."

The DJ stopped the music again, and Sam looked around, waiting for someone else to stand up and make an embarrassing speech.

"You guys. You guys," Rachel said, grabbing the microphone from the front of the room. "Shut up and listen. The mayor is dead."

"Oh, come on, Rach," Sam called out. "It may be my birthday, but murder's taking it a little far." A few laughs from people nearby slowly died out as Rachel shook her head and held up her phone.

"I'm not joking. It's all over Twitter. Looks like he was found unresponsive in his home a couple hours ago."

Sam exchanged a glance with Nathan. This was huge. He grabbed his phone and started scrolling through the #RIPMayorWhite hashtag. There was no more news than what Rachel had announced, but Sam felt his blood fire up. Things had been quiet the last few weeks, and that was the story he'd been waiting for.

"Looks like I've got to take off," said Rivera, slapping Nathan on the shoulder.

"Of course. Let us know what's going on, Tony."

"You bet."

Once Rivera was gone, the room erupted in conversation. At Sam's prompting, Rachel turned on the bar TV and flicked to the news channels. It hadn't yet reached the national level, but the local ten o'clock was reporting from St. Mary's hospital.

The reporter talking to the studio newscaster nodded as he listened into his earpiece.

"That's right, Ted. Mayor White was apparently found in his bedroom by his wife earlier this evening."

"Any word on cause of death yet, Brian?" the newscaster asked.

"No word yet, but there are rumors the mayor had been suffering from angina over the past few months. It may have been a heart attack."

"Very true," said Ted the newscaster. "We know he'd been trying to get in shape and lose some weight in the past few months—under doctor's orders. It's been slow going because of his age."

The mayor was sixty-three—a large man with a well-known love for greasy double cheeseburgers. Heart attack did seem the most likely scenario. After a few more questions with not much detail provided from the on-ground reporter, Rachel turned the TV off and the music started back up. No one in the bar had much love for the mayor, whose policies had always favored the rich suburbs of West Stonebridge over the grittier downtown. While Sam wasn't exactly fond of his deputy either, surely the guy couldn't be worse than White. And then, during the next election cycle, maybe some new blood would have a chance.

"So, what do you think? You want to get out of here?" Nathan asked as the party started to break up.

"Hell, yeah." Sam was itching to get back to his computer.

He said goodbye to everyone and followed Nathan into the pleasant May night. It would be another month or so before things heated up for the summer, and Sam enjoyed the temperate spring.

"I can't believe the mayor's dead," said Sam, falling into step beside Nathan as they walked the seven blocks back to their place.

"You couldn't have asked for a better gift." Nathan elbowed his side.

"Oh, come on. I'm not heartless. But after what happened on Halloween, the guy was clearly unfit for office. He should have resigned months ago."

"True."

After the bombing of the Episcopal Church, Mayor White had received a ton of criticism from all sides. Sam had written a scathing piece on his blog, and even the normally pro-White *Gazette* had written some op-ed pieces criticizing his decision to hold the Halloween block party, even though the arsonist terrorizing the city was still on the loose.

"Well, I'll tell you what," said Sam, "I'm not happy the guy's dead, but maybe this is a blessing in disguise for the city."

"Maybe so."

"I wonder if Judy White's down at the hospital. Maybe we can pop by quickly, see if she needs a shoulder to cry on?" If he could get the scoop straight from the mayor's wife, leave the *Gazette* in the dust….

"No. Not tonight. You're going to let it go for tonight."

"But—"

Nathan shook his head. "It can wait. But I can't." He opened his hand. There, on the flat of his palm, was a small key. A frisson of excitement ran up Sam's spine. He thought of the silver keychain.

"Is that for—"

"Yes."

"Well, I suppose the mayor will still be dead in the morning." Sam was buzzing with anticipation by the time they entered the building and hit the button for the elevator. He still got a kick out of living in a place that actually had one.

Upstairs, their white cat, Shadow, was lounging sleepily on the rug near the door. She immediately sprang to her feet and began meowing for her dinner. Then she narrowed her blue eyes accusingly when neither paid her any mind.

"All right. All right," Nathan said, picking her up. Then he looked at Sam. "I'm going to feed the cat first. You, go get into position and stay quiet. I don't want to hear a sound."

"With or without the blindfold?"

"With. Hold this key in your lips."

"Okay."

"Okay, *sir*."

Sam's belly swooped at Nathan's dominant tone. "Okay, sir." He quickly entered the bedroom and kicked off his shoes—the only nice ones he had—and yanked his shirt over his head. The blindfold was in the black box they kept under the bed, along with many of the other paraphernalia used for their play. Sam ran his fingers over the flat paddle Nathan had given him several months before. The smooth wood was cool to the touch, and he shivered remembering the first time they'd used it. He hoped they'd use it tonight.

After he'd grabbed the blindfold and undressed, he kneeled at the foot of the bed with his hands behind his head, cock already hard. The metallic taste of the key wasn't pleasant, but Sam wasn't about to disobey Nathan— he was too eager to see what it would unlock.

Don't miss how the story started!

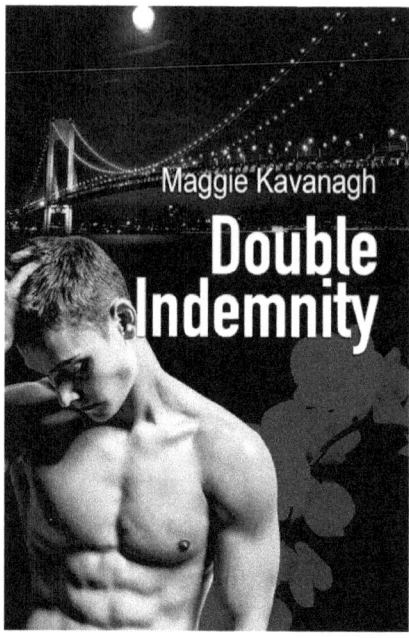

The Stonebridge Mysteries: Book One

Sam Flynn dreamed of being a journalist, until a car accident killed his parents and put his brother into a long-term coma. Now Sam spends his days as a landscaper, toiling in the New England sun, and his nights drunk in bed with the closest warm body. In his limited spare time, he writes about Stonebridge's local crime and politics on his blog "Under the Bridge."

Then Sam's favorite client is found dead in her home—shortly after telling him someone has betrayed her trust. Sam can't believe her grief-stricken husband, Nathan, would be a suspect, but the investigation focuses on him. Sam has always admired handsome Nathan from afar, but now he puts his libidinous feelings aside to help clear his name. But the closer he gets to Nathan, the more he's told to keep away from him and the investigation—by the fatherly police chief, by an officer on the case who's hated him since school, and by Nathan himself.

Sam is determined to expose the real reason his friend died and to clear Nathan's name—even if it's the last thing he does. Which, considering how fast the death toll is rising in Stonebridge… it might be.

www.dreamspinnerpress.com

MAGGIE KAVANAGH works full-time and steals moments to write; you can find her in the wee morning hours typing away on her laptop with a steaming cup of coffee in her living room. Her passions include traveling, eating great food, and writing stories about flawed, human characters finding love. She lives in New England.

Twitter: @maggie_kavanagh

Facebook: www.facebook.com/maggie.kavanagh.33

When Hunter decides he wants more from his relationship with Jake, the couple finds themselves at a crossroads. Never home for more than a few weeks at a time, Jake has been running from the pain of a rocky childhood ever since high school, when he first enlisted in the army. The thing is, he always comes back to Hunter's bed. It's not the kind of commitment Hunter wants, but it's the kind he's settled for—that and a dead-end job at the local bookstore in the small Southern town where he grew up. When Jake reveals his plans to make a full-time career in the army, Hunter wonders if he's putting his life on hold for a relationship that will never happen. He needs to say something now before he loses Jake. However, if Jake can't conquer his demons, Hunter's asking for more is sure to drive him away.

www.dreamspinnerpress.com

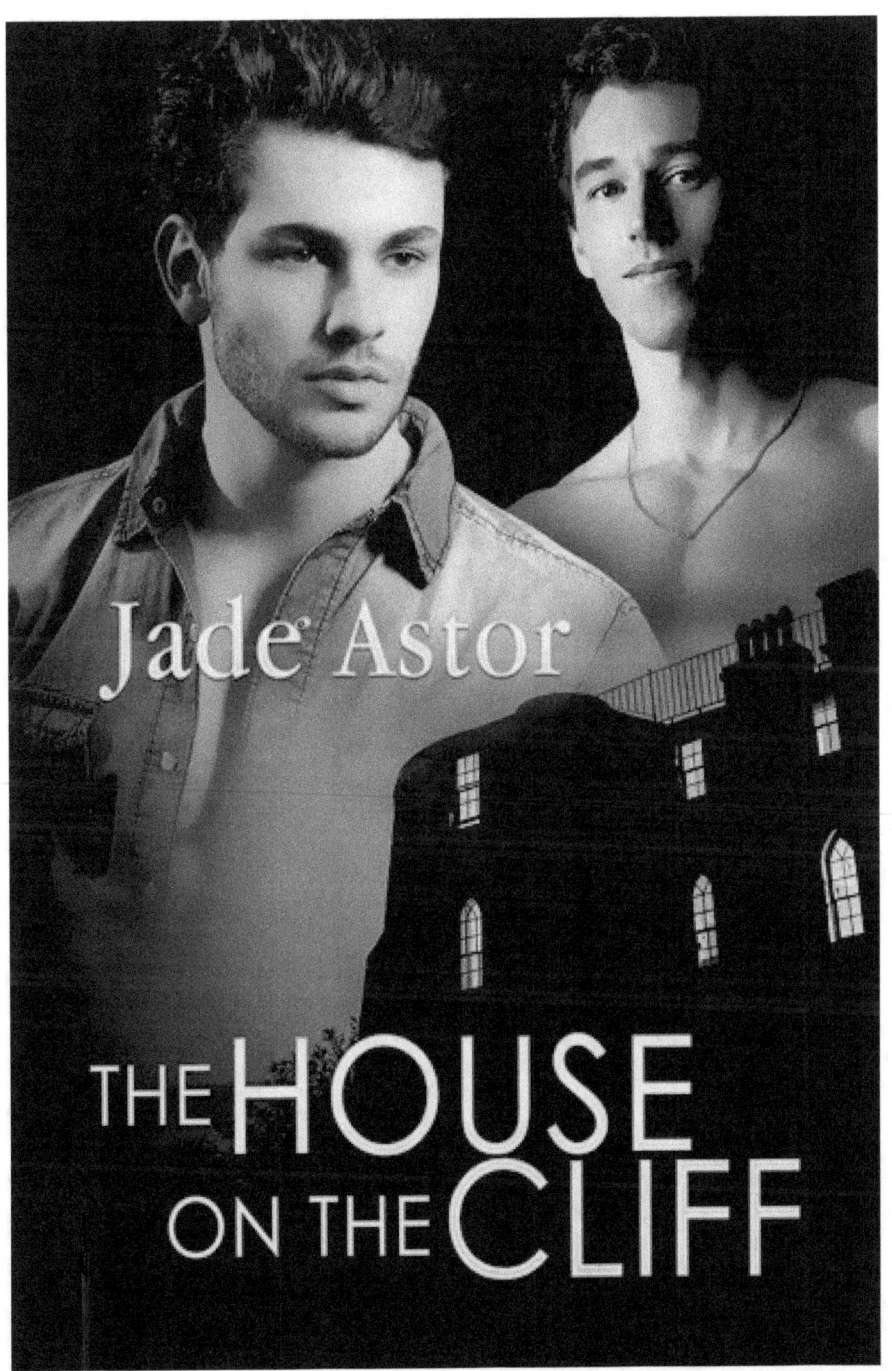

Also from Dreamspinner Press

LIV OLTEANO

A tooth FOR A fang

www.dreamspinnerpress.com

Also from Dreamspinner Press

NORA ROTH

AIDING
AND
ABETTING

www.dreamspinnerpress.com

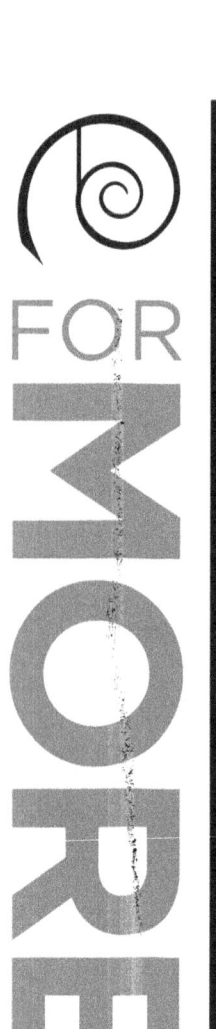

www.ingramcontent.com/pod-product-compliance
Lightning Source LLC
Chambersburg PA
CBHW060051260626
47160CB00005B/1650